THE BARRINGTON BOOK CLUB

SMALL TOWN ROMANCE

BARRINGTON SERIES

SUSAN MACKIE

For all the readers in all the book clubs.
This one is for you.
And to the members of the Barrington Book Club in real life, I
thank you (especially Joanne B).

Susan Mackie

ABOUT THIS BOOK

Twelve books, nine friends, four babies and one unimaginable tragedy that will change their small town forever.

The Barrington girl-posse is back.

With friendship ties stronger than ever and often hilarious girl-banter, the women we know and love spontaneously begin a book club. Yes, it's about reading books, but it's also a way to ensure they catch up, altogether, at least one night per month. Leaving little ones with their menfolk, book club becomes the place to share their hopes, dreams, secrets and fears. And fun and laughter, coffee, wine and food.

Over the course of a year, twelve books are read, four babies are born, relationships grow, businesses change and newcomers arrive. But when tragedy strikes one of their own, their small-town world is spun off its axis.

Now book club is more than girl-chat and paperbacks. It's where they share their grief and help each other recover.

THE BARRINGTON COMMUNITY AT THE START OF THIS BOOK

This is the eighth story in the series but it's the fourth full-size book. There are also three novellas and a short story.

While it's best to read the other stories first - in case you haven't, or you've forgotten who's who - here is a cheat sheet for you.

Rose Gordon Hamilton (writer) married to **Angus Hamilton** (Vet) – we first met them in **Charlie's Will.**
Own Barrington Homestead and farm & the Vet practice.
Son **Charlie** (pre-school).
Rose is pregnant.

Debbie Webb Tait (Café owner) married to **Jamie Tait** (grazier) – we met them in **Coffee is my Calling.**
Son **Warwick** (nickname **Woz**, day care).
Debbie & Jamie are exploring adoption due to pregnancy health risk.

Harriet Russell Murray married to ***Drum Murray*** (grazier, Councillor) – we met them in ***A Place to Start Over.***
Own Montrose Homestead and property.
Harriet's office is within Evans Real Estate.
Billie – Drum's daughter from first marriage (primary school).
Harriet is pregnant (high-risk).

Meggie Hamilton (Angus's sister, in business with Harriet) engaged to ***Max Masters*** (Vet, Angus's partner) – we met them in ***Meggie & Max.***
Recently moved into cottage on small acreage farm together.
Meggie's office is within Evans Real Estate.
Indiana – Max's daughter from first marriage, lives away.
Tommy – Max's son from first marriage (primary school).
Meggie wants to have a baby with Max.

Melanie Mitchell Evans (Vet nurse) married to ***Ben Evans Jnr*** (nickname ***Little Ben***, Evans Real Estate) – ***all books.***
Tiffany – Melanie's daughter from earlier relationship (primary school).
Melanie is pregnant.

Laura Harrison (farmer, bull breeder) dating ***Ben Evans Snr*** (nickname ***Big Ben***, Evans Real Estate, Councillor) – we met them in ***A Place to Start Over.***
Ben is almost retirement age.
Laura is in her early 50's.

Frances Barlow (office manager) married to ***Douglas Barlow*** (Solicitor) – ***all books.***

Own the old bank building the café is in, office upstairs.
Close to retirement age.

Nicola Reid Stewart (accountant, BnB owner) married to
Robbie Stewart (builder) – we met them in ***Ragged Mountain Ranges.***
Harry Stewart – Robbie's son (fencing contractor, builder, horse-breaker).
Lucy Stewart – Nicola's daughter (high school, shy, talented cook).

Frederica Campbell (***Freddie***) – 3rd year Vet Science at Uni, daughter of local grazier, works at Vet Clinic in Uni holidays – we met her in ***Charlie's Will.***

Cathy – works at the café
Kristen – Cathy's daughter – works at café in Uni holidays

1

DEBBIE

'I NEED YOU ROSE. NOW. PLEASE!' DEBBIE DREW IN HER breath as she navigated the sharp bend, before slowing for the single lane bridge across the Barrington River. 'Can you meet me? At the café? Please!'

She was asking a lot. It was late afternoon and Rose would be trying to wrangle Charlie into the bath, which was never an easy task. Angus wouldn't be home yet. Debbie hated asking, but it was urgent.

'Bring Charlie, it's okay. But I have to talk to you.' She was crying now, the tears running unchecked down her cheeks. She didn't care. Couldn't have stopped them, anyway.

There was no hesitation in Rose's response. 'I'll be there in ten minutes. Meggie is here, she'll mind Charlie for me.'

She didn't even ask what was wrong. Just said she'd come. Debbie cried harder, blinking to see clearly, as she clicked the phone off using the button on her steering wheel. She couldn't ask for a better friend than Rose. Gasping, she swerved to miss a single cow standing on the edge. Heart racing, she slowed as she entered the outskirts of Barrington.

Wiping her eyes, Debbie parked at the rear of the café. Cathy's car was gone, she would have closed up an hour ago.

Slipping in through the back door, Debbie didn't turn on any lights. It was gloomy, but not quite dark outside. She unlocked the front door and sat at a table to one side. She contemplated making coffee but didn't have the energy.

A few minutes later the front door opened. Rose stepped inside, closed the door, then turned the lock.

'Deb?' Rose peered into the café, her voice uncertain.

'Over here.' Debbie half stood, then slumped back into her chair. Rose was with her in two strides. Dropping her handbag on a table, she pulled a chair close to Debbie's and reached for her hands.

'Deb? What is it?' Rose face was full of concern, her brow creased. 'You've never, ever, called me with this,' she wiped the tears from Debbie's cheek, 'this urgency!'

Leaning into Rose, Debbie cried harder, grateful Rose didn't ask more questions. Instead, her friend held her, rubbed her back and murmured, 'it's alright' like she would with wee Charlie if he hurt himself.

Her tears gradually subsided to sniffles and Debbie slowly sat up. Rose produced a packet of tissues and handed her one. Or maybe it was a napkin from the table they sat at. Debbie blew her nose. Wringing her hands together, she tried to speak.

'Take your time.' Rose spoke quietly, yet firmly. Her presence gave Debbie strength.

Debbie blurted the words out, sobbing as she did. 'I don't know what to tell Jamie!' Shaking her head, she almost shouted the next words. 'I *can't* tell Jamie!'

2

ROSE

ROSE SHIFTED SLIGHTLY IN HER SEAT, THE BABY HAD moved and her lower back spasmed for a moment. Debbie's anguish affected her deeply. She'd never seen her like this, she was always calm and quietly confident. Debbie was <u>her</u> go-to-person.

Trying to maintain a sense of equilibrium by modulating her voice, Rose needed to establish what it was Debbie believed she couldn't tell Jamie. 'What is it Debbie? Jamie's one of the good ones, you can tell him anything.'

Debbie raised her head, then looked sadly at Rose. 'One of us will die.'

Rose blinked, then shook her head. *What? She can't have heard her correctly.* 'Debbie. You need to tell me what you mean!'

Taking a deep breath, Debbie seemed to lose focus for a moment, and a small smile played around her mouth. She whispered something, but Rose couldn't catch her meaning, her own mind was racing.

Debbie's smile faded and a deep sadness returned to her eyes. 'I'm pregnant, Rose.'

'Oh.' For a moment Rose wanted to hug her, congratulate her dearest friend. *Then she remembered.* They'd nearly lost Debbie when baby Warwick was born. She wasn't planning to have any more children naturally, they were looking into adoption.

'How long have you known? How far along are you?' Rose patted Debbie's arm for a moment, hoping the contact would reassure her, while she tried to recall the medical advice. Debbie *couldn't* have more children, or *shouldn't*? Rose's own baby bump was obvious, at five months, and she felt a pang of guilt for having such trouble-free pregnancies, and a relatively easy birth with Charlie.

'I'm ten weeks.' Debbie began crying again. 'It was an accident, but oh, when I realised, I just wanted to keep it to myself for a while, savour the feeling.' She beseeched Rose with her eyes, while blurting the words. 'But Jamie. He's adamant. Says we've done the right thing, looking into adoption. He told me today. That. If. He. Ever. Had to choose. He'd choose me. Not the baby.' Her words were punctuated by sobs and now she leaned over the table, head on her arms, with her sobs turning into a wail. A wail of grief that sent shivers up Rose's back.

'So I can't tell him. My baby will die.' She looked up, her face red and blotchy, and shook her head, before whispering, 'and we know that if I carry this baby to term, it's likely I will die. Jamie won't take the chance. He'll ask me to. To. To.' She shook her head, unable to complete the sentence.

'Deb. Debbie. Look at me.' Rose handed Debbie another napkin, waiting while she wiped her eyes. 'It's almost two years since you had Woz. And they know your problems, about the pre-eclampsia. Perhaps a full-term pregnancy can be managed.'

A glimmer of hope reached Debbie's eyes. She straightened. *At least she's listening,* Rose thought.

'Have you seen anyone Deb? A doctor? Your obstetrician? Before you make any decisions, you need to know the facts. As they are *today*.' Rose leaned back. She needed to stand. Her own baby was doing back flips, or tumble turns, and not only was it uncomfortable, she really needed to pee.

She watched Debbie nod, deep in thought.

'Think about it Deb, but I'm sorry, I need to pop out the back and use your bathroom.' Rose stood, waited for a second, saw Debbie give another very slight nod, then rushed through to the back area of the café.

Returning a few minutes later, Debbie had turned on a light and the pile of discarded paper napkins had been tidied away. She walked to Rose, who automatically opened her arms. They held each other tightly. Rose murmured into Debbie's hair, 'but you need to tell Jamie. He will support you. I know he will.'

'I had been thinking he would, but when he said those words today.' Debbie hiccupped, stepping back slightly. 'I wondered, if he *knew*, if he'd worked it out and was letting me know ...' She trailed off.

Rose chuckled and Debbie looked at her in surprise. Placing her arm around her friend's shoulders, Rose shook her head. 'He's a man, Debbie. He knows bupkis. Nothing. If he's noticed anything at all, I'd be surprised.' She lowered her tone. 'Tell him Deb. Tell him tonight after you put Woz to bed. I think you'll be surprised at his response. Sure, he's been saying that he'd choose you over a baby, but it's much easier to say that when there *isn't* a baby. Now there *is* and you need to tell him.'

'Thank you. Thank you Rose. For coming. For just being here.' Debbie lifted her chin. 'You're right. My husband *is* one of the good ones. I'll talk to him tonight.'

'Message me after if you want to chat. I'm here for you Deb. Always.' Rose hugged her again, then giggled. 'Meggie said she'd bath Charlie for me and start his dinner. I'm tempted to call Angus, get him to meet me at the pub for a meal, and just leave her to it!' Rose was relieved to see Debbie's quick grin. Wee Charlie was notorious. *A handful.* But also the light of Rose's life.

3

______

MEGGIE

DESPITE EVERYONE BELIEVING THREE-YEAR-OLD Charlie was a mischievous imp, Meggie delighted in her nephew. He was bright, inquisitive and behaved himself, mostly, when his parents weren't around.

After Rose rushed out, Meggie read Charlie a story. He found anything dangerous fascinating at the moment – sharks, snakes, lions and tigers. He could identify several dinosaurs by name and Meggie giggled when he picked one toy up, referring to it as a 'shtegashaurus', which was correct, despite the slight mispronunciation.

Max found them half an hour later. Charlie was in a very full bubble bath with a large number of plastic animals; including dinosaurs and sharks, and Meggie was kneeling on the floor, pretending to be terrified each time Charlie thrust a toy at her, making scary animal noises as he did.

'That looks like fun. Can anyone play?' Max drawled from his position leaning against the doorjamb, a broad grin on his face.

Meggie jumped at his voice, while Charlie stood up in the bath, a shark in one hand stretched towards Max. 'Max. Max. Grrr, shark!' Unsteady in the slippery bath, Meggie reached for Charlie just as he fell and landed on his plump bottom, sending a small wave of water and foam over the edge, now pooling around her knees. A blob of bubbles landed on one side of her face, and Meggie laughed and flicked it at Max as he stepped into the room.

'All your fault Max Masters. Now you can scoop the slippery little mite out of the bath, if you please.' Meggie stood, ignoring her damp knees, and held out a towel as Max hefted Charlie out, holding his wet little body under the arms. Meggie wrapped him deftly, capturing his arms in the towel, then handed him back to Max.

'To his room. I'll just wipe this mess up.' Turning back to the bath, Meggie grinned as Charlie shrieked loudly while Max galloped him into the next room.

Joining them, she dressed Charlie quickly, enjoying his chatter with Max as she did. 'Alright little mate. Which book would you like me to read?' Meggie set him on the floor, and Charlie ran to his bookshelf, pulling several books out. Instead of bringing them to Meggie, he took them to Max.

Raising an eyebrow, Meggie stepped back to allow Max room to lift Charlie into his bed. 'By the way, what are you doing here? Where's Angus? And Rose hasn't returned, she rushed out in a hurry after a call from Deb.'

Kneeling beside the bed, Max looked up. 'Strangest thing. Rose was getting into her car, behind the coffee shop, as Angus and I returned from a call-out. She asked me,' he laughed, 'no, she *told me* to come out here, bring you some dinner, so she and Angus could have a meal at the pub.'

'Read Max!' Charlie wriggled in the bed, pulling on Max's sleeve. Max settled on top of the covers, book in hand, his long legs and sock-clad feet protruding over the end.

Meggie walked to the door. 'And Tommy?'

'Where do you think Tommy is? I picked up pizzas.' Max turned a page, made a tiger-like growl, at which Charlie squealed, delighted.

Hurrying down the hallway to the kitchen, Meggie could smell the pizzas, and garlic bread. Nine-year-old Tommy had plates laid out on the kitchen counter, and two pizza boxes, unopened with a wrapped garlic bread on top.

'Hey Tommy.' Meggie gave her nine-year-old step-son a one-arm hug as she reached for glasses. 'You can start, your Dad's reading to Charlie.' She giggled. 'He might be a while, Charlie had quite a stack of books lined up.'

Tommy drew in a breath and nodded. 'It's okay. I can wait ...' But Meggie knew he'd be hungry, and keen to eat.

'Have some garlic bread, it needs to be unwrapped. I'll check on Max.' Tommy grinned at her words and reached for the steaming package.

Meggie returned down the hall, more quietly this time. She could hear Max's voice as she approached the room, but nothing from Charlie. Popping her head in, she saw Charlie had fallen asleep, his pudgy hand clutching a shark toy. Her eyes misted over at the image of Max reading to little Charlie which conjured an image of what might be, for them, one day. Max put his finger to his lips but continued reading the last pages of the book. Glancing at Charlie, he closed the book, slid off the bed and pulled the covers up, tucking in the hand with the shark.

He tiptoed to the door, following Meggie out, but left it ajar.

In the hallway, Max reached for her hand, spinning her into his arms. He kissed her mouth gently, quietly. Warmth filled her chest. She kissed him back, enjoying his closeness.

Looking up, she whispered, 'Tommy is waiting for us. But this.' She kissed him again, letting her teeth nip his bottom lip briefly. 'Later. More of this later.'

4

HARRIET

Harriet snapped her book shut and tried to slide it under the folder on her desk, but Meggie was too quick. 'Whatcha reading Harriet?' In two steps she was in front of Harriet's desk, reaching her hand over to the folder. Harriet laughed, but lightly slapped Meggie's hand away, who grimaced and flopped into the nearest chair.

'Is it another natural childbirth book?' Meggie's eyes twinkled. 'Um, something serious?' She tapped her fingers on the desk. 'Market your way to millions? Brand your business like the beast it is?'

Harriet laughed. 'Stop it! You weren't supposed to see that.' Sliding the book into the open, she pushed it across the desk with the tips of her fingers. 'I know I have stuff to do. Business stuff. But Meggs, I just can't put this one down! Have you read it?'

'Have I read it? Ha! Of course I've read it! This came out a couple of years ago and actually,' Meggie flipped to the inside cover, 'It's *my* copy. I loaned it to you at Christmas. See the little MH here inside the cover?' She thrust the book back at Harriet, one finger on the tiny initials.

'Oh, yeah. Now I remember. It's been on my To Be Read pile since then.' Harriet shook her head sadly. 'Why did I not read this before? It's sooo good that I'm now reading while pretending to work!' Harriet slipped the book back under the folder, then leaned forward, her hands steepled under her chin. 'But now that you're here, I have questions. At first all the different *character voices* threw me, but now I think I love it ...'

Meggie stood quickly, frowning at her fit-watch, and rushed to the door. 'Hold that thought. That's my phone, it's the wine guy ...' The last words were barely audible as Meggie sped into her own office.

Harriet reached for the novel again, then sighed and dropped it into her tote bag. She had work to do. They had two events in the next two weeks. An elopement and a small wedding. She held her left hand up, looking at the rose gold wedding band and matching diamond solitaire. She loved looking at the rings, the symbol of her marriage to Drum Murray. Their wedding had been their very first *Barrington Elopement* and it had been a beautiful day, with just close family and friends, at the homestead she shared with her husband and little step-daughter Billie. And now the business was taking off, they had no less than five elopements scheduled in the next four weeks and she and Meggie were busy pulling the events together. The great thing about the new business was that the events were small, intimate and unique and they now had a template to work from. She chuckled to herself. The old adage was true. *Work smarter, not harder.*

CHAPTER 4

Harriet rubbed her tummy gently. Despite her old injuries, and the advice she may not carry to full term, her pregnancy had been uneventful once the initial discomfort around her old scar tissue subsided. Her due date was after Rose and their other friend Melanie, but Harriet acknowledged she may require a caesarean delivery, before either of them. She'd known this from the beginning. Having a premature baby may be touch and go. But so far, all was well.

Meggie rushed back in. 'That was Finn Anderson from Barrington Ridge Estate. He can provide boutique wines - two reds and two whites. Good ones. At the right price. He loves the intimate weddings and elopements concept. His winery is small and independent, I think it's a good fit. We can go there for a tasting, or he can bring some here later this week. What do you think?'

'Oh, he finally called you back.' Harriet frowned. 'I thought you'd gone off him and his wares, that he wasn't quick enough to return calls and so on?'

'You're right Harri, I did think that. But now I understand the scope of his business and he understands ours, I think we'll work together well. The size of his output precludes him from big events and the commercial market. Working with us, on small events, creates a boutique opportunity. The few bottles Ben and Melanie picked up for your wedding Harri, were outstanding. Especially the Merlot.' Meggie looked like she was about to lick her lips and Harriet shook her head, giggling.

'I trust your judgement on this Meggie. I can't have more than a sip or two, and you have loads more experience in this space. Let's try him for the ones we have booked already and then reassess.'

Harriet looked at her watch, then patted her tummy. 'It's almost one and I'm hungry. Feel like a stroll to the café? I fancy that pesto gnocchi we tried last week.' She raised her eyebrows.

'Sure. I'll just let Ben know we're popping out.'

5

____

ROSE

Rose saw Meggie and Harriet arrive from her table near the back. She turned to Debbie, concerned. 'Okay if they join us?'

'Of course.' Debbie stood, waved to the arrivals, who began to weave their way through the tables towards them. Turning back to Rose, she said quietly, 'I'm not ready to tell anyone yet. Not even them.'

'Understood.' Rose moved to the next chair, making room for Meggie and Harriet.

'We're here for the pesto gnocchi, Deb, if you've got any today.' Meggie grinned. 'Harriet's *starving.*' She emphasised starving and Rose patted her own tummy, somewhat defensively.

'And we're eating for two. No judgement here Harriet.' She turned to Debbie. 'I'll have the same please.'

Debbie bustled over to the counter speaking to her staff quickly, before stepping behind the coffee machine.

'How's your day going Meggie?' Rose shifted slightly in her

seat. At five months she was already getting lower back pain when she sat in one position too long.

'Good, thanks Rose.' Rose gave an almost imperceptible shake of her head when Meggie raised a questioning brow towards Debbie. She'd asked the night before, when Rose and Angus returned to the homestead, if everything was alright. It was Debbie's news to tell, and Rose had been non-committal in her response.

Meggie picked up on the vibe and immediately changed the subject. 'Hey Harri, do you have that book in your bag? The one I caught you reading earlier?'

'Yes I do. And I still have questions, although I'm not quite finished.' Harriet pulled the book from the depths of her tote bag. It was a best-seller by an Australian author who'd had a television series and a movie made from previous books. Rose felt a quick pang of envy. Her own writing was progressing well, but gosh, she'd love to have the readership of *that* author. 'Have you read it Rose?'

Rose nodded, about to speak, when Debbie arrived back at the table with a tray of drinks. 'Oh, loved that one. Very twisty.' She passed the drinks around. 'Dirty chai for you Rose, caramel latte for Meggie, tea for Harri and a chai for me.'

'Well that's just it. It is twisty, in a good way, but I've never read a book with so many,' Harriet looked at Rose, 'Voices? Is that what it is?'

'P. O. V. Points of View. But yes, *voices* works too. And this one also has a lot of short chapters, with the POV of the hair-dresser, and the next-door neighbour, and others, interspersed with longer chapters from the main protagonists.' Rose raised her eyebrows. 'Essentially the whole family.'

Harriet flicked through the pages to where her bookmark sat. 'I'll be finished tonight. I'd love to catch-up and talk about this one.' She looked up. 'Anyone keen? You know, like an informal book club. And now I don't know what to read next, although Meggie has been feeding me books from her shelf.'

'Wait. Stop. What did you just say?' Debbie was leaning forward. 'An informal book club?' She looked at Rose, grinning. 'We should do it. I mean it. Start our own book club!'

Thrilled to see Debbie so pumped after her despair the night before, Rose grinned back. 'I love it. We should. Start a book club.' She turned to Meggie. 'I didn't know you were a big reader, but it makes sense now, you have a huge bookshelf at your place.'

'Always loved to read. Anne of Green Gables, Little Women, all the Harry Potters.' She was gazing into space, her expression dreamy, as she spoke, and Harriet nudged her.

'Alright Meggie. Don't make it weird now.' Rose giggled at Harriet's words. She loved the easy closeness Meggie and Harriet had developed..

Harriet picked up the teacup in front of her, brought it to her nose, grimaced, then set it down again.

'It's chamomile with honey Harriet. You loved it last week.' Debbie reached for the cup, smelling it tentatively.

'I know. My taste buds are crazy. This morning I really wanted scrambled eggs, but the first bite made me nauseous. So I had vegemite toast. Again.' Harriet reached over, picking up the cup in front of Meggie. She brought it to her lips. 'Aaah. Caramel latte. With real coffee. Not decaf.' She took a sip, both hands now holding the cup. 'This coffee. Mine.'

'If you weren't pregnant Harri.' Meggie laughed as she reached for the offending chamomile tea. 'I'll drink this. It's nice. And healthy. And I'm not even pregnant.' She let out an exaggerated sigh. 'The things I do, Harriet Russell-Murray.'

'Returning to topic. Book club? Really? I'm keen.' Debbie leaned in and Rose chuckled as they huddled in too. 'And you know what else, we can make it a *thing*. A regular thing so the blokes take care of themselves, and the little ones. It'll be a girls night. With books. Like we used to have with wine. Before babies.' She leaned back. Rose glanced at the others. They were all keen, giggling, smiling and giving each other knowing looks.

'Okay. I'm in. I think Melanie will be interested too, and maybe Laura and Nicole. Is that too many?' Rose was enthusiastic. Books were her thing. Writing them. But writers were also big readers. And she loved talking about books.

'Definitely ask the others. We'll make it a set night, once a month. We can do it here at the cafe, after closing. There's always leftovers for snacks.' Debbie was brimming with excitement and Rose felt a new contentment after her concern for Debbie the night before.

'We need rules though. About books. I'd love it if we could stick to Australian writers, women writers, for the first six or so. And what about genres? I like romance, historical, mystery, crime. But not horror. Any others?' Harriet was tapping into her phone as she spoke.

It's a thing, this book club. Rose was eager. 'Yes to Australian writers. Debbie, it's your idea so you choose the first book, then we'll make a list at our meeting. Let's make it two weeks from now.' She turned to Harriet. 'Can you shoot an email out to the others? Invite them. Get their book suggestions too, if they have any.'

They were all speaking at once and didn't hear Debbie at first.

'And it has a two-fold purpose. Sure, it's about books.' She reached her hands into the centre of the table. They all reached theirs in too. Rose saw tears in Debbie's eyes. 'But it's about women. Friends. Supporting each other.' They were silent for a second, digesting this, taking it in.

Then Harriet laughed loudly, and the mood shifted. 'And we'll call it The Barrington Book Club!'

6

DEBBIE

September - Barrington Book Club - Meeting 1
Present: Debbie, Rose, Meggie, Harriet, Melanie, Laura
Apologies: Nicole, Frances?
Book: *Apples Never Fall* by Liane Moriarty

MEGGIE AND HARRIET ARRIVED TOGETHER, STRAIGHT from work. Debbie thought Meggie looked unusually pale, but when she caught the determined look in her eyes, she didn't mention it.

'I'm happy to man the coffee machine Deb, I haven't forgotten how it works.' Harriet laughed, stepping behind the counter and tying on an apron.

'Oh good, thank you. That's a big help. I've got mostly finger food for snacks, and there's plenty of cake and slice for something sweet after.' As Debbie handed the cheese board and small plates to Meggie as the door opened, letting Rose and Laura in.

'This is a great idea girls!' Laura strode to the table, pulling a bottle of wine from her bag as she did. 'I have wine. Grab some glasses Debbie, we're celebrating!'

Debbie laughed then, but shook her head, waving her arm towards the rest of the women, which now included Melanie. 'Rose, Mel and Harri are pregnant Laura, they can't drink.'

'Hang on Debbie.' Harriet looked up from the coffee machine. 'If there's something to celebrate, a wee sip won't hurt.'

'Not me,' Rose rubbed her tummy. 'Not even a sip. Just don't like the taste these days.' She turned to Melanie, 'what about you Mel?'

'Oh, I'm in for a sip.' Mel stood beside Rose, and Debbie chuckled internally. Rose was tall, her baby due first, but Mel's bump seemed larger, although perhaps it was because she was more petite.

Debbie also had news she wanted to share with her friends tonight. But she'd wait until Laura told hers. Laura was older than the rest of them, by close to twenty years, but she'd been a good friend to Harriet since she'd arrived in the area and worked with Rose on the designs for her book covers. She'd never been one to frequent the coffee shop, until she started seeing Ben Evans Senior, Big Ben to his friends, late last year.

Finally all seated, Debbie glanced at Harriet. 'You're our unofficial leader here Harri. What do we do first? Book Club? Or general chit chat? And I'm dying to hear Laura's news.'

'Should we wait for Frances? She told me yesterday she was coming.' Rose looked at her watch, a small crease appearing between her eyes as she said the words, then answered her own question. 'No, I guess not. She'd be here by now if she was coming.'

Attention returned to Harriet who had her notebook open in

front of her. She smiled as she looked around the table. 'We meet here by six, but anyone arriving earlier can give Debbie a hand. I thought we'd settle, have a snack and chat for the first half hour, then spend thirty minutes to an hour on the book we've read, including choosing one for next month. Anyone who needs to leave will be able to go by half seven, but we can stay and chat until eight if you'd like to, and it's not a late night for anyone.' Eyebrows raised, she looked at each of them. Debbie was pleased Harriet had slipped effortlessly into managing the book club and setting parameters to put them all on the same page.

They all spoke then, agreeing with Harriet's guidelines, passing food to each other, some sipping hot drinks and Laura, Melanie, Harriet and Meggie sipping the wine in front of them. Debbie had declined alcohol, and no one questioned her.

'Alright Laura. Top up your glass and tell us what we're celebrating.' Rose's words brought the other conversations to a halt, and they looked expectantly at Laura.

'It's not what you think Rose Gordon.' Laura shook her finger at Rose, smiling.

'What do I think Laura?' Rose challenged her, the others giggled.

'You think Ben's popped the question. Or some such thing.' Laura looked smug. 'But it's not that. Well, not *exactly* that.'

'*Exactly* what then Laura?' Harriet couldn't hide her grin.

'I've sold the farm.' Laura's words shocked Debbie. She knew how much Laura loved the farm, and her animals.

'Really?' Rose and Debbie shared a look and Debbie saw concern on Rose's face.

'Yes. Really. I know you're shocked, and I was too when I first considered it. But there was an offer. A bloke-from-the-city-too-good-to-be-true offer. And you know I've always struggled, and I did it tough during the drought.' She turned to Harriet. 'The bull sale saved me, but it also made me realise how much living I'm missing out on because I'm tied to the farm.' Laura raised her glass, took a sip, then sat it back on the table. 'And Ben and I are, well, having fun. There are things he'd like us to do together. Short trips interstate, a holiday up north. I'm over fifty, he's almost sixty. And suddenly you realise that time is finite.'

Laura looked at Melanie then. 'And Little Ben has been brilliant, feeding the cattle and dogs for me when I've taken a day or two off. But these short trips have made me yearn for more.' Laura grinned. 'So here's to me. And Ben. And travel. And *living*.'

They all raised their drinks, talking over each other again, until Melanie, usually the quietest one, spoke loudly. 'That is wonderful news Laura. I admit, *my* Ben mentioned to me there was a chance of this.' She lowered her voice. 'His dad is mad about you. But where will you live? Are you moving in with Ben? Big Ben, I mean.'

'No. No I'm not.' Laura was firm. ' I've put an offer in on that gorgeous old heritage house in Gloucester Street, there's room for my dogs in the yard, and Ben will keep his place and we'll travel a bit and see what happens after that.' She looked at Harriet. 'You know what I'm like. I'm not sure if Ben is ready for all of my *eccentricities*.' She threw her head back and laughed and the others grinned and offered congratulations again.

Clearing their plates and clutter away, they sat copies of *Apples Never Fall* on the table. Debbie noticed that Melanie had a kindle and Laura an iPad. Meggie and Harri were sharing Meggie's copy. And Rose had a paperback with a different cover, but the same title. Debbie's had a torn cover, courtesy of her son, Warwick.

'Can I start? This is the book that started my questions and led to Debbie's brilliant book club idea.' Harriet moved the book closer to Meggie, then turned the page of her notebook.

Meggie snorted. Then put her hand over her mouth.

'What?' Harriet stared at her friend for a moment.

'You have notes?' Meggie smirked. 'This isn't a business meeting Harri. It's girl-chat-and-paperbacks, right?'

'Whatever floats your boat Meggie Hamilton. Me, I like to note down my thoughts. I want answers.' Harriet jostled Meggie with her shoulder and Rose looked at Debbie and laughed.

'This was us Deb. In high school.' Rose pointed at the other two, giggling. 'But we've matured.'

'Too funny! But I'm with Harri. I have questions too.' Melanie nodded at Harriet. 'Go ahead.'

'The big one, for me, is the large number of Points of View,' Harriet added in a stage whisper, 'an official writing term that I learnt from Rose.' Her voice returned to its usual pitch as she continued. 'At first I found them confusing and had to turn back and read the previous chapter, but then I got into the swing of it and loved it. Especially the really short ones from seemingly random people, like the hairdresser.'

'That was the bit I disliked. Almost didn't finish. I felt like the writer made me work for the answers.' Laura tapped her iPad. 'I've liked some of her other books, but this one isn't my favourite.'

Melanie spoke up. 'You know, I didn't really notice that, as much as the whole dysfunctional family narrative, and the misconceptions about each other that they'd all carried for years. Their whole lives.'

'And who invites a complete stranger to live with them? I mean, really? Sure, let them in, tend them, but call the police, people!' Meggie clapped a hand to her forehead, making the rest of them laugh.

'But you know, the bit about the mother, how she had to prepare all those meals, all those years, and then having someone doing that for her, removing a daily task she'd grown to hate. It would be tempting to let them stay.' Debbie looked at Rose. 'I *felt* that. I really did.'

They all looked at Rose. 'You're a writer. What did you think, Rose?' Harriet was really focussed, and the questions, the discussion, had lifted the energy in the room. It was good to talk about something other than their immediate world, their own issues, big and small. Debbie was enjoying this.

'Fascinating. I've loved most of her books. But this one, I read twice.' Rose chuckled. 'The first time for the story. The second time for the craft.' She shook her head then. 'Those random little points of view really moved the story on, and at times planted some red herrings. It was clever, really clever.' Her face lost is glow. 'I've written two books and have a third one almost ready to publish, and they don't have anywhere near this level of... of craft. Sometimes I read books like these, and I wonder what I'm doing.' She shook her head sadly.

'Stop it Rose!' Laura's voice was firm. 'Your books are my faves. I *love* them. You have twists and surprises in yours and reading them is pure pleasure.' Laura patted her iPad again. 'This one was hard work for me.'

'Different genre too, Rose. Your books are doing really well. Don't compare yourself.' Meggie blew her sister-in-law a kiss, then turned to Debbie. 'It's after seven but I vote we have something sweet.'

Debbie chuckled, picked up most of their used plates from the next table and headed for the kitchen. Harriet was behind her, having cleared the rest.

'We're using up leftovers, Cathy baked today. There are a couple of pieces of pecan pie, some strudel, carrot cake and three chocolate brownies. Can you just set them all on a tray Harriet and I'll take clean plates out.' Debbie picked up the crockery, then turned back. 'There's fresh cream in the other fridge, thanks. I'll see if anyone wants another drink.'

'Just take a carafe of water out Debbie, no one needs more coffee and I think the wine has been finished,' she hesitated, smirking, 'just as well Rose drove Laura here.'

7

———

MEGGIE

A TUGGING FEELING IN HER LOWER BACK SENT MEGGIE into a spiral. She knew what that was. She also knew what it wasn't. *It wasn't a baby.* Now she just wanted to go home. Home to Max. She'd been hopeful they'd have something to celebrate themselves. About to make her excuses and leave, Debbie and Harriet returned with a platter of various sweet things, making the rest ooh and aah. She gritted her teeth, internally, hoping she was hiding her sadness.

They chatted for a moment about the food, poured water for each other and threw around ideas for their next book club read. Meggie felt like she was melting into the background, disappearing into herself.

She sensed eyes on her and looked at Debbie. A tingle of *recognition* ran up her spine. Her eyes widened, then Debbie began to speak.

'Before we finish for the night, I'm glad you're all here because there's something I want to tell you. Need to tell you.' She looked at Rose. 'Only Rose knows, but you'll understand why.' She took a deep breath. 'I'm pregnant. Twelve weeks.'

When her eyes met Meggie's again, they were bright with tears. 'You know I'd been told, after Warwick, that I shouldn't have any more. Too dangerous, the pre-eclampsia affected my kidney function and it's possible it will be worse next time. This time.' She took a shuddering breath and Meggie watched Rose move closer, her hand on Debbie's back. 'We were looking into adoption. But. Well. I'm pregnant.'

Debbie sat back. The others were silent, surprised more than shocked, but trying to process what this would mean for Debbie. Rose spoke first. 'Yes, it's a high-risk pregnancy. For Debbie and the little one.' She patted Debbie's tummy, and the tension left the room. 'And Debbie will be monitored, closely, through every stage.' She looked at Harriet. 'It might mean an early delivery too. But so far all is well.'

A tear coursed down Debbie's cheek. 'There's more. It was hard to tell Jamie. Initially he wanted me to consider.' Meggie watched Debbie struggle to find the words. 'To consider *not* having the baby. But we're past that now. We're together in this. Now.'

Meggie's own cheeks were wet, but when she looked at her friends, this group of women she'd grown to love, she saw others crying too. And laughing. And hugging Debbie and each other.

8

FRANCES

Frances turned the kitchen light off and padded to the bedroom. Douglas had fallen asleep, his glasses still on his face. She removed them gently, and the book he was holding, and placed them carefully on the bedside table.

Sitting on the edge of the bed on her own side, she picked up the tin of Miracle Balm she'd bought from Ayla, the region's Bee Whisperer. She loved the smell of lemon grass that emanated from it and rubbed it thoroughly into the backs of her hands. She peered at them, certain the balm was making them *look less old*.

As she replaced the tin on her bedside table, she saw the book she'd been reading. *Apples Never Fall*. She frowned at it. Not even finished, it was a struggle and she seemed to need to re-read every other chapter. *Just not for her*. She pushed it to one side, almost disdainfully, clicked off the lamp and lay back.

Her eyes flew open. *Book Club! It was Book Club tonight and she'd forgotten. She'd promised Rose she'd be there!*

Brow wrinkled in concentration, Frances brought one hand closer to her face, inhaling the scent of the balm. Strange. *She never forgot anything.*

9

———

DRUM

D RUM ROLLED OVER AND REACHED FOR H ARRIET. Tentacles of early morning sunlight slithered through the shutters, and he cracked one eye open. Harriet's side was empty, but still warm. Probably in the bathroom. Five months pregnant, she was healthy and fit and thankfully no longer experiencing the pain she'd had in the first weeks.

He lay on his back, one arm behind his head, contemplating the day. He had a meeting at Council this morning. If he timed it right, he could drive in with Harriet and they could have lunch together when he was done.

The bathroom door swung open and a cloud steam issued forth. Drum rose on one elbow, and saw Harriet standing naked in the doorway, in silhouette, one hand proudly on her baby bump.

'You look beautiful.' The words caught in his throat. *So Beautiful.* He rose from the bed and padded towards her, as naked as she was. Bending down, he kissed her gently, and placed his hand over hers, on her tummy.

'Peanut is busy this morning.' She giggled as the baby gave their hands a nudge. He wished just then that time would stand still. This moment was as perfect as any he could imagine.

'Want to join me?' she cocked an eyebrow, then jerked her head toward the bathroom's steaming interior, her face alight with mischief.

Wrapping his arms around her, he chuckled, deep in his throat. 'We've had rain, but Harri, really, we should still conserve water.' He backed her into the bathroom, closing the door with his foot.

———

TWENTY MINUTES LATER HE WAS DRESSED AND HELPING Billie with breakfast. They were eating porridge when Harriet bounced in, stopping to drop a kiss on the top of Billie's head before helping herself to yogurt and berries.

'Harri! Dad wants me to catch the bus today, but you said yesterday you'd drop me to school!' Billie's voice rose on the last words and Drum was surprised. It had never seemed to bother Billie which way she arrived at school. Until today.

He shot Harriet a quick look, but she was focussed on Billie. 'I can still drop you Billie, but is there a reason you don't want to catch the bus?'

Billie looked down and shook her head, her mass of sun-kissed curls bouncing on her shoulders, saying quietly. 'No. It's just that you said ...'

'Finish your porridge and I'll pack your lunch box. Then brush your teeth and bring me your hairbrush. Plaits today?' Harriet's words were warm, matching her smile, and Billie's young shoulders seemed to relax. He still didn't know what *that* was about.

Drum admired the way Harriet managed Billie. Always calm, always loving. Twenty minutes later they dropped Billie at school, with Harriet stepping out of the car to ensure she had everything. He watched Billie give her a quick hug before running inside the school grounds, having spotted her friend Tiffany.

'Any idea what that was about this morning? She's never whinged about the bus.' Drum slowed at the corner, then drove on towards Harriet's office.

'I think she's getting a bit nervous about the baby. About it taking my, no, *our* attention. She needs reassurance.' Harriet lightly touched his arm. 'Her mum was pregnant when she left Billie with you, perhaps she thinks we'll do something like that. Send her back to her mum. I don't know for sure, she hasn't said.'

'Oh.' He sat for a moment, now stopped at the back of Harriet's building. 'Yes, of course.' He turned to Harriet. 'We need to include her more.'

He saw her smile falter, and she looked away for a moment. 'I know. I've been reluctant to, you know, really get her excited about Peanut.' Her hand automatically rested on her bump as she turned back to him, and her eyes seemed over-large, and wet with unshed tears. 'In case, you know, in case ...' She couldn't finish the words.

Resting his large hand over her small one, he smiled. 'I was the same Harri, but you're doing so well. You look great. Peanut is a little bit small but still growing. I vote we stop worrying about the worst possibility and start looking forward to the best.' Her smile told him she was beginning to feel they could do this too. Go all the way with Peanut.

'Then *I vote* we start setting up the nursery this weekend, and I'll ask Billie to help, get her involved in the planning.' She lifted an eyebrow. 'And maybe some painting.'

He mock-groaned. But inside he was excited. Yes, they'd start on the nursery.

10

ROSE

October – Barrington Book Club – Meeting 2
Present: Debbie, Rose, Meggie, Harriet, Melanie, Frances, Nicole
Apologies: Laura
Book: *The Quarantine Station* by Michelle Montebello

'WHO WANTS TO START? I READ IT WHEN IT WAS FIRST released in twenty nineteen but reading it again this month was a revelation.' Rose picked up her cup, tentatively sipping the chamomile tea, glancing at the others over the rim.

Frances cleared her throat and Rose smiled at her. 'Do you want to start Frances?'

'Me? Oh. No. Um, I did read it.' Rose thought Frances seemed flustered, which surprised her. 'But as this is my first book club I'd rather someone else go first.' Frances smiled, and a myriad of tiny lines appeared around her eyes. Rose wasn't sure how old Frances was but assumed early sixties. A petite woman, she always looked stylish and tonight she was wearing a cream silk blouse under a Chanel-esq navy jacket with burgundy trim and fitted navy pants, with low heels. She'd worked with husband Douglas in his law practice since they'd married and Rose wondered, for a moment, if they were edging towards retirement.

'I'll start.' Meggie tapped the cover of the book in front of her. 'One of my favourites. Love the dual timelines and I'm impressed by the research the author undertook to get this right. And the absolute power of the matron! Gosh, how strict were the rules for staff there one hundred years ago?'

'And the mystery with Emma's grandmother in the current timeline. I did not guess the ending. At all.' Harriet chimed in on Meggie's last words.

Several people spoke at once then. Rose let them go. It seemed all had read the complete book and had something to say.

Nicole had entered a lively discussion with Melanie and Debbie about the role of women in the early nineteen hundreds, and how arrivals were treated quite differently, depending on class. 'And I thought Australia was classless.' Meggie and Harriet were still discussing the author's research.

Rose turned back to Frances, who hadn't said much. 'What about you Frances? How did you rate this one?'

'I loved it and read it really quickly.' Frances glanced around the table, as the other conversations ended, and they were all listening attentively. She drew her copy of the book toward her. 'I found it easier to keep up, um, with the jump between timelines, by reading big chunks at once.' She smiled at Rose. 'I even read a few bits out to Douglas and we're going to do the tour of the Quarantine Station next time we're in Sydney. Absolutely fascinating.'

'We were just saying that too.' Meggie nudged Harriet with

her shoulder. 'Harri has an appointment with her specialist in two weeks and I've offered to drive her.' She grinned at Harriet. 'It clashes with a Council meeting for Drum.' Their laughter was infectious, and Rose laughed loudly, before leaning forward, an intense pain in her chest.

Meggie was instantly at her side. 'Rose! Rose! What is it? Do you have pain?' Rose tried to breathe through her nose for a moment, waving Meggie back. The pain resided. She looked around at her friends' faces, also registering concern.

Rose tried to laugh, then held her chest again. 'It's. Heartburn. Just heartburn.' She tried taking a few more breaths. 'Bubba gets up under my ribs. Been happening for two weeks or so.' She saw their faces relax. They were nodding to each other and recounting their own experiences with pregnancy and heartburn. Standing helped, so she got up and paced about in front of the table for a moment.

'Hang on.' Debbie was laughing, holding her own bump. 'Bubba? That's new.'

'Wee Charlie is calling he or she Bubba. I think the name has stuck. Angus and I are doing it now, too.' Rose sighed, walked a few more steps then returned to the table.

Harriet rubbed her belly. 'This one is Peanut. No idea what we'll do if it sticks after birth.' More laughter, then they looked at Melanie.

'Bronte.' Melanie grinned. 'I was going to tell you all tonight anyway. We're having a girl, and our favourite name is Bronte. Once we told Tiff, there was no going back.'

'Adore Bronte. Good choice Melanie.' Nicole grinned at Debbie. 'Does yours have a name yet?' Rose saw a soft flush infuse Debbie's face and drew closer.

'Did you just blush, Debbie Tait?' Rose looked at the others. 'Now I have to know what you call him. Or her.'

'It's a Jamie-thing. He's convinced it's a boy. And so far we have no complications, my doctor says this pregnancy looks fine. Normal. Uncomplicated.' Her eyes shone and Rose felt a tear of happiness slide down her own face.

'Really? That's the best news!' She hugged Debbie as her friend nodded.

Meggie handed them each a tissue. 'Uh huh. That is brilliant.' She narrowed her eyes. 'but the name, Debbie. You didn't tell us the name.'

Rose laughed with the others. 'You *have* to tell us now, Deb.'

Debbie giggled. 'Well, it started as Tiger.' They chuckled. 'Then it became Tenacious Tiger as the pregnancy progressed. And now it's TeeTee.' Exasperated, she sighed. 'For Tenacious Tiger.' Her hand was resting on her bump.

'TeeTee. Cute.' Rose smirked and Debbie poked her tongue out. 'It's no worse than Bubba. And let's face it girlfriend, probably less likely to stick, after it's born.'

Nicole chuckled, then looked at her watch. 'I need to get home, but this has been lovely. I've always been a big reader, but it's really nice to do it this way and chat about it after. Even better to get together and have some laughs, thank you.' She shook her head. 'Lucy reads a lot too, but at the moment it's all Hunger Games and such, which I admit, doesn't really float my boat.' They grinned, although Rose heard Meggie say quietly; *love the Hunger Games.*

'I'll be off too. Thank you, such a lovely night out.' Frances gathered her things. Debbie walked Frances and Nicole to the door, then returned, her face expectant.

'What about you? Staying a bit longer? I can make another hot drink.' Debbie was glowing and Rose was relieved her friend's pregnancy was proceeding without problems.

'I can stay.' Rose checked her watch. 'Is it wrong to want to stay until I'm sure Angus has put Charlie to bed?' She tried to look serious. 'Asking for a friend.'

'I have to stay, if you're staying.' Debbie wiped a tear from her eye, mid-laugh. 'I have to lock up.' In a stage whisper she added, 'And Woz will be tucked up by then too.'

"I'll stay if we can have another chocolate brownie.' Harriet smacked her lips together, eyes twinkling.

'Done.' Debbie returned with a slab of brownie and a knife and proceeded to just hack off pieces as required. Through a mouth full of brownie, she mumbled, 'Cathy's going to kill me, this is for tomorrow.'

Relaxed, they talked quietly together. Harriet about her upcoming appointment with the specialist, which should provide an idea of how long she could carry the baby, and about the conversation with Billie. Rose was glad she'd brought it up. Harriet's outcome was far from certain, but each week that passed provided more hope.

Meggie spoke quietly. 'Billie needs to be part of your pregnancy journey too, Harri. To celebrate the coming baby, bond with he or she from the very start.'

'I know Meggs. But we want to protect her from.' Harriet looked away, took a breath and returned her gaze to her friends. 'From the possibility of there *not being a baby*, at the end of this.' One hand was curled protectively over her tummy, and she reached over to Meggie with the other.

Meggie took Harriet's hand. 'If the worst happens Harri, and I pray it doesn't, Billie will need to grieve too. You can't protect her from this, but by including her, she can share your grief and recover with you. If you don't include her, she will be confused and upset anyway.'

'Wise words Meggie.' Rose gave her a nod of approval. Harriet also nodded, taking it in. *Good.*

What Meggie said next, surprised Rose. 'Rose knows this, and Max and Angus, but I've never shared with anyone else. Not even my mother.' Meggie paused then, and Rose was going to slide closer, but Harriet still had hold of Meggie's hand, her face registering surprise.

'I lost a baby at five months gestation, two years ago. It's one of the reasons I came home.' Tears began to fall, but Meggie continued. Bravely, Rose thought. 'It was a little girl. The father wasn't.' She stopped, dabbed at her eyes. With a napkin. 'Wasn't in the picture. Grieving by yourself is hard and I hope none of you ever experience this.' She sniffed, blew her nose, and gave Rose a watery smile. 'Coming to Barrington, sharing this with Angus and Rose, gave me strength.'

The other women seemed to move closer to Meggie then, almost circling her. *Circling the wagons, that's what friends do.* They murmured words of consolation, friendship and acknowledged Meggie's loss. Rose was crying unashamedly. *Damn pregnancy hormones.*

Meggie sat a little bit straighter then and smiled through her tears. 'And now I'm going to tell you something else, and it's really stupid of me to do this right now.' She squeezed Harriet's hand, then let go.

'You all know I want to have a baby with Max. We're not married yet, and we've only just moved into our new place. We decided a couple of months ago that we wouldn't *try* for a baby. Instead, we would stop trying *not* to have a baby. And last month, at book club, I was late. Only a day or two.' She held up her hand as the women began to speak. 'And I got my period that night. Sitting here. I felt it. Knew we hadn't made a baby.' Rose saw the others nod. They all knew that feeling.

'And this month I'm late again. Three days late. And I didn't want to feel like I did at the last book club.' Looking at the others Meggie added, 'I'm sorry, but once I got that dragging feeling in my lower back last time, I just wanted to go home. Wanted to cry.'

Rose waited, almost holding her breath. She was sure there was more.

'So I did a test. Just before I left home tonight. I wasn't sure if it would register. Anything.' Meggie's face lit up and Rose's tummy flipped over. 'But I am. Pregnant. And I haven't even told Max and its silly to tell you because, you know, it's so early. But there you have it.'

I hope it holds. I pray it holds. Rose looked around at her friends, laughing, crying and hugging each other. *But if it doesn't we're here for her. For each other. These women.* Rose felt her chest expand. Happiness could do that.

11

LITTLE BEN

BEN CLICKED THE PHONE AND COCKED AN EYEBROW AT Melanie. 'That was Dad. They're in Broome, *riding camels*. I'm not sure whether I should be happy for him, or worried.' He returned to the sofa, stretched his legs out and took another sip of beer. 'Don't get me wrong, I'm all for him travelling, and the whole thing with Laura.'

'Then what is it?'

He leaned his head back and gazed at the ceiling for a moment. 'it's making me think about the future. More specifically, about the business if he cuts back, takes more time off.' He looked at his wife. At six months she was glowing. Not so big yet that she looked awkward, and still in that radiant, healthy phase. 'He's past retirement age, but I've never seriously considering him actually doing it. Retiring. But now, I can see that he's *thinking* about it.' He sat up. 'You know he asked me to consider running for Council in the new year just before he left on this trip. Said he won't stand again.'

'He didn't say, but I thought he might.' Melanie snuggled against him. 'What does it look like, the business I mean, if your dad retires or takes extended leave?'

'I'm there, of course. But you know I like the stock and station side of real estate. More than residential. And he's on the Chamber of Commerce and does all the town and community engagement. I mean, there's Harriet, but she's busy with the new venture with Meggie. She still oversees the property management and thank goodness she set up great systems, it's less staff intensive.'

Melanie moved away from him, and he missed her warmth, for a moment. 'I'm going to tell Tiffany to turn her light out, it's almost nine and she's still reading. I'll put the jug on so we can have a cuppa and chat a bit more.' Melanie was already at the living room door as she said the last words.

Ben strolled into the kitchen, turned on the jug and began making the tea. Melanie had been having a concoction of lemon juice, honey and hot water in the evenings lately. He'd just have a tea bag, no point making a pot just for himself.

He heard her come in but was concentrating on the honey and almost dropped the teaspoon when she pressed up against him from behind, winding her arms around his waist.

'Hey you.' He dropped the honey filled teaspoon into the cup and turned around. On a whim he picked her up, sitting her on the kitchen counter. He dropped a kiss on her mouth. 'Should I go and say goodnight to Tiffany?'

'No, she was asleep with the book in her hand.' Melanie chuckled, shaking her head. 'Do you think you'll need some support in the office. Another sales agent? Or property manager?' He watched her nibble her bottom lip. He was done with talking, wanted to pick her up and carry her to bed, but he could see she had more to say. 'I could help a bit, you know, with admin and such.'

'You're the best Mel, thank you. But no. You love working at the Vet clinic and the hours suit you. And you know Angus and Max will be flexible when the baby comes.' Shaking his head, Ben continued. 'No, as much as I'd love to have you in our business, I think staying where you are, at least for now, is best. And I've said this before Mel. You don't *have* to work. We don't need the wage.' He lifted her down and finished making the tea, handing her a steaming cup.

Back on the sofa he was rewarded with a smile. 'I love the clinic, I really do. And you know I like having a bit of financial independence too.' She sipped her cup, screwed up her nose. 'Very lemony.'

He reached for the cup. 'I can add more honey.'

She closed her eyes and sipped again. 'It's fine. What are you thinking? For the business?'

He returned his focus. 'I'll talk to Dad when he gets back, but I was thinking about a trainee. Maybe someone who's done a bit of marketing and business, you know, a certificate or diploma. If we found someone before Harriet takes maternity leave, she could train them in the systems we have.'

Melanie put her cup down, now half empty. 'I think you need to think more broadly Ben. It's not just *your* business. The Vet clinic will need help while I'm on maternity leave. I think they've been talking to young Freddie Campbell, she's in her second year of Vet Science and if the timing is right she could work from December until March next year. But I've also been wondering about Debbie and the café. Cathy and the other staff are great, but it will need some management too.'

'I'll ask Dad to call me in the next few days. And I'll speak to Angus and Max, and Debbie. Actually, the Chamber should do an audit of local job opportunities. Perhaps we can run a bit of an employment promotion for town for the summer period.'

'Hmmm, good idea.' Melanie nestled into his side again. He placed his cup on the coffee table, scooped his wife into his arms, and walked through to their room. Business could wait.

12

DEBBIE

'How long are you going to work Deb?' She spun around at Jamie's words. He had little Warwick in his arms, and she reached for him, holding his wriggling body close for a moment. He was a miniature version of Jamie, in jeans and tee shirt. The mornings were becoming warmer.

'Chooks.' Her son pointed to Jamie, who held six eggs in his upturned hat.

'He was awake, so we went to collect the eggs while you finished in the bathroom.' Stepping inside, he kissed her on the mouth, looking at her intently. 'How are you feeling?'

She didn't answer his first question, wanted to understand his motivation for *that* one, first. 'I'm great, but I think I'm in that *nesting* phase. I've got a long list of things to do at the café today, but I'm also keen to set the single bed up for Woz and get the smaller room ready for the baby.' She saw Jamie's face break into a grin as he set the eggs on the kitchen counter.

Taking Warwick from her arms, he replied. 'I can set the bed up for this one.' He ruffled his son's hair, causing him to giggle and squirm, before putting him down. 'And move the cot into the little room. Do you want to paint it first? You mentioned that a while ago.'

'Not sure. It's a neutral colour.' She stepped closer, rewarded by his arm around her waist, his large hand rubbing the small of her back. 'Are you sure you don't want to know? The gender? I'd have more confidence painting the room if we knew.'

Drawing her into a hug, he seemed to think about it for a moment. 'No. Everything is going so well. Don't jinx it.' He released her and scooped Warwick under his arm, galloping him from the room. 'Let's wash our hands mate, then breakfast.' Over his shoulder he called out to her. 'I promised dippy eggs, can you put a couple on please love?'

A sense of contentment filled her soul, as she put the eggs to boiling on the stovetop and cut some bread for toast. Just minutes later they were back, and Warwick was in his high chair. She placed a finger of vegemite toast in front of him, the eggs had another minute to go.

'I was speaking with Ben yesterday, Deb. Bumped into him at Rocky Crossing. It seems Big Ben and Laura are still travelling, taking longer than planned. He thinks his dad is hinting at retirement.' Jamie put another finger of toast in front of their son.

'Really?' Debbie was surprised. 'I've never imagined Big Ben doing anything but running the business. He's an institution in this town.'

Jamie chuckled. 'Yup. He is. He also told Ben he wouldn't run for Council in the new year. Wants Ben to run instead.' Debbie put the eggs on the table, along with the egg cups and more toast already cut into fingers.

'Little Ben is ready. He's as well known, and respected, as his dad. He gets my vote.' Debbie sat with them, taking the top off an egg for Warwick and letting it cool for a moment.

'Mine too.' Jamie appeared thoughtful and Debbie knew better than to press him. They ate in silence for a moment, Warwick happily dipping his toast into the soft-boiled egg. She poured tea for Jamie. She still liked a coffee in the mornings and would wait until she got to the café.

'Actually Deb, Ben mentioned something else, and it's got me thinking. He wants to catch up with you and perhaps have a get together with Angus, Max and Harriet too. We could get your mum to mind Woz and maybe arrange a dinner at the pub later this week, what do you think?' Jamie scooped the last of the egg out for Warwick, then took the top off another one for him.

'I'm keen to have dinner at the pub with the gang anytime. But you've lost me. What else did Ben mention.' She laughed.

'His dad is already away from the office a lot, retirement or not, and Ben is concerned about staffing. Harriet is due before you, but could go early, and she handles some of the property management stuff. And Meggie is flat out building the new business.' He chewed his toast for a moment. 'And Melanie taking maternity leave around the same time will affect the clinic, although Angus and Max are already talking to young Freddie Campbell to help out.'

'Of course. It's fabulous we're having our babies close together, but I totally get it, we'll all have to make changes in our businesses.' Debbie sat back. She was almost five months now, and still working every day. She'd planned to cut back on her hours at the café, but really hadn't put anything in place yet. 'Where has the time gone? I need to talk to Cathy and arrange extra staff too.

Summer is always busy, and in the past we've managed to get young people home on their university break to help out.' She frowned.

'I know Deb. You've got such a good handle on your business, I never interfere.' He walked over to the sink, picked up a wash cloth and returned, wiping Warwick's hands and face before lifting him out of the high chair. She watched her son run to the toy chest in the corner, where he lifted out a tip truck and began pushing it across the kitchen floor.

'But?' She waited for Jamie to articulate what was on his mind. But she could see where he was going.

'After *Tiger* arrives, do you want to continue working the same hours? I'll be guided by you love, but it might be nice for you to have a bit more time at home.' She saw him look fondly at Warwick. Jamie was great with him, and both their mums helped too. He'd be going to day care in the new year. But yes, sometimes she did feel she was missing out. Missing important milestones.

'I'm a bit embarrassed actually.' She sniffed, suddenly close to tears. Jamie was by her side in an instant. 'I haven't really thought it through. The baby, Woz and the business.' She turned to him, pressing her face into his shoulder. He made soothing noises and rubbed her back.

'It's your call Debbie. Let's have this pub dinner with the others. You're all in small business, talking it through might help to decide how you'll each operate through the next six months, maybe longer.'

She smiled through her tears. 'I love you Jamie Tait.' He wiped the tears from her cheek with his thumb. 'You have always trusted me to run the café my way. No pressure, no judgement.' She sighed. 'I'm so bloody lucky.'

'Bluddy lukky.' Warwick had toddled over to them. Looking at each other, they laughed. Jamie sat on the chair next to Debbie and pulled Warwick onto his lap. 'We don't say those words mate.'

Warwick nodded, squirmed to get down, then ran around the kitchen shouting, 'bluddy, bluddy, bluddy!'

13

MEGGIE

MEGGIE WAS RUSHING AROUND THE HOUSE, PUTTING the dishwasher on and hanging out the wash. Tommy had come to breakfast in school shorts with a torn pocket and a large green-brown smear down one leg. She'd asked him to change and had thrown a few things in the wash. She laughed to herself. Just in case the shorts he'd changed into came home from school in the same state today. *Boys.*

Picking up the basket, only half-full, Meggie carried it out through the laundry door to the clothesline. She adored their new home, and looked skyward, as she had done on many occasions, silently thanking Fred Saunders for offering them first option to buy it. She could hear the chickens scratching around on the other side of the hedge, but she knew Max had fed them before he took Tommy to school, on the way to the clinic.

Humming to herself, she reached down into the basket, then stopped. A sudden queasy feeling made her head spin, for one brief moment. About six weeks pregnant, so far there'd been no real morning sickness. Hanging the last pieces, she picked up the basket in one hand. Her tummy lurched again, but she ignored it. *Normal pregnancy stuff.* She returned the basket to the laundry and locked the outer door.

Back in the kitchen, Meggie checked she'd done everything, then reached for her handbag. *Damn, now she needed to pee. Again.* But she was excited to be pregnant at last and frequent peeing was only a small inconvenience.

As she sat on the toilet, her tummy flipped again, and she frowned. *Too early to feel baby movement.* She looked down, then whimpered. Her heart sank. There was blood in her underwear. Bright red blood. Hands shaking she turned her head, looked over her shoulder into the bowl. Blood. A lot of blood. Her earlier energy left her, and she sat there, slumped on the toilet with her head in her hands and cried, as the new little life drained from her body.

14

ROSE

November – Barrington Book Club – Meeting 3
Present: Debbie, Rose, Harriet, Melanie, Frances, Nicole
Apologies: Laura, Meggie?
Book: *The Stationmaster's Cottage* by Phillipa Nefri Clark

ROSE WAS FIRST TO THE CAFÉ AND HELPED DEBBIE SET up. She'd had a great day writing, Angus had worked form home and taken Charlie with him to move cattle to another paddock. Seeing him sitting on the saddle in front of Angus made her heart melt. He had no fear of the horses. Or the dogs and cattle for that matter.

Melanie, Frances and Nicole walked in together, chatting about the warmth of the day and the likelihood of rain later in the week. After quick hellos, they gathered around their usual table.

'Is anyone else reading more than usual?' Melanie sat down, smiled at the others, then pulled her kindle from her bag. 'I usually read two to three a month, but since we've started book club I'm reading one a week.' She opened her kindle, turning it so the others could see. 'And I've found more books by Michelle Montebello, last month's author. She has a series of romance-slash-women's-fiction that I'm loving.'

'Tell me their titles, I'll see if I can get them on my iPad.' Nicole peered at Melanie's kindle, then took a photo of it with her phone. 'Thanks Nicole.'

Debbie brought drinks to the table. 'Laura is back later this week, she's an apology.' She looked up as Harriet arrived. 'Is Meggie coming separately?'

'No. She didn't come in today. Said she was unwell and would work from home.' Harriet smiled. 'I think she's finally got some morning sickness. Now she can suffer with the rest of us.'

'Not me. No morning sickness.' Rose looked smug. 'Nothing to speak of anyway.'

'Honestly Rose, don't look so smug. You've had heartburn.' Debbie nudged her.

'Oh yeah. I do get heartburn, mostly when I go to bed. I'm sleeping half-sitting-up.' The others began chatting about their pregnancy symptoms.

'Every pregnancy is different. Lucy was small, I hardly showed until seven months.' Nicole reached for a piece of carrot and walnut cake, taking a big bite. 'So good Debbie! I need to send Lucy in for this recipe.'

Debbie spun around. 'How old is Lucy now, Nicole? She's a great little cook herself.'

'Fourteen next month. Loves cooking, and she's quite creative too. She's talking about being a chef or interior designer. She's really got an eye for design, probably better hours than cooking.' Nicole flushed. 'Sorry Debbie, I didn't mean ...'

Debbie waved Nicole's words away. 'I'm lucky that there's been no real need to open after five. The pubs and other restaurants get that trade. And Cathy always opens for me early in the mornings, she likes to get the baking done, then leave after the lunch rush. It doesn't always have to be unsociable hours.' Debbie slid a plate of assorted slices towards Nicole. 'But I have a reason for asking.'

'Really?' Nicole leaned forward and Rose wondered where Debbie was going with this.

'Do you think Lucy would like some hours over the summer break? Working here? I'm going to cut my own hours back a bit, and I'm beginning to think about staff arrangements.' Debbie patted her baby bump.

Nicole seemed hesitant. 'I think she'd love it Debbie. But she's very shy, with strangers. I know she'd enjoy working in the kitchen, and maybe learning to make coffee, but serving at the counter would challenge her. At least in the beginning.'

'I think she'd be great in the kitchen, cooking with Cathy. And yes, we could train her in coffee and have her clear tables and such, once she was comfortable.' Debbie looked Nicole in the eye. 'We'd look after her Nik. Can you ask her if she's interested to have a talk with me? Bring her in after school one day if she's keen.'

'Thank you, I will, I'll ask her tonight.' Nicole beamed, then looked around and made an eeek-face. 'Actually, she keeps asking if she can come to book club. But I've put her off. This.' She waved her arm around indicating the others at the table. 'This is just for me. My time. With grown up friends. Best. Idea. Ever.'

The others smiled, nodded and laughed in agreement. Rose felt the same. These women, this one night a month. Just for her too.

'It's been years since I've had a regular night out, like this.' Frances spoke quietly, and Rose turned to her. 'Working with Douglas for more than thirty-five years means we're always together. It's lovely. He's lovely.' She smiled then and her face broke into lots of little creases. 'But last month, laughing with you all, it was a tonic. A real tonic.'

'We love that you join us Frances.' Rose squeezed the older woman's hand briefly and saw Frances' face flush with pleasure.

Harriet pushed her plate aside and lay her book on the table. 'Did everyone finish? I devoured it in a couple of days, then I was cross that I hadn't made it last. So Good. I'm looking for more stories with dual timelines now.'

'Me too. I fell in love with Thomas and all the small-town characters. And the dog, Randall. He had a whole personality of his own.' Debbie spoke quickly, waving her hands around as she did. Rose loved seeing such genuine enthusiasm for a story.

'I was sort of confused about how Christie could fall for the other guy. The bad guy. I forget his name. She's such a smart, talented girl!' Frances furrowed her brow.

'I think he was only just starting to show his true colours, his selfishness, when her grandmother died. And she'd had a difficult childhood. Sometimes women hang on to a perception of their partner, without seeing the reality. I get it.' Rose flicked through her book. 'And if you're a person that wouldn't do underhand, illegal or immoral things yourself, you're less likely to believe that others might. I think we all view others through a prism of our own values, at least to begin with.'

'*A prism of our own values.* I like that Rose Gordon-Hamilton. You should be a writer.' Debbie giggled at her own joke and put a hand to her forehead, laughing.

'Stop it.' But Rose was pleased to hear Debbie's words. *Yes, I am a writer.* 'I really enjoyed this book, and there's more of these. She's turned it into a series. I'm halfway through the second one.' Rose pulled a second book from her bag, passed it across to Debbie, who turned to the back cover, reading the blurb aloud. Nicole snapped a photo of the cover.

The conversation flowed, all had read the book quickly. Rose enjoyed listening to the different perceptions of the group, as readers. Maybe she would get them to read her current work-in-progress for book club, when it's released in the new year. It would be good to hear their feedback. *And a little bit scary.*

15

HARRIET

When Meggie wasn't in the office again the next day, Harriet wondered if she should call, but didn't want her to feel compelled to come to work if she was suffering from morning sickness. She decided to send a message after work, just to check in.

The day sped by. Harriet was writing a procedures manual for the property management functions for Evans Real Estate. She wanted to be organised in case her baby came early. She wasn't sure what might trigger an early delivery and so far she'd been fine. Some small discomfort, but when she thought about it, less than in the first few weeks.

Tummy rumbling, Harriet checked her fit-watch. Almost noon, but by the time she walked down to the café it would be twelve. She was finding it was better to eat more frequent small meals than three large ones.

Tote bag in hand, Harriet strolled down the street, the midday sun warm on her face. She caught a glimpse of her reflection in several shop windows and smiled inwardly. She really was starting to pop out. And not just her tummy. Her booty looked bigger too. *Hope that returns to normal when Peanut arrives.*

After ordering a chai latte and quiche Harriet asked the café staff where Debbie was. 'Taking a day off Harriet. She said Jamie was going to paint the baby's room and she needed to supervise.' Cathy grinned as she spoke. 'It's been so busy lately, she deserves a day off.'

'Of course. I don't know how she does it, on her feet all day.' Harriet looked down. 'I think mine are beginning to swell. A combination of baby and warmer weather, I expect.'

A table near the footpath was available, just out of the sun. Harriet strolled over, staking her claim. Engrossed in a message on her phone from her parents, Harriet was startled when Angus spoke.

'Angus! Sorry, I was miles away. What did you say?' She smiled up at him.

'I asked if I could join you. Cathy's making me some lunch.' Harriet saw him hesitate. 'But if you're busy ...'

'No, not at all. Please join me. Mum and Dad are travelling at the moment, sending really bad selfies.' She held her phone out. 'What do you think that thing is?' Harriet giggled, the picture was out of focus and there was a furry little creature in the foreground, her mum in the background and part of her dad's legs.

Angus drew out a chair and sat, while studying the phone. He raised his eyebrows. 'I think they're in Western Australia. On Rottnest Island.' He handed the phone back.

'How did you know that?' Harriet studied the picture again. 'Oh! Now I see. That's a quokka.' She snorted. 'It looks huge from that angle. But yes, you're right, that's exactly where they are.'

Laying her phone down, she shook her head with mock sadness, 'My parents are really bad photographers. Really bad.'

Angus laughed loudly. 'They really are.'

Their drinks arrived and Angus checked his watch. 'I've been flat-out today, Max hasn't been in for two days.'

Harriet's ears pricked at his words. 'Did he say why? I'm asking because Meggie hasn't been in either. And she missed book club last night.' A knot of worry formed in her chest.

'Max called yesterday just after dropping Tommy at school. Said Meggie was unwell, and he was heading home. I didn't ask any questions. I'm a bloke, we don't go there.' Angus leaned back as a steak sandwich was set before him, and the quiche and salad in front of Harriet. His expression sobered. 'But maybe I should mention it to Rose? She can call Meggie.'

'Let me, I'll finish here, then call her.' Harriet cut into the quiche, then closed her eyes for a second. 'So tasty.'

'Yep, Debbie has this place running well. The food's consistently good and the service is quick and friendly, even when they're flat out.' Angus gazed around for a moment. The café had filled up while they'd been talking. 'Has Ben spoken to you about having a pub meal together to talk about staffing, later this week? The clinic, real estate office and café will all be affected when your babies arrive.' He waggled his eyebrows. 'Did you girls plan this?'

'Ha, ha Angus Hamilton. You know we didn't, but any excuse for a pub meal with the gang is good for me.' Harriet grinned at him. She was happy their babies would be close, even happier that her own pregnancy had been trouble free. She frowned then, thinking about Meggie. She wasn't sure if Angus knew his sister was pregnant.

As if he could read her mind, Angus leaned in, his voice

lowered. 'I know about Meggie. Max hasn't said much, but it's obvious he's excited. He did tell me that Tommy and Indiana don't know yet.' Angus furrowed his brow. 'Given Meggie's history, I think that's wise.'

Harriet met his eyes then and paled. Perhaps it wasn't morning sickness at all. She pushed her plate away, her quiche only half-eaten. 'Angus, will you excuse me? I'm going to drive out to see Meggie. I need to check on her.' Sudden tears filled her eyes and Angus stood when she did.

'Should I call Rose? Ask her to drop by too?' He caught her meaning straight away and his eyes darkened, his concern obvious.

Harriet shook her head. 'I'll call Rose. Once I've seen Meggie.'

Angus wrapped an arm around her shoulders, quickly giving a light squeeze. 'Thank you Harriet. But I hope our concern is unfounded.'

———

'I'm sorry Harriet, Meggie's resting at the moment.' Max spoke quietly as he opened the front door when Harriet knocked. He stepped outside and closed it gently behind him.

'Max?' Harriet searched his face. He looked weary. And sad.

'Meggie will tell you herself Harriet, but yes, we lost the baby.' Harriet wanted to hug him then, comfort him, but he wrapped his arms around himself as he spoke.

'I'm so sorry Max, please tell Meggie that.' Harriet touched his arm briefly. 'Is there anything I can do? Perhaps Rose and I ...' She was searching for the right words, hoping to offer support.

He shook his head. 'I called Angus just now. Melanie will pick

Tommy up after school again and keep him for a sleepover.' He sighed. 'I'm going on instinct here Harriet. I don't really know what I should do, but being by ourselves a second night seems best.'

'I'm sure your instincts are spot on Max.' Harriet stepped back then, suddenly feeling like an intruder. 'I'll message Meggie in the morning, see if she wants to talk, or catch up.' She blinked a couple of times, not wanting to cry. Max had enough to deal with. 'And there's no pressure. Whenever she's ready. I'm here. Rose too. All of us. Whatever she needs, we're here for her. And you Max.'

Max lunged forward suddenly, and hugged Harriet tightly for just a moment, before letting her go just as quickly. 'Thank you Harriet, I'll tell her.' He turned, reaching for the doorknob, before speaking again, his voice suddenly hoarse. 'It means a lot, to both of us.' And he was gone, the door quietly closed.

Harriet walked to her car crying. For Meggie and Max, for their loss. She wiped her eyes, then picked up her phone, messaging Rose.

I've just spoken to Max. We need to talk. x

Come straight here Harri. x

16

———

FRANCES

STANDING IN THE BEDROOM, FRANCES PAUSED. *What did she come in here for?* Hesitating for a moment, she sat on the edge of the bed, opened the jewellery box on her bedside table and began systematically removing her wedding, engagement and eternity rings, and then her watch. Lastly she removed the small pearl earrings that had been a wedding present from her parents, placing them all in their usual spots, before closing the lid of the burnished rosewood box, just as she did very night when she got ready for bed.

Humming to herself, she picked up her tin of Miracle Balm and began rubbing it into her fingers and nails. Leaving the tin open on the bed, she looked at the backs of her hands. *When did she get these old-lady-hands, they don't look at all like her own.* She screwed up her nose at them.

Her reverie was broken when Douglas called out to her. 'Frances! Are you almost ready? We'll be late.' He appeared at the door, his face kindly. 'You came in to get a jacket.' He tapped his watch, then smiled. 'Quick love, we need to leave now if we're to be there at six.'

Douglas left the room and Frances stood, suddenly embarrassed. *What was she doing?* She opened the jewellery box and quickly put her rings back on, checking the time on her watch as she did up the clasp. She must have been miles away. It wasn't bedtime. They were going to the pub for dinner with the young ones. She'd been excited about it all day.

Alert now, she finger-combed her hair and gave it a light spray, then dabbed her favourite perfume on her wrists, and with the jacket over her arm she picked up her handbag and hurried from the room.

17

LITTLE BEN

It was such a large group that Ben had booked the small function room at the pub. There were six couples plus Tiffany, Billie and Tommy. Wee Charlie Hamilton and Warwick Tait had been left with Debbie's mother, Rachel.

Melanie had told him about Meggie's loss early in the week, and he hadn't been sure she would make it to the dinner, so he was pleased when Meggie arrived with Max and young Tommy. He thought Meggie looked pale, but she laughed when Tommy read the specials board menu aloud to her and had a lively discussion about what they would choose. Max looked relieved to see Meggie so animated. Ben understood it had been a difficult week for him too.

Douglas and Frances were the last to arrive, and they accepted a glass of wine each as they said their hello's. Melanie, Harriet and Meggie ordered for the children straight away, plus a platter of garlic bread for the adults to share.

Ben cleared his throat and raised his glass. Like most of the men, except Douglas, he was having a beer before their meals arrived. 'I'd like to welcome you all here to this informal meeting of...' He looked around, grinning. 'Something between the chamber of commerce and Barrington book club, with partners.' This raised some smiles and laughter.

'Really, it's great that you all came out tonight. But we'll order our meals first and then throw some ideas around about staffing solutions for the summer.' Ben took a sip and turned to speak to Douglas, but out of the corner of his eye he noticed Meggie lean into Max. Ben hoped the evening might be a distraction for them.

The conversation flowed and Ben, not for the first time, wished his father and Laura had been home in time to join them. As their meals arrived, Angus informed them that he and Max had secured Freddie Campbell as a veterinary intern from December until April. With Melanie's baby due after Christmas, it would give her time off before the baby arrived, as well as after. Freddie had worked with them in her term breaks in previous years and knew the office systems quite well.

'Are you planning to return to work Melanie, once Freddie goes back to uni?' Rose asked the question of Melanie but included Ben and Angus in her gaze.

'I know this sounds a bit nerdy, but I really love my job. I've always been able to work school hours and Angus and Max have been very flexible. Mum would love to look after the baby while I'm working, like she did when Tiff was small.' She lay a hand on Ben's leg under the table. 'And Ben is keen to be a hands-on dad.'

'So the clinic is sorted now that Freddie has confirmed. That's good news.' Ben was excited about the arrival of his first-born, and although he adored Tiffany, his step-daughter, he hadn't been around when she was really small.

Billie, Tommy and Tiffany had finished their meals, and were playing a card game, somewhat noisily, at their end of the table. Drum jerked his head in their direction, saying quietly to the other adults. 'Can they have ice cream tonight? Billie asked on the way in.'

Max laughed. 'Of course.' He turned to his son, saying more loudly. 'Tommy, would you like to go and order ice-cream for the three of you?' He had their attention immediately and they slid out of their chairs, gathering around Max.

'Can I have your card, Dad, to order?' Tommy was taller than the girls and Ben thought he stood a bit straighter as he spoke. He held his hand out to Max.

'No mate, just tell them it's for our table. We'll settle up at the end. The three of you can order over there.' Max put his hand on Tommy's slim shoulder, saying firmly. 'No running inside please.'

The three of them shot across to the servery and the adults chuckled. Drum said, 'Not quite running, but mate, those kids can move when they want to!'

Harriet placed her napkin over her plate. Ben noticed she hadn't eaten all of her meal. They had all worried about Harriet at first, as her medical team advised she might not carry to full term. But she looked happy and healthy to Ben, and Melanie had said she understood Harriet's pregnancy was progressing better than expected.

'I want to keep working, as long as I can. But returning to work will depend more on the baby than me.' Harriet self-consciously touched her baby bump. 'If I go early, Peanut might have to stay in hospital. It's really hard to say, and we'll go to Sydney for the birth, if there's time.' She looked at Ben. 'But our office has the extra issue of Big Ben wanting to retire. And if Little

Ben,' she nodded at him, 'stands for his father's seat on local Council in the new year, then he'll be out of the office more too. I can run the property management side, almost remotely, but we may need someone to help with residential sales.' She turned to Meggie then. 'And don't say you'll step into the breach Meggie, because you're already running Barrington Elopements and it's very heavily booked for the next few months.'

Meggie nodded. 'I agree Harriet, although I can help with the property management if needed, your systems are well set up.' She turned to Ben. 'You must have some thoughts?'

'I've been talking to Dad. I think we're okay with the admin side, thanks to Harriet and you. But we really need another agent. Someone who understands residential sales. The market has been buoyant, and properties are moving quickly. If we're not able to inspect, appraise and list the stock, we'll lose it to other agents in town. I think we'll have to advertise because Harriet's maternity leave isn't the issue for us. We need a long-term solution. And we can't poach a sales agent from one of our competitors, this town is too small to get away with that.' He laughed then.

'You wouldn't do that anyway Ben Evans.' Douglas joined the conversation, his tone jolly as he shook his head at Ben, before looking at Debbie. 'What about you Debbie? What are your thoughts for the café? Can your current team step up to give you some time with your little one?'

Debbie looked at Jamie, then at the others around the table and shook her head. 'I had two days off this week. Partly to get the nursery ready at home, but also to step away and think about the café and what I want for its future.' Ben saw Jamie slide his arm around Debbie's back. 'To be honest, for the first time since I opened the business I realised I wasn't excited to be going to work after my short break. Spending two days at home with Jamie and Woz was, well, nice.' She looked over at Rose. 'Really nice.' She sniffed, and Ben leaned forward, hanging on her words. 'Woz will be at school in a couple of years, and I realise now that I've missed a lot of stuff. Milestones and so on. I've decided I'd like to be a stay-at-home-mum for a this one. For a year at least. Have time with both of them.' She looked at Jamie, then across at Douglas and Frances. 'I need some advice Douglas. Do I hang on to the café and come back to it once Warwick's at school? Or once they're both at school? Cathy loves working with me, and she's great at cooking and ordering and so on, but she really doesn't like the front-of-house side. She doesn't want to be the manager. Do I hire a manager and go in a couple of times a week? Or should I sell the business?'

'Sell?' Rose spoke quite loudly, then covered her mouth with her hand. 'Sorry Deb, but that takes me by surprise. You *love* your business!' Ben saw the others were murmuring too, most of them looking shocked at Debbie's declaration.

'I *do* love my business. It was my dream, and I made it come true. But Rose, I love my family more.' Debbie wiped a tear from her eye. Ben was surprised, but totally understood her reasoning.

Douglas took his glasses off and laid them on the table, then looked at Debbie kindly. 'You've created something that has become a local institution, and the whole town should be grateful.' He looked at Frances then. 'I know we are.' Ben saw Frances nod. 'If you're sure you want to walk away from it completely, for at least a couple of years, selling the business might be the solution. But if you want to wait for six to twelve months, to make sure, then hiring a manager is the better way to go. Cathy's already indicated she doesn't want to be the manager, so that means attracting someone with experience, from the city or another country town.'

'Yes. The business is running well, and I can offer a reasonable salary package. It means not making much myself, but it keeps my option open to return in some capacity later on.' She nudged Jamie. 'I've never done it because I *need* to work off-farm, it's my passion and Jamie has been super supportive. I think I'd like to support *his* passion for a while, and I have skills that can be used for the farm business too as Jill and Ross are also talking about stepping back.'

Ben chimed in. 'Gosh, big changes in Barrington. We're looking for a real estate professional and a café manager.' He looked at Harriet. 'Can you help with some creative advertising for both businesses Harriet?'

'Of course. Let's talk more about that. One of the key things here will be accommodation.' She looked at Drum. 'We've been renting my little cottage as short-term accommodation, but perhaps we can package it for one of the roles, offer a six-month lease, for example.' Ben noted Drum was quick to agree.

'And the flat over the post office is still empty. Australia Post is talking to the tourism office about short-term rental there too, but they don't really want to manage it.' Meggie looked at Debbie. 'Perfect location for your new café manager, if they're not a local.'

'And Freddie has already indicated she's happy to use the flat at the clinic as a base, but she'll stay at her family farm most nights so she's sorted for accommodation.' Angus spoke up quickly. 'She likes to come out home and ride Rose's horses on her days off.'

'Okay. Good. It's almost December, I think we should adver-tise soon. Harriet, Meggie, Debbie and I will have a catch-up, next week if that suits, to get the ad wording right and where to place them.' Ben turned to Douglas. 'Can we talk to you about drawing up employment contracts?'

'Of course Ben. We have a pro-forma I can email to you tomorrow. We can work from that.' Frances answered the question for Douglas, although Ben noted his nod of agreement. They'd always been a great team, Douglas and Frances. Had helped Ben Evans Real Estate on many an occasion.

'I have a question Ben?' Meggie spoke, laughter in her voice, which he hoped was a good sign. Coming out with them tonight may have been good for her.

'What's that Meggie?' He raised his eyebrows.

'We'd like dessert too. Run and grab the menus please!' He grinned at her. He'd happily pay for dessert, to see the sparkle stay in Meggie's eyes.

18
____

MEGGIE

Meggie pushed the keyboard away then ran her fingers through her thick hair, lifting the weight of it from the back of her neck. She shuddered as a rivulet of sweat made its way down her back, between her shoulder blades. Still a few days before it was officially summer, and the temperature had soared. She glared at the front office air-conditioner. It had broken down last week and local tradesmen were so heavily booked, they said it might be new year before they could have a look at it.

Pulling the keyboard within reach, she completed the spreadsheet for events booked in the next three months. So many. *Too many?* She wondered if she should have turned some away, but the business was going so well she didn't want to lose momentum. Meggie was manning the front office of the agency while the two Ben's interviewed prospective real estate agents. Harriet was working from home this morning, she had a zoom consultation with her Sydney obstetrician, but would come in around lunch time.

Little Ben strolled in from the back room, the last applicant with him. He was mid-fifties, and rather stout with a florid face. Meggie hadn't been impressed when he'd arrived, something about the way he looked at her had made her uncomfortable. She hoped Ben wouldn't hire him, he was her least favourite of the three applicants. *But they need to hire someone soon.*

Meggie raised her eyebrows at Ben as the front door closed. 'Any luck?'

'I'll answer that dear Meggie.' Big Ben had appeared from the back as she spoke. 'Definitely not the last one, there was something *slippery* about him. What do you think son?'

'Honestly Dad, you're right. Eight applicants in all. I spoke to each of them on the phone and invited just three in for an interview. The first one was okay but when she said she wanted an answer straight away as she had another offer on the table, I just turned off. If that's an example of her negotiating skills, she's a bit high-pressure for the way we like to do business. And the second one, the young bloke from Taree, said straightaway he'd only stay for six months, that it's a stepping stone to a job in the city.' Ben leaned against the other desk. 'We'd do all the training, and then he'd take his *transferrable skills* to a city agency. No thank you.' He chuckled when he said that - it was a term Harriet had used in the advertising campaign.

'I hope Debbie's having better luck,' Big Ben straightened as the door opened and Laura stepped in. He walked towards her, but she held her hand up and he stopped, looking confused.

Meggie studied Laura while her attention was on the men. *Something was different.* She wore smart navy pants instead of her usual jeans, and a button up blouse with a collar. Meggie looked at it again and almost laughed. It was a pinstripe *man's shirt*, but it looked good on her lean frame, tucked into the tailored pants. And it wasn't just the clothes. Laura's short dark hair was sort-of *done*. Styled. And she had on mascara and lip-gloss. Meggie wondered if this was to do with Laura's growing relationship with Big Ben.

'Laura?' Big Ben's voice held puzzlement.

'Laura!' Little Ben grinned. 'You look great!'

'I'm here for the job.' Laura never beat about the bush and Meggie sat back, surprised. She glanced from Laura to the Bens and back again.

Little Ben blinked, then asked, 'The job?'

'Yes Ben. The job.' Laura spoke quickly, with a slight hint of impatience. *No, of nerves.* Meggie was intrigued.

'It's like this. Yes, Ben wants to retire.' She cocked an eyebrow at him. 'But it's because he wants to spend more time with me. We both want that.' She waved her hand in front of her face. 'It's bloody hot in here, you need to get the air-con fixed.'

Galvanised into action, Big Ben stood aside, gesturing for Laura to come further into the office. 'Come into the meeting room love. I mean Laura. It's cooler there. Let's talk.' He began to usher her towards the hallway at the back of the room.

'I'm serious. Interview me.' She turned to Little Ben. 'Both of you.' She pulled two documents out of the slim briefcase she held. Meggie hadn't noticed it earlier. 'My resume. Yes, I've been a farmer. But I'm also a graphic artist, running my own business. I had a bigger business in Sydney before I came here, with several staff.'

Both Ben's were opening and closing their mouths, not sure what to say. Meggie walked to the front door, locked it, and turned the sign to 'Out to Lunch'. Then she touched Laura on the arm. 'Follow me Laura, I'll interview you if they don't want to.' She strode down the hallway, letting herself and Laura into the meeting room. The Bens were right behind them.

In her usual forthright manner Laura said, 'I'll start. Firstly, let's discuss the elephant in the room.' She turned to Big Ben. 'We've had a few weeks off and travelling with you has been brilliant. And I'm keen to make more trips. A week or two here and there. But Ben, I'm younger than you and I realise now, since selling the farm and travelling, that I'm *not ready to retire*. In fact, I'm not sure you're ready either. But that's a decision for you to make.'

Turning to Little Ben, she continued. 'I've done my research, and I can undertake study online for my sales and property management licence, while working in the industry as an assistant. Ben, I know the area, the community and I know property. I'm straight forward and honest. Those who know me, trust me. I have a good understanding of technology and systems, and I'm happy to learn the property management side of the business first, if that's your priority. I can be flexible with hours. I can work under my own ABN if that's easier.'

Meggie clapped her hands. 'I love it Laura. You're perfect.' Pointing to Little Ben, she added, 'Why didn't we think of this?'

'Because we thought Dad and Laura were going to be away a lot. Travelling. And stuff.' Ben still seemed unsure.

More quietly, Laura spoke directly to Big Ben. 'This is a way we can be together, see each other most days. I want that Ben. And I'd really love to work here. With you and Little Ben, Meggie and Harriet. And I'm still keen for more trips away with you, but shorter ones I think.'

This time she addressed Meggie. 'It was hard leaving my two

dogs for so long. The neighbour was great. But they fretted. I think I did too.'

Little Ben stepped forward, put his arms around Laura and hugged her. 'You're perfect Laura. For the business. And for Dad. It's a yes from me.' Laura hugged him back and Meggie saw her shoulders drop slightly. She realised how much Laura wanted this, and how nervous she must have been. But it didn't show. Meggie shook her head. No one would ever be as cool as Laura. Her admiration soared. *Wait until Harriet hears about this! She'll be so excited.*

'I'm stunned.' Big Ben gently took one of Laura's hands in his. 'Just when I think I know you, you surprise me.' He lifted her hand to his mouth and kissed it and Meggie saw Laura blink twice before withdrawing her hand.

'So is that a yes, Ben?' Laura had lifted her chin, and her back was ramrod straight.

'It's a yes. Definitely. But I'd like to discuss a part-time arrangement, maybe three or four days a week.' He gestured to his son. 'And I'll be here too, the same hours as Laura. But Ben, I'm still standing down from Council, that hasn't changed.'

The phone rang then, and Meggie rushed to pick up the handset in the meeting room. Turning to them, the phone to her ear, she mouthed *it's Harriet*. Out loud she said, 'You have to get in here Harri. We've chosen a new agent for the business. Meet us at the cafe.'

Putting the phone down, she laughed. 'We've already got the out-to-lunch sign on the door. Harriet's on her way in. Let's go to the café.'

Big Ben placed his hand in the small of Laura's back, gently ushering her into the hallway. 'Lunch. We'll celebrate.'

Back in the front office Laura stopped. 'Hold on Ben. I need to make a call' She spoke firmly.

'Um, of course.' He nodded his agreement. Laura pulled her phone from her briefcase, tapped into it, then put it to her ear. 'Barrington Electrical? It's Laura Harrison. The air-conditioning unit in Ben Evans Real Estate needs repair or replacement. This week please. Yes, call me back.' As she replaced the phone Meggie and Little Ben began to laugh.

'I bet they'll do it this week.' Meggie giggled.

'They wouldn't dare not doing it.' Ben agreed, his chuckle deep and hearty.

Laura frowned. 'I'm not sure it's funny. But of course they'll do it.' She walked ahead of them all, to the front door. 'I'm hungry. Let's go to lunch.'

'I'll divert the office phone Dad, you go ahead.' Ben stepped across to the reception desk phone and quickly hit the keys to divert calls to his mobile. Meggie watched, and when he turned around they laughed loudly, until Meggie had to wipe the tears from her eyes.

'Quick!' she whispered. 'Or we'll miss them telling Harriet!'

19

DEBBIE

Ringing the order up, Debbie moved to the coffee machine and grinned at young Lucy Stewart, hovering behind her.

'Three lattes, a dirty chai and an iced tea, Lucy. Want to give this order a go? I'll get the cold drinks.' Debbie moved aside and watched Lucy surreptitiously as she started the lattes. The girl was a natural on the coffee machine. Shy with customers, but fabulous with the orders. She'd been working after school and weekends for almost three weeks and was in today because there was something at school she wasn't needed for. Debbie was grateful. Lucy was a keen baker and had picked up most of Cathy's recipes easily. And Cathy was thrilled. Last week she'd been able to start a bit later because Lucy had baked the scones and brownies after school that were usually a first-thing-in-the-morning job for Cathy. Debbie felt sure that Lucy would gain confidence dealing with customers, over time.

The order was for the Bens, Laura, Meggie, and Harriet, who'd just arrived. Debbie rubbed her lower back. Standing at the coffee machine seemed to make it ache more than usual. Moving around was better, so she would deliver the drinks to her friends herself.

The drinks were ready, assembled on a tray when Cathy popped her head out of the kitchen. 'Hey Lucy, want to make the lunch orders up in here while I man the front?' Lucy nodded eagerly and shot into the kitchen, around Cathy.

'Make yourself a drink Deb and go and sit with your friends. We'll be alright until the tennis crowd comes in, and that's not for another forty-five minutes.' Cathy bustled out to stand beside Debbie.

Debbie groaned gratefully. 'Thanks Cathy, you're the best.' She made herself a chai latte and added it to the tray, then walked it down the back to where the others were sitting. They were laughing and chatting loudly, and Debbie was curious about their obvious excitement.

'May I join you?' Debbie passed the drinks across the table.

Big Ben immediately moved to the next chair, pulling his out a bit further for Debbie to sit down. 'Of course Debbie, join us.'

Meggie turned to her, eyes bright with merriment. 'We've been interviewing all morning and we've just hired the perfect recruit.'

Eyebrows raised, Debbie chuckled. 'Lucky you. Tell me about him. Or her.'

Harriet took a sip of her iced tea. 'Our new recruit is right here. At this table.' She waggled her eyebrows over the rim of her glass and Debbie giggled. She looked at each person at the table. Meggie? No, she already had her own business. She saw Laura, seated at the other end of the table, sipping her latte. She seemed different. More dressed-up than usual. Not dressed-up-fancy but dressed-up-business-ey.

'Laura, of course.' Debbie tried to sound nonchalant, like she'd known the whole time, but really her mind was racing. What about Big Ben and his retirement plans?

Laura spoke up. 'See, it's not strange at all. Debbie got it straight away.' Laura winked at Debbie before continuing. 'Decided on our travels that I'm not ready for retirement. Too young.' And she threw her head back and laughed. Debbie's mood lifted. Laughter could do that.

'And Dad's not quite ready either.' Little Ben nudged his father with his elbow. 'They're both going to work part-time, and still have some short getaways, you know four-day weekend-love-ins and so on.'

Big Ben glared at his son and cleared his throat. 'With Laura starting now, Harriet can show her the systems and she can undertake her licence studies online. Once Harriet is ready to return.' He smiled at Harriet and said the next words straight to her. 'For whatever hours may suit her, then we'll adjust our schedules, and Laura and I may reduce our hours from time to time. It's a perfect solution.' He leaned in a bit. 'But I'm definitely not standing for Council next year. Ben will be doing that.'

'So happy to hear your news, and congratulations Laura. It's an excellent solution for you all.' Debbie set her cup down as Cathy arrived with lunch for the group, and kindly placed a salad in front of Debbie too, touching her lightly on the shoulder as she left. 'And the applicants you interviewed?'

'We weren't happy with any of them, for varying reasons, but before we had a chance to regroup, Laura appeared with the solution.' Ben laughed, then said more quietly, 'Bloody good timing Laura, I must say.'

'I wanted to wait until you had interviewed everyone, then ask you to interview me too. You know, make it a fair playing field. I've been thinking about it since we returned last week, and I almost didn't speak up.' Laura play-hit Little Ben on the arm. 'But you know me. I'm not one to not-speak-up.'

Debbie giggled. That was true.

Ben turned his attention to Debbie. 'What about you Deb, any likely applicants for your manager role?'

'Not really. Only one stood out on paper, but I'm not sure about her. I haven't asked her to meet me yet.' Debbie frowned slightly. 'But on a brighter note, young Lucy Stewart is a dream. She's very capable in the kitchen and learning to barista as well.' Debbie waved her hand in the general direction of the food and drinks on the table. 'She made your lunch, including the coffees.' She was pleased to see their eyebrows raise and nods of appreciation.

'It gives Cathy a bit more flexibility to be out the front, and she's happy to do it short term. But long term she doesn't want the manager job.' Debbie sighed then. She really needed to get something in place before Christmas, it was getting harder and harder to come in herself, if only for a few hours a day over the busiest period.

Meggie spoke up. 'So the one applicant that looks good on paper, but you haven't decided to interview? What's that about?'

'On paper she seems perfect. She's been running her own café for a few years, over on the coast. With her husband.' Debbie felt uncomfortable continuing.

'Is it because a husband-wife team is more staff than you need?' Harriet spoke quietly and Debbie felt she understood there was more to this.

'That's not the problem, although it is true. I asked one of my suppliers if he knew the café. He said he'd heard the marriage was breaking up and they were planning to sell the business, at first. But then he heard from other suppliers that he shouldn't offer credit, that they may declare bankruptcy. It made me nervous.' Debbie drew in a breath. She knew her friends could be trusted not to repeat this information, but she felt uncomfortable even mentioning it.

'Hmm.' Harriet looked thoughtful. 'There are always two sides to a story. The marriage breaking up could be due to their financial pressures. Or it could be something else altogether, like a large increase in rent, or being too highly geared. With interest rates climbing it may not be the café that's failed, it may be other commitments they're struggling with that has forced them to pull money from the business. Your call Debbie, and I certainly understand your hesitation, but maybe you should interview her and then decide.'

'Harriet's right. You might be doing this woman a disservice.' Little Ben agreed. 'Would it be helpful if one of us sat in the interview too, and asked the hard questions? I'd be happy to help.' Debbie brightened, she hadn't thought of that.

'Yes.' Feeling more decisive she turned to Harriet. 'You know this business well, Harri. You managed it when I had Woz. Any chance you could interview her with me?'

'Of course, I'd love to. Sensible approach.' Then Harriet put her hand to her mouth, saying, 'Oh, but we need to do it in the next ten days. I spoke to my doctor this morning and he's booked me in for a c-section in two weeks, in Sydney. Peanut will be thirty-six weeks and they don't want me to go any longer.' She laughed and shook her head. 'I haven't even told Drum yet!'

20

___

ROSE

December – Barrington Book Club – Meeting 4
Present: Debbie, Rose, Harriet, Melanie, Frances, Nicole, Laura,
Meggie
Apologies: none
Book: *The Work Wives* by Rachael Johns

'Who's ready for Christmas?' Rose settled herself gingerly into a chair. 'I'm huge. So much bigger than I was with Charlie.' She sighed, one hand on her large belly. 'Angus says I can use this like a shelf - you know, set a few drinks on there, maybe a pizza.'

'Stop it, Rose!' Harriet was laughing, already sitting at the table. 'I get the hiccups when I laugh.' Harriet had just one week to go before her c-section delivery and Rose felt a twinge of envy. To have it all over now would be wonderful. But she wasn't due herself for another three weeks.

Meggie stepped out of the kitchen area of the café, carrying to the table a tray of cold drinks. 'We put the tree up yesterday. Tommy helped me decorate, but everything is hanging on the top half because he keeps letting the puppy in and he jumps up at the shiny stuff, baubles and such.'

'Ours is the same. We have to keep everything out of Warwick's reach. Toddler, puppy. Same same.' Debbie reached for an iced tea, taking a sip. 'So refreshing. The heat has been awful the last few days.'

'There's a cool change coming later in the week, and rain too.' Laura had followed Meggie from the café kitchen, a tray of small Christmas puddings in her hands. She placed the tray in the centre of the table, then raised her eyebrows. 'Anyone keen for a glass of wine? I have a bottle of red, a pinot noir, from the Hunter region.' Her eyes settled on Frances. 'Frances? Melanie drove you in. Meggie?'

'Yes please Laura, that's one of my favourites.' Meggie waved her hand toward the bottle. 'I'll get glasses. Anyone else?'

'Thank you Laura, yes please.' Frances responded quickly.

'Me too Laura.' Nicole stood. 'I'll help with the glasses.'

Finally, they were all settled around the table, the puddings eaten, wine glasses and coffee cups almost empty. Rose leaned back, rubbing her tummy. 'This has been just perfect, girls. It's finally beginning to feel like Christmas.' The others agreed, laughing and chatting easily with each other.

A few of them cleared the table, then Rose pushed her copy of their book club read, The Work Wives by Rachael Johns, into the centre of the table. 'Such a talent, I honestly think this author can turn her hand to any genre. But this one hit a chord for me. It reminded me of my bestie and I when I worked in Sydney.' She chuckled. 'And maybe a little bit of Deb and me.'

Laura quirked an eyebrow. 'Really? Without the difficult back story, of course.'

'Despite their affection and support of each other in the work place, they had never revealed *all* their secrets.' Nicole grinned as she spoke, emphasising *all*. 'Don't get me wrong. A really entertaining read but it certainly raised questions for me. Do we ever truly reveal ourselves to another, no matter how close we are?'

Meggie laughed loudly, clapping her hands as she did. 'We're women Nik. We have to have some secrets. I think it's good to keep a little bit back, just for yourself.' She nudged Harriet beside her. 'Harri is my bestie and Rose, you're practically my sister, but we've all had moments when we've surprised each other. It's healthy.' Her last words were emphatic. 'And Debra, in the story, had her daughter to protect. And herself. I totally get it.'

A series of expressions flit across Melanie's face, before settling on something that looked like acknowledgement, or perhaps relief. Rose leaned forward. 'Mel? What did you think?'

Melanie shook her head slightly, then smiled, somewhat sheepishly at Rose. 'I was on Team Debra the whole time. As much as she wanted to confide in Quinn, she just couldn't. It resonated with me quite deeply.' She paused for a moment. 'Fear and the need to protect your child are strong motivations to stay silent. I've been there. But the reality is a life half-lived. And now that everything is in the open, and I have Ben and our own baby on the way, I realise how much I was missing. And in a way, my desire to protect Tiffany also made me a poor role model for her. There was a place in the book where I was shouting, in my head, 'trust Quinn. You can trust Quinn'. Her words trailed off and as if sensing her slight discomfort the others moved to other themes in the story and the writing style.

Then Frances spoke up. 'I've been with Douglas for almost forty years. Not work wives, as in the book, yet married and working together all that time. And yes, there were pieces I held back, perhaps unconsciously. But as each year passes, I find myself unravelling, little bit by little bit. Revealing more of myself. My secrets. My fears.' Rose watched Frances as she looked away for a moment, her eyes shiny with tears. 'But now here I am, on the verge of retirement, trying to gather some of those pieces back, to hold on to, lest there's nothing left.' Her last words came out almost as a sob, and they were all silent, for a moment.

Rose spoke quietly, directly to Frances. 'You're in a safe space here Frances. Is there anything going on that we can help with?'

Frances' demeanour changed instantly. She laughed, picked up her wine and threw back the last mouthful. 'No. You misunderstand but thank you dear girl. This book sent me off on a whole other journey. Made me think of my marriage and business partnership with Douglas, that's all. We're good. Everything's good. Some nostalgia perhaps. But this book.' She tapped it with her fingers. 'My favourite so far.'

Rose leaned back in her chair, pleased. Looking around at the eclectic group of women, her friends, she said a silent prayer to her grandfather Charlie. Without him she would never have returned to Barrington to live. And met Angus. And reunited with Debbie. While reading the book she had remembered fun times working in Sydney. But it would never compare to the life she led now.

'I have a book recommendation for next month.' Meggie set her wine glass down, empty now. 'Will we still meet? Harriet will have had her baby. Rose and Melanie will be close to having theirs.'

'I say we meet.' Laura smiled at Frances. 'Frances and I will be here. How about you Nik? And Meggie?'

Frances agreed, murmuring, 'yes', with Meggie nodding vigorously in agreement. Nicole chuckled. 'Of course I'll be here.' She turned to Debbie. 'If you can't make it Debbie, could Lucy stay on to let us in, then close up at the end. The book will have to be Lucy-appropriate, of course.'

Clapping her hands Meggie grinned. 'That's perfect. Totally Lucy-appropriate. I want to suggest *Runt* by Craig Silvey. And before you say anything, it is a children's book and Tommy adores it. We've been reading it together. It's just won the children's book of the year and I hear it's going to be made into a movie.'

'Great suggestion. Tiffany loves it too. The writing is brilliant. Every Aussie child should read it.' Melanie was enthused. Rose was surprised, but keen to check it out.

'And Billie.' Harriet smirked. 'At first she said it was a kid's book and way too easy for her, but everyone in class had to read it. She loves it too! And I confess, I've read the first few chapters already. It's brilliant. It really is quintessentially Australian.'

Meggie grinned. 'My thought was, with Christmas approaching and the babies almost due, we mightn't have time for a big book, or a deep one. And this would be fun for those that can make it next time. But I suggest you *all* read it, I'm telling you now, this one is destined to be a classic, in every sense of the word.'

'*Runt* it is then.' Rose stood, stretched a little, then arched her back. 'I can't stay in one position too long these days. My back gets so uncomfortable.'

Nicole looked across at her. 'Are you sure you have three weeks to go Rose? Honestly, you seem about ready to pop right now!'

'So the mid-wife tells me.' Rose turned to Harriet. 'Are you excited Harri? You'll have yours this time next week!'

'I am. And a bit nervous. Peanut is small, but he has a strong heartbeat.' Harriet blushed suddenly and held a hand to her mouth.

Rose was all over it. 'Did you just say 'he' Harri? I thought you didn't know the gender?' Hands on hips she laughed as the others huddled closer. Whispers of 'really?' and 'a boy!' flew around the group.

'You got me. Drum doesn't know. He's insisted on that.' Harriet giggled. 'But I saw something at the last scan. His little bits. One hundred percent it's a boy.' Eyes shining she looked at the others. 'But I better be careful at home now, that I don't let it slip.'

Turning to Debbie, Harriet added, 'I'll see you here tomorrow morning at eight Deb, to sit in on the manager-interview. What's her name again? I'll write it down.'

'Millicent Tucker. Thank you so much Harriet, I'm not sure what I think but I really need to get something in place, and she's indicated she can start before Christmas. She's coming in at half past eight, so we have time for coffee and a quick chat first. Thank you.'

21

—————

MILLIE

GOLDEN FINGERS OF DAYLIGHT CREPT ACROSS THE fields from the east, as Millie drove her old Corolla through the tiny hamlet of Stratford, now only ten minutes from Barrington. She was early but wanted to take a walk through the town before her interview. It would help calm her nerves.

She drove along the main street slowly, noting where the post office was for the accommodation the café owner, Debbie, had mentioned. The road was tree-lined and the footpath wide. Many of the shops had veranda awnings, providing both shelter and shade, and the whole town was neat, clean, and had a country-heritage look. *A Tidy Town winner, I bet.*

There were a couple of pubs and interesting retail offerings. An old-fashioned bakery with its doors open lured her in, the smell of fresh bread wafting out to the street. Millie had seen her destination, the café – *Coffee is my Calling* – further along the same side of the street. It was too early to go there. She ordered coffee and a croissant from the bakery and sat outside to eat it, watching the town slowly come to life. She tried to relax her shoulders as she basked in the early morning beauty. Closing her eyes she imagined the future, stepping out of the door from the post office accommodation, walking across the street, smiling at a local, waving to another, patting a dog, before opening the front door of the café. *You can do this. They'll love you.*

By twenty past eight a lot of the shops were beginning to open. A gift shop set a small table on the footpath with Christmas decorations on it. Further along, near her destination, a florist set buckets filled with flowers just outside the door and a random selection of quirky garden ornaments.

Taking a deep breath Millie stood, then patted down her outfit. The day was already warming up, but the tailored black pants she wore were made from lightweight material, as was her white blouse with three quarter sleeves and boat neck. She wore the blouse out, to hide the extra kilos she'd put on in the years since the children had arrived. So slowly that she hadn't noticed. Not really. *But he had.* Rudy. Her husband. *Ex-husband now.* It wasn't what had ended her marriage, it was more of a symptom really. And she'd already lost a bit of the weight. The outfit she wore today wasn't new, but it was excellent quality, the style timeless. It hadn't fit her for more than a decade.

Millie began walking along the street, taking deep breaths as she did. This was her chance. Today. Her chance to start again. For a moment she faltered. It was her *last* chance. If she didn't get this job she had nowhere else to go.

The café was even prettier than it looked on its social media pages. Millie already knew it was busy and popular. This was a maternity-leave position, for six months to begin with. She hoped for a more permanent role, but this would be a start. *If she got the job.*

Stepping through the cedar and glass door, she walked to the front counter, glancing around quickly at the layout, number of chairs and glass display cabinet filled with sweet and savoury delights. *I could be in Melbourne. This place has something.*

About to speak to the woman behind the coffee machine, a movement from the back of the café caught her eye. An obviously pregnant young woman, maybe ten or more years younger than Millie, walked towards her, smiling. She smiled in return and waited as the woman drew nearer.

'You must be Millicent?' the younger woman thrust out her hand. 'I'm Debbie. Thank you for coming in today.'

The words, her friendliness, the tone of her voice was almost too much for Millie. She couldn't get any words out, just for a moment, to respond. She was still shaking Debbie's hand, when the words finally came. 'Thank you. Thank you Debbie. I'm delighted to be here. And please, call me Millie.'

22

——

HARRIET

From her spot at the table in the back, Harriet saw Millicent's reaction to Debbie's friendly greeting. Relief came through strongest. But she looked around with interest as she followed Debbie back to their spot, seemingly taking mental notes. She was medium height and well dressed. Harriet could see her clothes were good quality. Classic styles. And she knew the woman was forty-three, from her application. Attractive, perhaps a bit conservative, but that could be her interview persona.

'This is my colleague Harriet Russell-Murray. Harriet, meet Millicent Tucker.' Debbie paused then, grinned at the woman, and added, 'but she prefers to be called Millie.'

Harriet stood and shook the hand the newcomer proffered. A good strong grip. If she was surprised at Harriet's pregnancy, she didn't show it.

They chatted for a moment about Barrington generally and Millie's drive in this morning before Debbie began asking about her experience and the recent years owning the café on the coast.

Millie answered all the questions easily, but hesitated when Debbie asked why she was looking for work as a Manager, after owning her own café for years. It was the question Debbie and Harriet had chosen to be the most important. If she answered honestly – they knew it had been sold to pay off creditors, only just escaping receivership – then they would give her the job. If she hesitated, or denied any liability, they would reconsider their position.

Millie sighed, then looked at them each, directly. 'There is no easy way to say this. We had financial pressure and a marriage unravelling. There's a chance we might have saved it if we had taken steps sooner. But we weren't on the same page. Rather than go into receivership we sold the café and paid out the creditors. The marriage is over, and I am effectively starting again.' She drew breath, Harriet waited. She could see Debbie's face was a picture of empathy, so she wanted to keep her own feelings hidden, for now. Harriet raised her eyebrows, indicating Millie should continue, if she wished.

'While the story is more complicated than that, it's not one to air at an interview. We had a good business and loyal customers, but we made mistakes that had nothing to do with the business - but impacted it in the worst possible way. The financial mismanagement was personal, not business-related.' Her chin lifted slightly, and she said this in a very direct manner and suddenly Harriet *knew*. The personal financial mismanagement was caused by the husband, yet Millie was shouldering the blame equally. There was more to the story, definitely, but Harriet's instincts were strong. This woman had been wronged, but she was also proud, and Harriet suspected, smart and business savvy. Except for a possible blind spot when it came to her husband. *Ex-husband.* Harriet knew exactly what that was like.

Debbie seemed about to speak, but Harriet spoke first. 'You mentioned children. Will they come with you if you move here Millie?'

Millie shook her head. 'My son is at University in Sydney, and my daughter is working in Western Australia. At a bakery in the Margaret River region. They may visit, of course, but I would move here on my own.'

'I have one more question for you, if you don't mind.' Debbie's words were friendly, and Harriet saw Millie's eyes blaze with hope. 'Do you think you could live here, in this small town? It's not what you're used to.'

Nodding enthusiastically, Millie smiled and her whole face changed. She looked younger, prettier and Harriet saw a glimpse of the person she may have been before her marriage and business woes. 'Yes. I arrived quite early and had a good look around. It's a lovely town with an interesting heritage and a whole lot of community pride.'

'Community pride?' Harriet asked with interest. 'How do you get that?'

'It's the streetscape, the heritage trail, the presentation of the main street retail sector.' She laughed, then leaned in, 'and I'm one hundred percent sure Barrington is a regular Tidy Town winner.' She leaned back, chuckling and more relaxed than she had been throughout the interview.

'You're right! You nailed it Millie. Barrington is *always* a Tidy Town winner.' Debbie laughed and looked happily at Harriet. Harriet knew then that Millie would get the job.

Debbie looked at her watch. It was nine-thirty, and the café was getting busier. Millie noticed and began gathering her things, then stood up as Harriet did.

'Are you driving straight back Millie?' Harriet asked, Debbie beside her.

'No, I'd like to drive out to a couple of tourist spots, see The Bucketts Mountains from the western side. I'll come into town for lunch, then head back.' Millie smiled, some of her confidence appeared to have left her. 'It's been lovely to meet you both. And good luck with your little ones, when they come.' She picked up her handbag.

'I'm pleased you're having a look around and not leaving straight away.' Debbie looked at Harriet, who nodded. 'We'll talk about you after you leave.' Debbie grinned and Harriet saw Millie's eyes shine with hope. 'But please come here for lunch later. I'd like to chat further.'

23

MEGGIE

MEGGIE ARRIVED JUST AS A WELL-DRESSED WOMAN stepped out through the café door. Meggie guessed she was the applicant. They smiled at each other. Meggie scooted down to the table at the back where Debbie and Harriet stood, deep in conversation.

'Hi. How'd the interview go?' Meggie asked, looking from one to the other. 'Was that the candidate just leaving? She has a nice smile.'

'We were just discussing her. Millie.' Harriet nudged Debbie as she spoke.

'She's gone for a drive and is coming back in for lunch. I'm going to offer her the management role.' Debbie grinned. 'She has loads of experience. I think she'll be great for the business.' Debbie glanced at the counter, where a short line had formed. 'I've got to go back to work, but Harriet can fill you in. Would you like a coffee?'

Meggie raised her eyebrows at Harriet. 'Do you have time

Harri? When are you heading to Sydney?'

'Thanks Deb. Caramel latte for both of us.' Harriet sat down as Debbie rushed back to the counter. 'We're picking Billie up from school at twelve, and we'll head to Sydney then. My procedure is scheduled for tomorrow, and I need to be at the hospital by seven in the morning.'

'I wasn't sure if you'd take Billie with you.' Meggie sat across from Harriet, her tone questioning.

'I know. We only decided last night. Melanie offered to have her, but she's been feeling a bit left out, with the baby coming. So we decided we'd take her with us. She's more excited than we are!' Harriet paused. 'Even though I'm only thirty-six weeks, the baby's heartbeat is strong. So Billie will be with us to celebrate. To be part of the excitement.' She lowered her voice. 'She won't attend the surgery, of course. The baby may need to be in a humidicrib for the first days. Weeks even. But we'll be there together.'

Meggie watched as Harriet looked down for a moment, then her gaze returned. 'And if anything goes wrong, we'll be together for that too.' Harriet frowned as she spoke and Meggie reached across, placing a hand over her friend's.

'Stay positive Harriet. When you first fell pregnant there were no guarantees you'd get through the first couple of months. And look at you! Close to full term.' Meggie saw Harriet's expression lighten and continued. 'And it's a good decision to take Billie. She's quite mature for her age and being there for the birth will only strengthen your connection.'

Their coffees were delivered by one of the staff. Debbie was chatting to a couple, they looked like tourists, as she worked the coffee machine. Taking a sip, Meggie spoke again. 'If you do have to stay in Sydney for a bit, if the baby needs to, will Drum and Billie stay too?'

'If it's not touch-and-go they'll come back after a few days, then visit each week until we can all come home. Drum needs to be on the farm and Billie shouldn't miss more than a week of school.' Harriet sighed then. 'I'm excited but scared at the same time. There won't be another chance for me.' Then she raised a hand to her mouth, her eyes full of compassion, adding in almost a whisper, 'Sorry Meggs.'

Meggie swallowed her own feelings, her pain, with her next sip of coffee. 'Don't be sorry Harri. I'll have my chance.' She smiled then. 'And I am so happy for you! You're a walking miracle.'

Harriet looked at her watch. 'I'd better go home. I still need to pack for Billie and sort a few things out before we leave.' She finished her coffee then pushed her chair back, standing. Meggie rose, stepped close and wrapped her arms around her friend. 'Wishing you all the very best for tomorrow Harri. Get Drum to call or message when he can.'

Harriet squeezed her back, murmuring, 'Thank you darling Meggie.'

24

FRANCES

STEPPING INTO THE LARGE OFFICE WHERE DOUGLAS SAT, Frances noted his glasses had slid to the end of his nose as he worked. *Douglas is starting to look old.* She acknowledged him when he looked up and smiled, his expression an unasked question. With no explanation she walked briskly to the table filled with files tied up with red tape.

Not wanting to invite comment, Frances turned and began sifting through the files, lifting each one, reading the cover quickly, then placing it down again. *It wasn't here. She couldn't find it. She was sure it would be here.*

'Frances?' She turned to see that Douglas had laid his pen down and small creases had appeared on his forehead.

'Not to worry Douglas. I was looking for that file, but it's not here.' She began to tidy the table up again but found her hands shaking. *Where could it be?*

'File? What file? Perhaps I can help?' His voice was kindly, as always, but she felt unaccountably annoyed.

CHAPTER 24

'I said. Not to worry.' Wincing at the sharpness in her own voice, she turned and left the room, waving a hand at Douglas to indicate she didn't need to discuss it. *She didn't need help either.*

There was no one waiting in reception, so she stepped into the kitchen and turned the jug on. Then she thought about how sharply she'd spoken to Douglas and decided to pop downstairs to buy coffee at the café instead. A quick chat with Debbie was just the tonic Frances needed. She'd been feeling out of sorts all day.

Returning to the office she carried the coffees through to Douglas, intending to sit with him for a moment while they drank them, but the phone rang and the moment was lost.

25

MILLIE

Millie enjoyed the couple of hours she spent driving around the region. She'd pulled over at a place called Rocky Crossing and taken photos of the river, the Bucketts Mountains and the Barrington Tops in the distance. She'd stopped at a little general store on the outskirts of town to fill up with fuel. The owner had pumped the fuel and cleaned the windscreen for her, and chatted about the region, the weather and a little bit of history. She'd almost told him she was hoping to get a job locally, but she didn't want to jinx it.

Now it was twelve-thirty and the main street was full of cars and bustling with people. *Locals and tourists*, she thought. Millie found a car park behind the town hall and walked through to the main street via a laneway.

She peered at listings in the window of a real estate shop. Cheaper here than the coast, certainly, but higher prices than she'd anticipated. It would be a long time before she could buy again. About to continue on her way, she saw someone wave from inside.

Millie took another look. It was the striking young woman she'd almost bumped into at the door of the café after the interview. She smiled and waved back. *Everyone knows everyone in a small town.* There were pluses and minuses for that, but perhaps the woman's friendliness was an indication that the job at the café was hers. *Or she's just friendly and thinks I'm a potential home buyer.*

Not wanting to assume, Millie dampened her emotions as she walked back to the café. It was busy, with most of the tables inside and outside full. She could see Debbie at the coffee machine and another staff member clearing tables. There was someone in the kitchen too. She wondered how Debbie was going to have time to speak with her, but Millie was in no hurry. She would order lunch, sit up the back, and wait.

Debbie took her order, and despite the obvious busy-ness of the café, smiled and asked Millie if she'd had a good look around.

'I stopped at Rocky Crossing and took some pictures to send the kids. It's a beautiful region.' Millie handed her credit card over and Debbie waved it away.

'If you have time to wait, maybe half an hour or so, we can sit together and chat.' Debbie grinned. 'I won't take your money, Millie, I want to offer you the job.' Millie took the coffee Debbie passed her, knowing her own grin was a match for Debbie's. She walked back to the table, smiling at anyone who looked her way. *I got the job! I got the job!* Finally something to look forward to after months of stress, arguments and at times not knowing if she'd come out of her old business with anything but the clothes she wore. *Today couldn't get any better.*

Millie sat at the back, watching how the staff worked together. Debbie was incredible. Despite being six or seven months pregnant, she made time to smile and speak to every customer as she served them. She'd have to ask her story. Debbie was a professional and absolutely perfect for the hospitality business. Another lady, somewhat older than herself, popped in and out of the kitchen with plated up lunches and a younger waitress was delivering them and clearing tables as she went. Every time she delivered a food or coffee order, she cleared another table and returned to the kitchen with a tray of dirty plates. Not once did she return empty handed. *Good training. No. Excellent training.* Three people managing the heavy flow of customers dining in, plus a high number of take-away orders, was a pleasure to observe. Millie had thought her own work practices and staff training would be needed here, but no. She would make sure she kept everything up to *Debbie's standard.* Thirty minutes later the lunch rush had slowed, and customers began to empty out.

Debbie joined Millie carrying a bottle of sparkling water and two glasses. 'Thank you for waiting Millie.'

'It was my pleasure Debbie. You run a well-oiled machine. I'm curious. Where did you train? Melbourne?' Millie took the bottle from Debbie's hand as she spoke, opened it and filled the two glasses, sliding one closer to Debbie.

'Not Melbourne. London. Notting Hill to be precise.' Millie saw Debbie blush as she spoke.

Modest too. Chuckling, Millie nodded happily. 'Notting Hill! Well that explains it. Your team works well together. Congratulations on your work culture and training.'

'Thank you.' Debbie looked delighted. 'Not everyone gets it, Millie. You know, recognises good work practices. I'm so happy you came in today and confident I'm making the right decision to offer you the management job. I've still got a couple of months to go, before this one is due.' She patted her tummy. 'This is my second one, and I worked right up to the day last time, and long-story-short there were complications. I won't make that mistake this time. I want to ease back for a couple of weeks, then take some proper time off to prepare for this one and spend time with Woz.'

'Woz?' Millie tried not to chuckle.

'Warwick. Everyone calls him Woz. I'm kinda hoping he'll grow into his full name.' Debbie's eyes twinkled. Millie looked at her admiringly, hoping she would be able to stay long enough to get to know Debbie and her family.

'When we spoke you said you wanted the job to start before Christmas?' Millie tried to get back on track. It felt more like chatting with a friend than a job negotiation.

'Yes. If that suits you? Debbie looked hopeful and Millie said, 'Absolutely,' with no hesitation in her voice.

Debbie continued. 'The town fills up with tourists for about three weeks over Christmas. The week before and two after. Then it becomes steady until the end of the school holidays at the start of February. My plan was to bring you on now, just before we're smashed for Christmas, and to work with you during the busiest part. Then, after three or four weeks, I'll cut right back, and just come in as needed.' Debbie paused and took a sip of her water. 'I'd like to get everything ready at home and spend time with Warwick, and my husband Jamie, before the birth. We're on a farm just out of town.'

Millie nodded as Debbie spoke. Yes, having both of them on during the busy period was a good idea, but she secretly hoped Debbie could cut back sooner than three to four weeks. Maybe straight after Christmas. And not because she wouldn't like working with Debbie. She already knew she would. But Debbie deserved the break, of that Millie was sure. Out loud, she said,

'Sounds like a good plan Debbie. I hope to hit the ground running, as they say. But I welcome the opportunity to work with you and understand your processes, get to know your suppliers and so on. And the customers, of course.' Millie smiled. She felt excited. This was exactly what she needed. 'You mentioned in the original advertisement, a three-month trial and six-month placement.'

'I did say that, didn't I?' Debbie sighed. 'Honestly Millie, I think I'd like longer. I've missed out on a lot with my first one. My mum and mother-in-law have helped with him. And Jamie of course. And now he's started day-care. Jamie's asked me to consider stepping back from the café for a year.' She frowned then. 'I haven't even asked what your plans are Millie. What timeframes you need.'

'I have no plans Debbie. My plans were ripped out from under my feet. I'm starting over. A few months is doable, but I was hoping for more. A year would be wonderful.' Millie smiled but still felt tears spring to her eyes as she spoke. She tried to blink them away. Didn't want Debbie to think she was a drama queen. But this opportunity had saved her.

'I understand.' Debbie spoke quietly, but Millie felt the connection. *Debbie understood.* 'I have the paperwork here with the letter of offer. You might like to read it before you go, and if everything is alright, sign it, here.' Debbie pointed to a space at the bottom. 'There is a contract too, but I want to amend the wording regarding the trial period and timing. I can email that to you tomorrow.' Debbie pushed her chair back and stood. 'Don't go yet. Read the offer and let me know if you need anything amended. I'll just check I'm not needed at the counter.'

'Thank you.' Millie spoke sincerely. She knew Debbie was

giving her time to read the offer by herself. Millie watched Debbie walk away. She spoke to several customers as she went by their tables and stopped to chat for a moment with a smartly dressed older woman as she stepped up to the counter. Millie observed all that Debbie did. She knew she was at least a decade younger than herself, but she doubted there was much she could teach her. The young woman was amazing. No wonder she was in her own business at such a young age.

Reading the contract, Millie did her sums and realised how generous the offer was. And there was an attached sheet of paper with the details of the apartment above the Post Office that was for rent. Millie had thought she might need something more modest, but the salary was generous and the rent cheaper than on the coast. She could make this work and still save a bit each week.

Finishing her drink, she re-read the details, then signed and dated the bottom of the offer. Picking up the document, and her bag, she walked to the counter. Handing it across to Debbie, Millie said, 'The only change I'd suggest, is that I can start next week, on Monday, rather than the following week. If it suits you. I'm going to speak to the real estate agent now, about the post office apartment, but if it's not ready I can stay at the caravan park to begin with.'

'Really? Next week?' Debbie's voice rose, her excitement evident. She held out her hand and Millie shook it. She had the strangest feeling that Debbie had been on the verge of giving her a hug. And she wouldn't have minded one bit. 'Yes, go down to Evans Real Estate. See Meggie. She's my friend. You'll love her. I think you almost bumped into each other this morning. I'm sure she can get the apartment ready for you by the weekend.'

They spoke for a few more moments, and then Millie left,

walking along the street to the real estate office. Debbie's friend Meggie was the one who'd waved to her earlier. *Small towns,* Millie thought. Almost like a whisper in her ear, she heard, or maybe *felt,* the words, '*big hearts.*' She looked around. It was her imagination. She pushed open the door to the real estate shop.

26

ROSE

ROSE WOKE WITH A START AND REACHED FOR ANGUS IN the dim light filtering in through the blinds. His side of the bed was cold. Groaning, she rolled onto her side and reached for her phone. Almost half six. Wee Charlie would be awake soon. If she wanted to grab a shower she'd have to be quick.

With one hand on her aching lower back, she walked across the hall and peeked at Charlie. He was asleep with one chubby leg on top of the covers and a plastic shark clutched in his hand.

Trying to move quickly, but quietly, Rose yawned as she returned to the ensuite and started the shower. Her back was really sore this morning. Posterior baby. Charlie had been the same. Even the labour pain had been in her back. She soaped herself up quickly and rinsed off, then luxuriated for an extra minute, the warm water soothing her lower back. The baby was due in two weeks and Rose hoped the back pain wouldn't get any worse. She didn't recall it being this bad with Charlie. *Or have I just forgotten the pain?*

Charlie shot into the bedroom, giggling, as she finished dressing. He threw himself up on the bed, jumping up and down as he asked the usual questions.

'*Where's Daddy?*'

'At work.'

'*What's for breakfast?*'

'Pigs trotters.' As tired as she was, she delighted in this little routine.

'*Not pigs trotters! What's really for breakfast Mummy?*'

'Weetbix and toast.'

'*And juice? Can I have juice?*'

'What do you say?' Rose chuckled.

'*Please and thank you Mummy darling.*' Angus had taught him that. Got her every time.

'Yes, you may have juice.' She was dressed now and stepped to the edge of the bed. He threw himself into her arms and she almost fell back with the force of it. Sometimes she galloped to the kitchen with him on her hip. But she just couldn't today.

Rose set Charlie down, diverting him with a question of her own. 'Where's Woof? If he's at the back door you can feed him.'

Charlie shot off as fast as his little legs would carry him, calling out 'Woof! Hey Woof!' Rose heard the young dog bark. He was just outside the back door on the veranda. She followed Charlie and helped him open the door. He knelt down and the young cattle dog, wriggling with excitement, licked his master's face. Bending to access the sealed container of dry dog food out on the veranda, Rose had to pause as a ripple of pain flowed through her back. Different to the usual dull ache she felt. The hairs on the back of her neck stood up. *Labour already?* She was early. Or maybe it was false labour. She noted the time on her watch.

Leaving Woof to eat his breakfast, Rose led Charlie through to the kitchen and helped him up on a tall chair at the kitchen counter. She used a washcloth on his hands and face, then placed a bowl of cereal down for him.

With one hand on the fridge door, another burning pain hit her. Hard and deep. She looked at her watch. Six minutes. *This could be it.* Grasping the edge of the sink with both hands, she leant into it, puffing through her mouth in short bursts as she did.

The pain receded and Rose straightened, swivelling her gaze to check on Charlie. He held the near empty cereal bowl to his mouth with both hands, noisily slurping the milk. She sighed, about to admonish him, but thought better of it. He was happy for the moment. Charlie was due at day care in just over an hour. That would give her time to find Angus. *Was he on the farm or had he been called out?* Rose sent him a text.

Are you far away? I may be in labour.

Not wanting to panic (after all she'd already had one baby), she made a list of things to do while she waited for Angus to get back to her.

Pack a bag for hospital. She should have done that already, but she'd gone past her due date with Charlie and thought this pregnancy would be the same.

Organise Meggie to pick Charlie up. Meggie had offered to wrangle Charlie when the time came.

Message Debbie. She'd want to know. And Angus's Mum.

'Mummmmyyy!' Charlie's tone was strident. Rose looked up. He was standing on the chair, milk and cereal mush down the front of his shirt. She looked closer. And in his hair.

Murmuring to him, she stepped over and lifted him from his chair, almost dropping him as another pain forced her to her knees, breathing through her nose. Charlie patted her face. 'Mummy ouch?'

Holding his small hand against her lips, Rose nodded as she continued puffing until the pain receded. Checking her watch she registered it was only five minutes since the previous contraction. Still kneeling on the floor, Rose stripped Charlie's damp shirt off and sent him to his room to get another. She had no idea what he'd choose, but right now it seemed of little importance.

Using the chair and then the counter as leverage to regain her feet, she reached for her phone. Nothing from Angus. If he was on the farm somewhere, feeding stock, he'd have it in his pocket. More likely he had been called out. His phone probably in his vehicle while he tended to an emergency. Gritting her teeth, she checked the time again, dropping quickly onto the chair Charlie had vacated as another wave ripped through her. Briefly moaning she felt Charlie at her side again.

'Poor Mummy.' He handed her his favourite teddy. She pulled him into her arms, hugging him tightly, trying not to cry.

The contraction tailed off and she took Charlie by the hand, turning the television on to ABC Kids and quickly clicking to his favourite show.

Back in the kitchen she turned the jug on. She'd make herself a green tea while she waited for Angus. Bustling around in the kitchen she acknowledged that this baby may be coming faster. *They say that about second babies, don't they?*

Her phone rang. Meggie, not Angus.

Relieved, she answered. 'Meggie. I'm glad you called.'

'Rose? Are you okay? I was going to ask if you want to have lunch today.' Meggie's tone was questioning, and alert.

'I'm in labour Meggie. I'm not sure where Angus is, he left before I was awake. Can you please help with Charlie today? I'll take him to day care but I may need you. To. Pick. Him. Up.' The last words were spoken through clenched teeth as another spasm rolled through her body, forcing her to put the phone on the counter while she grabbed it with both hands.

Fumbling with the phone, as the sensation eased, Rose turned it to speaker.

'I'm on my way Rose. Don't move. And I'll track Angus down.' Relieved at the confidence and firmness of Meggie's tone, Rose nodded. Then realising Meggie couldn't see her Rose managed to say, 'Yes. Thank you,' as she exhaled.

27

DRUM

Billie wanted to come into the surgery too, but Drum wouldn't allow that. Couldn't allow it. He felt strongly that Harriet would deliver a healthy baby. Small perhaps, but healthy. The process would be difficult enough for *him*. And Harriet. If something went wrong, or the room became chaotic, he didn't want Billie to be there. He was anxious enough for all of them. The hospital offered a private waiting area close to the surgical suites and he left Billie there, reading one of the many books she'd brought on this trip. He trusted her to wait there for him.

About to leave the room he turned back to look at Billie. As if she sensed him, she looked up. He was beside her again in two long strides, wrapped his arms around her and squeezed, saying quietly, 'it will be alright. They'll be alright.'

Arms around his neck she pressed her cheek against his. Her words were louder than his. Firmer. 'They will be alright Daddy. I'm sure of it.' Her confidence carried him from the room.

A theatre nurse helped him scrub up and led him through to Harriet. Slightly sedated, they were waiting for the epidural to take effect. He sat near her head, holding her hand. They didn't speak as they stared into each other's eyes. They needed no words. He could see tears in Harriet's eyes and tried to control his own emotion, to support her through this.

The surgeon arrived and the moment was lost. Machines beeped, midwives bustled around the room, and the voice of the surgeon, almost hidden behind a medical barrier, murmured instructions to his team.

He only had eyes for Harriet, blocking out everything else. He watched her carefully for signs of pain. Or fear. But she kept her gaze focussed on him. He held her hand, not too tightly, but squeezed it every now and again. Time passed. Quickly or slowly, he didn't know.

It wasn't until he saw her expression change, a smile flit across her face and her eyes widened, that he realised the midwife was speaking to him.

'You have a son Mr Murray.' *A son? Really?* He was dazed. The midwife moved Harriet's gown down, laying the tiny naked baby on her chest. Harriet placed her other hand on his little bottom while Drum stroked his boy's back with one large finger. *So tiny.* He looked up at the midwife, scared to ask.

Seeing his look, the woman chuckled. 'He's a fine boy. We'll take him from you in a moment, we need to do all the usual checks. He's small, but he's breathing without help.' Hope that he'd held onto so tightly spilled over and he wiped tears from his eyes with the back of his hand. Pulling his surgical mask to one side, he bent and kissed Harriet gently on the mouth.

'We have a son Harri. A son.' He saw her face was pale, but she was smiling through her own tears. She nodded, then whispered something. He leaned in, trying to catch her words.

'I know. I've known for months. We have a son.' Her words were quietly spoken, but he saw a glint of merriment in her eyes.

'Of course you knew! How did I not?' He laughed then, with abandonment. 'We have a son!' His last words were loud, triumphant. Although the medical team wore masks, he saw the laughter in their eyes as they chuckled with him.

The midwife placed a hand on his shoulder. 'Mr Hamilton, it might be best if you leave now. We'll come for you once we have Mrs Hamilton settled in recovery. Go and give your family the good news.'

'Billie. Our daughter Billie.' He stood then, released Harriet's hand and with a fond look at his baby son, left the room.

After shedding the surgical clothes, almost tearing them in his haste, he pushed open the waiting room door. Billie looked up from her book, then stood, letting it fall to the ground from her lap. Her eyes looked fearful, but he stepped over, scooped her into his arms and turned in a full circle before setting her down.

'You have a brother. He's small but breathing on his own. That's a good sign. They're checking him now and as soon as Harriet is back in the recovery ward we'll go and see them.'

'He's alright? Harri's alright too?' Her gorgeous little face beamed with delight. He felt so blessed. *His daughter Billie, and now a boy.*

They sat side by side then, and Billie retrieved her book.

'Billie?'

'Yes Dad.'

'You don't seem surprised that it's a boy.' He watched a range of emotions cross her face as she considered her answer.

'Nooo. I'm not surprised.' She shook her head, her golden curls bouncing as she did. 'Harri let something slip a few of weeks ago. She said 'him', and then she put her hand over her mouth and made me promise not to tell you.' She looked up at him, glanced around the room, then whispered, 'she said she saw his boy-bits on the last scan.'

'I didn't see any boy-bits. I was at that scan.' Drum furrowed his brow, trying to recall the baby shaped mass on the screen.

Billie laughed then, the sound warming his heart. 'Harriet said you wouldn't know. Because you only had a man-look!'

Shaking his head, delighted with his girl, he nudged her with his shoulder. She nudged him back just as the door opened. It was the same midwife.

'You can come through now.' She looked at Billie. 'Are you excited to meet your brother.'

'You betcha!' Billie grinned and almost danced out the door in front of him.

28

MEGGIE

MAX HAD JUST LEFT TO TAKE TOMMY TO SCHOOL. Meggie sent him a message to track Angus down. He called her within moments.

'Angus was called out to Cobark early this morning. One of their horses was startled into a barb-wire fence.' His tone was questioning.

'Rose is in labour, I'm heading over to her now. I'll look after Charlie and get her to hospital if it's moving along quickly. Angus needs to know.' Meggie was already walking to her car, the phone on speaker.

With no pause at all, Max responded. 'I'll drive out to Cobark and take over there. I'll send him straight back. He should be with you in just over an hour.'

Instantly relieved, Meggie exhaled loudly. 'Phew! Brilliant. Thanks Max, you're the best.' She started the car, the phone automatically switching to her car speakers. 'Want me to call Melanie, fill her in?'

'I'll call Melanie, and we'll let Laura and the Bens know where you are too. Just go Meggs. Take care of Rose and Charlie.' Max seemed to hesitate then. 'And let me know when you have news. About Rose. And if you hear about Harriet, from Drum.'

Meggie chuckled then. 'I will. Love you. What are the chances Harriet and Rose's babies will share a birthday?' His hearty laugh in response warmed her.

Meggie thought about that as she navigated through Rocky Crossing, taking the shorter route to Barrington Homestead. Harriet should be delivered before lunchtime, and unless Rose's labour was overly long, she'd deliver sometime today too. Cute. Then a pang of sadness hit her. Would she *ever* have a baby of her own? She wanted a baby with Max so badly. But he hadn't broached the subject since the miscarriage. He'd been loving and attentive as always. But they hadn't *made love*. The first couple of weeks she'd just wanted him to hold her, and he had known that. No words had been needed. But now? Now she wanted them to resume their love-making. Was he waiting for her to indicate she was ready? She slowed to turn into Rose's driveway. Maybe Max needs a signal from her.

Greeted by Woof as she got out of the car, she gave him a distracted pat on the head. The front door was open, so Meggie walked in, dropping her bag and keys on the hall table.

'Rose?' She called out as she walked from the kitchen to the living area. Charlie was dressed in pyjama bottoms and a tee shirt, playing with blocks on the living room floor. She noticed his shirt was on backwards. He waved at her, but remained focussed on the tower he was building. Seeing Meggie in the house was nothing out of the ordinary for Charlie.

Meggie felt panic rising in her chest as she walked quickly

down the hall towards the bedrooms. Rose wasn't in the master room, but there were a few clothes strewn across the bed and her overnight bag lay open beside them. Increasing her pace, Meggie rushed to the main bathroom, she could hear water running.

Pushing the door open she stepped into the steamy room. The bath was half full, the water still running. 'Rose?' Meggie turned the taps off.

'I'm here Meggie.' Spinning around, Meggie saw her sister-in-law sitting on the floor beside the toilet, her face screwed up in pain. Kneeling beside her Meggie took one of Rose's hands in hers.

'Contraction?'

Rose nodded, breathing through the pain as she did. Meggie moved closer, placed one arm around Rose's back to support her. Rose relaxed as the pain eased and looked at Meggie, her face anxious.

'Angus? Have you found Angus? Only three minutes between the last ones.'

'He's out at Cobark, no phone signal. Max is on his way there to take over and send him back. But he'll be an hour yet.' Meggie thought to herself, *that's if Max finds him straight away.*

Her answer seemed to provide some comfort and Rose gave her a tremulous smile. 'Dear Meggie. Thank you.' Meggie leaned in, holding Rose close for a moment, then sat back on her heels.

'A bath Rose? Really?' She pointed to the bath, steam still rising languidly from the surface.

'I had a shower already. But I thought I might have a bath. I don't know why.' She frowned then. 'That's silly, isn't it?'

'Not silly Rose. But also not necessary. I'm going to let the water out. We can't leave water in there with Charlie wandering around. Can you stand? Walk?' When Rose nodded, Meggie helped her to her feet.

'Let's go back to your room, you can sit on the bed while I finish packing your overnight bag.' They made it back into the bedroom as another contraction hit. Rose leaned over the bed, supported on her arms, while Meggie rubbed her lower back.

The contraction over, Meggie helped Rose turn to sit on the bed. 'Ah, Meggie. My back. The pain is always in my back. Thank you.' She breathed out through her mouth noisily. 'Charlie? He's very quiet.'

'I was just thinking the same thing. I'll check on him.' Meggie sped from the room, trotting quickly back to the living area. No Charlie. Then she heard scrabbling noises in the kitchen. Standing at the counter, she tried not to laugh. Charlie was sitting on the kitchen floor in front of the open fridge door. He had an array of food around him. Mandarins and an apple had rolled to one side. But he was focussed on a jar of Nutella. The lid was in his lap and one chubby little hand was in the jar. He looked up at her, guilt and chocolate all over his face. Grinning cheekily, he pulled his hand out and began to lick the chocolate from it.

'Charlie, Charlie, Charlie. Whatever shall I do with you?' Meggie picked him up and sat him by the sink. She put the lid on the jar and returned it and the fruit to the fridge, closing the door. Returning to Charlie, she liberally dampened a wash cloth and began to clean him up, but not before he left a chocolate hand-print on the front of her peach-coloured blouse. Taking him in her arms, she rushed back to Rose. She was sitting on the floor, her back against the bed, face red. But she held out her arms for her son, and he wriggled into them, putting his face against his mother's.

'Another one Rose?' Meggie looked at her watch. Under three minutes. And Angus still forty minutes away. At least.

'Yes. Another one. But my water hasn't broken, so I'm hoping I've got a bit more time. For Angus to get here.' Rose looked pale now. And tired.

'I'm going to pack your bag Rose. I'll grab what I think you'll need. I can come back later if I've forgotten anything.' Meggie began to do just that, quickly throwing in the items on the bed, then dashed quickly into the ensuite to fill a bathroom bag. Her phone vibrated in her back pocket. Angus.

'Angus. I'm with Rose. And Charlie. She's okay, but the contractions are close together.' Meggie tried to be brief, knowing he was driving, probably too quickly.

'I've been trying to call her! I'm still forty-five minutes away.' Angus sounded anxious.

'You've got time, I think. Her water hasn't broken.' Meggie paused, smiling. 'But brother, I think you'll have a baby today.'

Standing in the bedroom, she passed her phone to Rose.

She heard Rose murmur, 'Angus. Don't rush. There's time. Meggie is here.' Meggie didn't hear her brother's response, but Rose smiled as she handed the phone back.

'Thanks Meggie. When Angus gets here, we'll go to the hospital and you can drop Charlie to day care.' Rose began puffing and Meggie quickly took Charlie, rushing him back to his play area, before returning to Rose who was now pacing from one side of the room to the other, before flopping on to the bed.

'That was a strong one.' Rose spoke through clenched teeth.

'What can I do Rose?' Meggie sat beside her and Rose leaned into her for a moment. Meggie stroked Rose's hair.

'Meggie. I want to ask you something. To do something. Two things actually.' Rose's expression was serious.

Meggie moved sideways, so she could look directly at Rose. 'Anything Rose, you know that.'

'Firstly. Would you, could you, consider being with me today? With me and Angus? In the birthing room?' Rose chuckled then. 'Oh he was great last time, don't get me wrong, but he doesn't have the instincts, you know? Where to rub, what I need. And he needed reassurance. About the pain. Was I okay.' Rose snorted. 'A woman in labour doesn't have energy to reassure the father. I almost ordered him from the room, he was getting in the way!'

They laughed then and Meggie held Rose's hand. 'It would be my honour Rose. And you know I'll tell that hulking big brother of mine what to do if he gets in the way this time!'

'I'm counting on it.' Was all Rose managed to say before another contraction hit. The pacing helped, so they walked up and down the hallway, Meggie with her arm around Rose, until it subsided.

They returned to the bedroom and Meggie spoke gently. 'And the other thing Rose? There were two things.'

'We want to ask if you and Max will be godparents, for this one.' She couldn't seem to finish and Meggie brought Rose's hand to her face, resting it against her cheek.

'Oh Rose. I'm honoured. And yes, of course.' They nestled together, briefly, and Meggie recognised, not for the first time, how close she felt to Rose. More like a sister than sister-in-law. And she knew Angus and Max were close too.

The next half hour flew by. Meggie made a snack for Charlie, found him a clean tee shirt and shorts, packed his snacks for day care and ensured he was playing happily. In between she supported Rose through contractions, still three minutes apart and tried to maintain a sense of calm.

It all changed when Angus pulled up outside with a screech and a slammed door. Charlie met him at the door, crying at all the commotion, and Angus bounded down the hallway with his sobbing son in his arms.

'Rose! Meggie?' Angus paused at the door, still holding Charlie, who now leaned away from arm, his arms stretched towards Meggie. Rose breathed through the last thirty seconds of a contraction and sat on the bed, while Meggie scooped Charlie and galloped him back to the kitchen on her hip with the promise of a banana. She wanted Rose and Angus to have a few moments together. She no longer thought Rose would deliver quickly as the contractions and time between had remained much the same for the last hour. *She could be hours yet.*

The banana finished, she turned as Angus walked into the hallway, one arm around Rose and her bag in his other hand. He settled Rose in to a grandfather chair in the hallway.

'Rose says I have time to have a shower. What do you think Meggs?' His words were spoken quietly, his expression one of concern. And worry. Meggie glanced behind him to Rose, then laughed. Rose was pinching her nose with her fingers, pointing to Angus and making a stinky-face. She looked again at Angus, he was bemused by their laughter.

'What?' He spun around, but Rose was all innocence now, then back to Meggie. 'Do I have time? To shower?'

'It's a yes from me brother. You stink of horse. And something else. Manure?' Meggie screwed up her nose and took a step back.

'Fertiliser. The paddock we were working in had just been fertilised. We had to sedate the horse, get the wire away from it, before we could …' He didn't finish his sentence as Rose shouted, between clenched teeth. 'Shower Angus!'

He seemed to hesitate, but when Meggie rushed to Rose's side, got her on her feet and began pacing with her in the hallway, he bolted. He returned minutes later, wearing clean jeans and shirt, his hair damp. Rose patted his face. 'Better.'

Looking at her watch, Meggie saw it was already after nine. 'I'll take Charlie to day care. Rose, I'll take your car, it has the child-seat.' She threw her keys to Angus. 'You take mine. I'll meet you at the hospital after I drop Charlie and check in at work.' She hesitated for a moment.

'Rose?' Her sister-in-law turned to her.

'You know Harriet is scheduled for surgery this morning too. She had to be there by seven but there was no indication of the actual time of the caesarean. So I'm going to check with Ben in case he hears something first. He can message me.' Meggie took Charlie by the hand, his little back pack over her shoulder, and walked to the door. Looking behind her she saw Angus was helping Rose to her feet. Her eyes met Rose's. Angus was distracted, juggling the car keys and the overnight bag.

'I'm thinking of Harriet too Meggie. Please tell me, when you hear.' She smiled then. 'It will be okay. We'll all be okay.'

29

DEBBIE

DEBBIE FELT A PANG OF JEALOUSY WHEN SHE SAW THE message from Meggie.

> Rose in labour. I'm with her. Meggs xx

She'd always been Rose's person. Debbie placed a protective hand over her belly and shook her head. *Don't be silly. Of course Meggie should be with Rose.* But Debbie still had the strangest feeling that something was changing. Had the earth tilted, ever so slightly, on its axis?

> Wish her luck and love. Deb xx

She walked across the room to clear a table just vacated, smiling at new customers as they entered the café. Her mind was still racing with Meggie's news. *Rose was early. Not much. But she'd gone over with Charlie.* She'd thought to herself only yesterday that Rose looked ready to pop.

Still self-talking, her back was to the door and she was startled by a deep male voice. 'Excuse me. Um. You're Debbie?' She turned to the voice, her smile at the ready. His face looked familiar, but she couldn't place him.

'Yes, I'm Deb. Hello.' She waited. His eyes didn't leave hers, but she knew he was very aware of her protruding baby bump. 'Have we met? You look familiar.'

He held his hand out at once. 'Yes. Well, not formally. I'm Finn. Finn Anderson. Barrington Ridge Estate. I provided the wine for Harriet and Drum Murray's wedding.'

Debbie brought the palm of her hand to her face and rolled her eyes. 'Of course, silly me. You're Meggie's wine guy.' She shook his hand. 'How can I help you?'

He laughed, loud and heartily. The laugh a perfect reflection of his looks. Taller than Debbie, but not a giant, he had a stocky build and very broad shoulders. Dark hair, greying at the temples and a friendly, open face. 'The wine guy, yes.' He leaned closer. 'But I don't think I'm Meggie's. I've met Max,' and he laughed again. Debbie chuckled too. She liked this man.

'Actually, Meggie sent me a message, and if I understand it correctly, she's attending a birth.' He raised his eyebrows, then went on. 'I have a wine delivery for an elopement at the weekend. But her office is locked up. She asked me to bring it here.'

'Oh! Did she?' For a very brief moment, Debbie was annoyed. Meggie hadn't asked her about this.

'Um, if it's not okay, I can come back in the morning.' Finn had picked up on her momentary uncertainty. Then Debbie shook her head, laughing at herself. *Of course Meggie wouldn't think to ask. We're friends. Good friends. And she's with Rose at the hospital.*

'Where are you parked Finn? If you drive around to the back, I'll walk through and open the cool room for you. We have plenty of space.' Debbie waved her arm as she spoke. 'You can come down the side lane.'

'Oh that's perfect, thank you. I'm parked in front of Meggie's office, so I will be there in less than five minutes.' He began to walk to the door, then turned. 'I've heard a lot about your café Debbie Webb. After I unload the wine I'd like to come in for a coffee. And snack.'

'Debbie Tait now.' She laughed and pointed to her belly. 'But coffee and snacks we can do.'

———

HALF AN HOUR LATER, AFTER SERVING FINN HIS SECOND coffee, Debbie felt her phone ping in her apron pocket. Stepping behind the counter, she pulled it out, hoping for news of Rose. But it was Drum.

> It's a boy! Hamish. Tell everyone. Both well. Drum

> Congratulations! Will spread the word. Sending love. Deb xx

Debbie breathed a sigh of relief. *Harriet!* She'd almost forgotten she was having the caesarean this morning, with everything else going on. She popped into the kitchen and told Cathy, then sent a message to Meggie.

> Harriet has a boy, Hamish. Both well.
> How's Rose?

30

ROSE

ROSE WAS ANNOYED. SHE WAS STILL IN THE HOSPITAL emergency cubicle with Meggie and Angus, waiting for the midwife. The contractions were three minutes apart. She should be up in the labour ward, at the very least.

There was a crying child in the next cubicle and all attention was on him. He'd broken his leg on the way to school, falling off his push-bike. She exhaled noisily, aware her irritation was on display. Angus was on one side, holding her hand, and Meggie was alternating between sitting on the chair on the other side, to standing, supporting her back through the contractions.

The curtain opened and the midwife, Kerrie, came in. She'd attended Charlie's birth and Rose was relieved to see her.

'Rose. Hello.' She smiled at Rose and murmured hello to Angus and Meggie, before pushing the button for the blood pressure cuff to inflate, two fingers on Rose's pulse. Seemingly satisfied by the readings, she spoke to Rose again. 'So your water hasn't broken?'

Rose shook her head, mouthing 'no' just as another contraction took hold. Kerrie supported her back, saying calmly, 'just breathe Rose. You've done this before. Just breathe.'

When the contraction subsided Kerrie moved to the bottom of the bed. 'I'll have a quick look Rose, but if your water hasn't broken and you're only a centimetre or two dilated, you may be more comfortable at home for a few more hours. You can come back in when the action really starts.'

Kerrie busied herself at the other end of the bed and Rose was grateful both Meggie and Angus were at her head. She felt a bit silly, rushing in to the hospital so quickly. She could have waited at home a bit longer. This wasn't her first baby, she should have known. She frowned then. But it had *felt* urgent. She was acting on instinct, not logic.

Kerrie popped her head up. 'You can put your legs down now Rose.' She looked slightly flustered. 'I'm just going to consult with Doctor Rao.' She stepped out of the cubicle, drawing the curtain behind her.

Angus looked anxious. 'First she said we should go home for a bit. But then she said she wanted to speak to the doctor!'

Rose didn't know what to say, but Meggie seemed calm. 'She'll just be checking whether to send you home or admit you to the labour ward. She might not have the authority herself.' Angus visibly relaxed.

Within minutes Kerrie was back, the doctor with her. He smiled at Rose, shook Drum's hand and acknowledged Meggie. 'You're Angus's sister? I've heard about your new business venture, congratulations.'

He went to the bottom of the bed. 'Raise your legs please Rose. Slide your bottom down the bed slightly. That's it.' Rose felt uncomfortable, and another contraction was building. She squeezed Angus's hand and began puffing. The doctor stood then, picked up her chart and stepped out of the room with Kerrie.

'What the ... arrgh!' Rose gritted her teeth as the pain rolled through her lower back and across her belly like a vice. She could vaguely hear Meggie puffing with her, their faces close. Angus was standing now, supporting her into a half sitting position, one large hand rubbing her back, the other holding hers. Being squeezed by hers.

As the pain subsided the doctor was back. 'We're going to admit you Rose. It's unusual your water hasn't broken, you're eight centimetres dilated. We'll get you upstairs, and if necessary, I'll break the water and we can get this baby out.' He was cheerful and calm, but Rose's head was spinning. *Eight centimetres! What?*

She looked from Angus to Meggie. Angus seemed anxious still, until Meggie grinned at him, punching him lightly on the arm. 'You're gonna have a baby today, Gus.' His face lightened. He grinned at Meggie, then leaned down and kissed Rose loudly. She laughed.

In a flurry of activity she was transported to the lift, Angus beside her the whole time, and wheeled into a labour room. It wasn't a big hospital but had two modern birthing units. Meggie must have followed because she reappeared with Rose's bag.

'Music Rose?' Meggie asked, her phone in her hand. But Rose shook her head. She had a whole playlist planned, but the thought of music now was excruciating. What she wanted was some pain relief.

As if he could read her mind, Doctor Rao stepped back into the room. 'How's the pain Rose? Do you need something? Gas?'

Rose nodded. The Doctor waited. *Damn. She had to use her*

words. Through clenched teeth she snapped. 'Yes. Something for the pain. Gas. Yes.' Kerrie stepped forward, setting up the gas. She gave the mask to Angus, instructing him to help Rose *like last time*.

'Like last time!' Rose knew she was shouting, but she was in pain, eight centimetres dilated and her bloody water hadn't broken. 'Nothing about this. Is. Like. Last. Time!' Rose grunted, as the pain took hold again, Angus and Meggie taking their places while Kerrie looked momentarily shocked, before she smiled, patted Rose on the arm and left the room.

Returning, she spoke quietly. 'There's no time for an epidural Rose. It's gas for now. Pethidine if you need it.' She handed a glass of ice chips to Meggie. 'Doctor is going to break your water and then things should start to move quickly.'

Still feeling unaccountably annoyed, Rose snarled, 'I bloody hope so!'

While the doctor and Kerrie organised what they needed to break the water, Rose saw Meggie check her phone. She grinned. 'Harriet has a boy, Rose. They've named him Hamish. They're both doing well!' Hearing the words, Rose began to cry. Angus immediately leaned forward, wiping her eyes gently and murmuring to her. She held his hand to her mouth and kissed it gently. 'I'm so happy for Harri and Drum. Really I am.' Another pain began and she half grunted , half shouted her next words. 'But I want this baby. Out. Now!' She could hear herself. Knew she was being unreasonable. But didn't care. The pain was a vice around her torso, then she felt a gush of fluid from between her legs.

'Alright Rose, you're fully dilated. Push when you feel you

need to.' Kerrie checked her blood pressure and pulse as she spoke. Rose nodded, sucking on an ice chip.

The next contraction seemed softer, less painful. *Maybe it's the gas.* A few minutes later and another contraction came, but again it was soft. Rose didn't feel the urge to push. At all. She relaxed, listening to the quiet conversation between Meggie and Angus. At some point the doctor had left, but Kerrie seemed to be with them most of the time. Minutes passed. The contractions had subsided. At one point Rose dozed off.

She woke with a start. The doctor was in the room, examining her again. Kerrie had moved another machine into position and they were putting clips of some sort across her belly. Angus was standing beside Meggie, looking worried.

'What? What is it?' Rose tried to sit up. Meggie rushed to her side, supporting her. 'What's happening?' She gestured, suddenly angry again, at the clips on her belly. Louder now, she asked, 'What. Is. This?'

Doctor Rao moved to her side, leaning over her. 'Rose, we're monitoring baby's heartbeat. We're worried baby might be getting distressed.' He paused, looking across at Angus. 'Your labour seems to be, um, paused. If it doesn't progress soon, we may have to consider...' He stopped, looking again at Angus. 'Caesarean section.' He seemed to check himself. 'A last resort, of course.'

Rose's mind was spinning. *Caesarean? No!* She wasn't prepared for that. Gritting her teeth, she glared at the doctor. 'I've had one baby. I can have this one!' He was still leaning over her, his tie had somehow come loose from his white coat and was sort of *dangling* over her belly. Rose grabbed the tie with one hand, yanking it until his face was close to hers. She snarled, 'what's your hurry doctor? Got a golf game to get to?' Somehow Angus extracted the tie from her hand, releasing the doctor. She lay back. The doctor left the room.

Still furious, Rose heard a giggle. She looked up at Meggie. She was trying hard not to laugh out loud, one hand clamped across her mouth. Rose frowned, then looked at Angus, then Kerrie. Angus looked like he wanted to laugh but didn't want to upset her. Kerrie busied herself with something at the end of the bed. Rose looked at Meggie again.

Hiccupping and laughing, but trying not to, Meggie spoke. 'Grrr. Doctor. Do you have a *golf game* to get to? Grr.' Then she threw her head back and laughed out loud, tears running down her face. 'I'm sorry Rose. You're always so nice. So polite.'

Rose chuckled then. 'Stop it Meggs. I'm the bridezilla of birthing. I can get nasty.' She said *nasty* with an American twang and Angus snorted.

He looked at Meggie. 'I should have warned you. She gets a bit potty-mouth in labour. Well, she did with Charlie.' He grinned at Kerrie. 'There was a succession of fuckity-fucks last time.' Kerrie laughed with them.

Rose turned to Angus. 'I get it. It's funny.' She sniffed. Once. Then began to cry. 'I don't want to have a caesarean. I won't be able to pick Charlie up. For weeks. He won't understand.' She turned back to Kerrie, her expression intense. 'I can do this. I know I can.'

Kerrie murmured gently. 'Relax Rose. Let me check how baby is.' Kerrie checked the output on the machine. 'Still okay here. But Rose, if you feel the need to push, just do it.'

Nothing seemed to progress over the next forty minutes or so. The doctor popped in briefly and Rose tried to say sorry. He laughed it off, saying he'd heard worse.

Close to lunch time, Meggie said she was going to pop to the café to get coffee for her and Angus. Rose nodded. *Coffee. Coffee would be nice. Or wine. Or maybe she was just using the gas too much.*

As Meggie stepped back into the room, pain suddenly radiated from Rose's back, to her belly. She grunted and Angus quickly gave her the gas while Meggie abandoned the coffee and perched on the bed, Rose half sitting, half leaning on her. A strong contraction, like early this morning. Rose was heartened and pushed into it.

Two more and Kerrie was now at the foot of the bed. Doctor Rao returned and took over. 'Baby is crowning Rose. Another push and we'll have the head out.'

Taking deep breaths, keeping her eyes on Angus the whole time, she pushed into the next pain and felt the baby slither between her legs. Another push and she lay back, feeling the baby leave her body.

Doctor Rao lifted the baby for Rose to see. 'You have a girl. But she's a bit blue around the mouth, so Kerrie will take her now and give her some oxygen.' Rose wanted to focus on that. She reached for her baby, but the doctor was telling her to keep push-ing, she needed to deliver the placenta. Meggie and Angus on either side, Rose concentrated, and pushed.

'Alright Rose. Good. Well done.' The doctor grabbed a tray from a side table. 'You need a couple of stitches Rose, there's a small tear. I'm giving you some local anaesthetic.' He turned to Kerrie who was busy with the baby on the other side of the room. 'How's our little patient, nurse?'

Beaming, Kerrie carried the baby over to Rose, placing her on her chest. Her little mouth was rosebud shaped, and no longer blue. And she had a thick head of dark hair. Like her father. Pain forgotten, Rose marvelled at her daughter. She saw Angus wipe a tear away, and Meggie was crying openly.

'She's beautiful Rose. Just beautiful. Do you have a name for her yet? Did you even know you were having a girl?' Meggie's face was full of love and Rose's chest welled. *A girl. We have a girl.*

'We didn't know. I tried to peek.' She placed Angus's hand on their baby's little back, her face now red and screwed up. She let out a wail, but it was more like whimper. 'I've always liked Harper. You know, after Harper Lee, the author?'

'Harper.' Meggie and Angus said it at the same time. Angus spoke then, his face full of wonder. 'A daughter. Harper. Yes, Harper. It suits her.'

31

MILLIE

It was early, barely six, but Millie was awake. She padded out to the kitchen, peering out of the window overlooking the street as she filled her water bottle. It was already warm but she was keen to go for a quick walk before getting ready for her first day at the café. There were one or two cars parked in the street, outside the pub. Probably there from the night before and as she watched a four-wheel-drive moved slowly along the street, then parked outside the Vet clinic. She squinted. The Ute had signage on the side, like the sign in the clinic window. *The Vet, then.* He was a very tall, well-built man, about her own age, she thought, as he unlocked the door and entered, leaving it ajar. Millie was still watching a minute later as he stepped out again, a package under his arm. She jumped back, shocked, as he looked directly up at her, and waved. She blushed, suddenly embarrassed. Rushing back to her room, she picked up her keys and phone, putting them in her pocket. She glanced out of the living area window again, but the vehicle was no longer there. Phew!

Bounding down the back stairs, Millie felt energised. *A fresh start.* Since the breakup and closure of her own business, she'd been focussing on herself, for the first time in two decades. She walked at least five mornings a week, had found time to read again and was an avid movie-goer. She'd been doing this by herself and found it liberating. Doing what she wanted, when she wanted, for herself. Rather than feeling tired by exercising, or finding it a chore, she enjoyed it. There was a spring in her step and she felt healthy. And strong. She'd even bought some small hand weights and had been doing basic strength exercises at home, using a clever fitness app. There was no downside. She'd lost weight too, not as much as she'd like to, but it was *distributed differently* after just a few weeks of regular exercise.

While working in her own café was busy work and she exceeded her daily step count, the ever-present temptation to nibble their fare had been her undoing. She recognised she was a comfort eater, and as the marriage and business had become more stressful, she'd eaten more. Almost to the point where she would eat surreptitiously, hiding her treats. No amount of exercise shifted the weight. But it had all changed once she was free of the business, and her unhappy marriage. She didn't need the comfort of food and had no one to hide it from. And she had realised something else too, equally as important. She always put every-one's needs before her own. Her husband, the kids, the staff. Even the creditors and her friends.

But now it was *her* time. This move to Barrington, even if just for one year, was about her. She knew she'd love the work, and she wasn't worried about snacking at work. It wasn't *her business, her food.* It belonged to Debbie Tait. And Millie was honest and ethi-cal. Always. She was slightly disappointed that Barrington didn't have a movie theatre, but Taree and Forster did, and they weren't that far.

Using her phone GPS Millie navigated her way to the main park in town. There was a walkway that followed the river before turning back to town. Lengthening her stride, she followed the path, marvelling at the beauty of the well-maintained grounds. A few runners came past her, calling out 'good morning' as they did. She smiled and greeted them too, feeling already part of the community.

Almost seven, she ran up the back stairs lightly. *When did she last do that, after a walk?* Giggling to herself, she ran down the stairs, then up a second time. *Forty-three and feeling good.* As she let herself in the door she sang *I feel good,* and hummed the words she didn't know as she headed for the shower.

Debbie had asked her to be at the café at eight, but Millie was keen and walked through the door fifteen minutes before. Cathy was serving at the front counter, chatting to a customer and making coffee, and a young girl in school uniform with an apron over the top bustled out from the kitchen, placing baked goods in the display cabinet. She smiled shyly at Millie before dashing back to the kitchen.

Cathy finished serving the customer then turned to Millie. 'Hi Millie! Welcome. Debbie's not here yet, but come on in, put your bag out the back. Can I make you a coffee?'

'Good morning, and yes, thank you. Skinny dirty chai latte please.' Millie could see more customers coming in and she quickly put her bag in the locker Debbie had shown her last time and stepped back out to the counter, tying an apron on over her black pants and white shirt. She said hello to the young girl in the kitchen, who shyly said her name was Lucy.

Cathy knew all the customers by name. *Early morning regulars,* Millie thought. And introduced Millie to each of them as they ordered. Cathy was taking the orders now, and Millie was on the coffee machine. They worked well together and Millie tried to commit the names of the customers to memory.

Debbie breezed through from the back, just as Lucy waved goodbye. 'Lucy walks up to the High School. She'll be back this afternoon. School finishes this week and Lucy will be with us full time through the holidays.'

Cathy retreated to the kitchen and Debbie and Millie worked alongside each other until the early morning rush subsided, around nine thirty.

'Wow Millie. You just stepped in there, never missing a beat. Anyone would think you'd worked here for years.' Debbie 's voice was full of admiration and Millie was warmed by her praise.

'You have lovely customers. Got to love those weekday regulars!' She turned back to the coffee machine, wiping the nozzle and put more beans in the grinder.

'And here's one of our favourites.' Millie smiled at the warmth she heard in Debbie's voice. 'Hi Max. This is Millie, our new manager.'

Millie turned to greet the customer, then flushed. It was the man she'd seen this morning, at the Vet clinic. The one who'd caught her staring and waved. 'Oh hello. Max.' She held out her hand.

Shaking it, he grinned at her, then said to Debbie. 'I caught Millie's eye early this morning when I dropped by the clinic.' Then to Millie he said, 'I was watching out for you. I'm Meggie's partner. She used to live in your flat. She told me you'd arrive over the weekend. She'll be in this morning for coffee.' Millie was relieved. He didn't think she'd been staring at him or checking him out. And Meggie had been really helpful with her accommodation, she hoped they'd get to know each other while she was in Barrington.

Max left with two coffees. For himself and the Vet nurse, he'd said. Millie's mind was racing, trying to organise all the people she'd already met into compartments, working out who was who.

'Come out the back Millie, and I'll run through where everything is. Cathy takes care of the food and ingredient orders. I handle the drinks, coffee and consumables. We have it on a system linked to our accounting package.' Debbie led her through the kitchen to the office. She opened the cool room and freezer doors as they went by and pointed out the dry goods storage area too. Everything was well placed. Millie was impressed.

'It's a great set-up Debbie. Professionally designed. Who did this for you?' Millie was curious.

'Actually, the shell was already here when I took the lease, but the fit out hadn't been completed. The building is owned by Douglas Barlow, the Solicitor in the upstairs rooms. He had it designed by a Melbourne firm.' Debbie touched her tummy and sat suddenly.

Millie was on alert. 'Are you okay Debbie? Pain?'

Debbie laughed. 'No pain. Heartburn, and a foot under my ribs, I think.' She got back to her feet after a minute, but Millie wasn't convinced.

'You don't have to show me everything today Debbie. Why don't you head off. I'm sure Cathy and I can cope.'

Laughing, Debbie waved her words away. 'I'm fine. We'll get busy again mid-morning. I'll stay until after lunch.' They began walking back to the main area of the shop. 'But I'll arrange a catch up with Douglas Barlow, and his wife Frances for you this week.'

Back at the counter, they fell into their earlier rhythm, with Debbie taking orders and Millie making coffee and serving food. When Debbie picked up a tray, to head onto the floor to clear tables, Millie took the tray from her. 'Stay here Debbie. I'll do that.' With no argument, Debbie handed the tray and damp cloth to Millie.

———

MID-MORNING HAD BEEN BUSIER THAN FIRST THING, IF that was possible, and the day passed quickly. Another rush for lunch, then when Lucy arrived after school, Debbie and Millie went to the table in the back, sharing a plate of sandwiches and a bottle of water.

'Your first day is almost over Millie and you've done well. You know what to do without being asked and you're great with the staff and customers. I'm giving myself a little pat on the back for hiring you.' Debbie laughed, then raised her water glass to Millie in a toast, of sorts.

Clinking glasses with Debbie, Millie hesitated before speaking. 'I love it already Debbie. You've established such a great business here. I just hope I can fill your shoes while you're on leave.'

'Fill my shoes! Millie, you're very experienced and I have every confidence I can leave you to it, once we have Lucy full time next week and then Cathy's daughter Kristen will be with us too, she's coming home from university for the summer.' Debbie sighed and put her feet up on the chair across from her. Millie couldn't help noticing they were very swollen.

Debbie suddenly grinned. 'You remember Harriet? My friend at your interview? She had her baby a few days ago. Four weeks premmie but doing well. They'll be home at the end of next week. A little boy, Hamish. They already have Drum's daughter, Billie, from his first marriage.'

'That's wonderful news, I did wonder. She seemed lovely.' Millie chuckled to herself. 'And also a competent business woman, if I'm any guess.'

'You're right. She is. She works with Meggie, they have a business together, and Harriet has an arrangement with the Bens from the real estate office. You'll meet them all.'

Debbie finished her sandwich and patted her belly. 'That's it for me. I'm going to waddle off to my car after I say goodbye to Cathy, if you think you're okay now?'

'Run Debbie. Save yourself!' Millie joked and they walked back to the kitchen, laughing together.

32

———

FRANCES

With the tea tray in her hands, Frances walked through to Douglas. She smiled brightly at him.

'I've made a pot of tea. Do you have time for a chat?' She slid the tray onto his desk, her eyebrows raised in enquiry.

'Tea. Lovely. I was just thinking it was that time.' Douglas moved his notepad and pen to the side. She knew he'd been working on new wills for Angus and Rose Hamilton. They'd planned to have them signed before the birth. *That ship has sailed.*

Frances relaxed in the chair across from Douglas, sipping her tea. She glanced at the fine china cup she held. Her favourite from a set her parents had given them as a wedding present. She'd chipped a couple over the years and had brought the remaining four teacups and saucers into the office. It was the Arcadia design by Royal Doulton, now discontinued, so she hadn't been able to replace the broken pieces. *Pretty.*

'Frances.' Douglas was staring at her, his face concerned.

146

'Where did you go just now? I was asking if you'd heard anything more from Rose, how she and baby Harper are doing?'

Chuckling, she set her teacup down, but her hand shook slightly. 'Don't look so worried Douglas. Yes, I was miles away, just thinking about the beautiful tea set we're using. You know this was a wedding present from my parents?' *She hated him questioning her.*

'Ah yes. You are right. Royal Doulton if I recall correctly. It's very fine.' His words were warm and Frances relaxed. Douglas continued. 'I notice you never use these cups for clients.'

This time she laughed out loud. 'Could you imagine Drum Murray or Angus Hamilton trying to pick one of these up? With their giant hands?'

Douglas laughed with her. 'Of course. You're right.' He sipped the last of his tea. 'But they are lovely to drink from.' He replaced his cup and saucer on the tea tray. 'Was there anything particular you wanted to discuss, Frances?'

Frowning, Frances tapped her fingers on the desk for a moment. 'There *was* something.' Shaking her head she stood then, picking up the tea tray. 'It will come back to me.'

As she walked toward the door, she turned. 'Oh yes. Debbie's new manager, Millie, started yesterday. Debbie messaged and asked if there was a time she could bring her up to meet us? But I thought it might be nice if we went down to the café for lunch today, to meet her informally first.'

Frances blinked. Douglas looked so happy. *Really? Why was he so keen to meet her?* She paused in the doorway.

'Good plan Frances. And lunch at the cafe will be lovely. Two birds and all that.' His words put her at ease and she returned to the kitchen area, where she carefully washed up their tea things.

33

HARRIET

H ARRIET TURNED IN THE PASSENGER SEAT, FOR AT least the hundredth time, to check on Hamish. She'd fed him just before they left Sydney and he had slept all the way. *Only two weeks old and already heading home.* He was strong, fed lustily and had regained his birth weight, and more. She caught Billie's eye, sitting in the back beside the baby carrier, one hand resting lightly on her brother's chest.

Billie grinned, then put a finger to her mouth and pointed at Hamish. He was beginning to squirm. Harriet looked at Drum. He was concentrating on the road, but a small smile played around the corners of his mouth. She'd never seen him happier.

Harriet spoke quietly. 'I'm not sure we'll get all the way home, Drum. Your son's getting restless.' His grin widened and she smiled inwardly. Hamish left no one in doubt when he was hungry, which seemed to be whenever he was awake. He bawled loudly, but as soon as she put him to her breast, he'd stop, nuzzle, then latch on and suck with all his might. Her nipples had been

148

tender for the first few days, but now she really enjoyed the sensation. Loved the closeness of his small body against hers.

Drum tilted his head to one side, while still watching the road. 'Do you want to stop in Stratford, or wait until Barrington? It's ten minutes, but we can drop into the café and you can feed him there.' He glanced in the rear-view mirror and nodded as Billie said in a half-whisper. 'The café, yes please Dad.'

'Alright. But be prepared for screaming if he wakes up before we get there.' Harriet laughed as she spoke. His screams weren't really *that* loud. Settling back into the seat Harriet looked around as Drum drove slowly through Stratford, then accelerated as he left the township. She saw Billie was reading. She'd started the Anne of Green Gables series in Sydney and was loving them. She'd googled where Prince Edward Island was on Harriet's phone and asked if they could consider a holiday to Canada one day.

Hamish opened his eyes and whimpered a couple of times, but Billie rocked his little body gently with her hand and he seemed happy to look around him. But when Drum slowed in the main street, then reversed into a car park near the café, Hamish cried loudly. Harriet stepped out of the car carefully as soon as it stopped, her caesarean stitches had only been removed two days before, and opened the back door, crooning to the baby as she did.

Drum was beside her then and reaching into the car he undid the straps and lifted the baby out. 'Carrier too, Harri? Or will we just take him like this?'

'Like this I think. We won't be too long.' Turning to Billie she was about to ask her to get the baby bag from the car, then saw she already had it over her shoulder. *Good girl.*

Drum closed the car up, Hamish in his arms, but wide awake. He snuffled his face into Drum's neck. *So cute.* Harriet leaned down to Billie, saying quietly, 'wonderful girl, thank you. You're already the best big sister.'

Billie nodded, then said firmly. 'Six weeks Harri. You're not supposed to do *anything* for six weeks.'

'I'm sure I could carry the baby bag. Or Hamish.' They were almost to the café now.

Billie shook her head. 'The baby bag is too heavy. My book's in there.'

Harriet laughed. 'I was like you Billie. I took a book everywhere when I was your age.'

Billie nodded, her face serious. 'Just in case.'

'Yes. Just in case.' Harriet's happiness metre rose another notch.

———

Debbie rushed to greet them, oohing and aahing over Hamish, then led them to the table at the back that Harriet thought of as *their* table. They ordered morning tea and Harriet settled in a chair. She unbuttoned her blouse and Drum placed Hamish carefully into her arms. Harriet thought she'd feed him first, then change him, and top him up with another feed before they left.

Drum ordered coffee, and a glass of water for Harriet, and Billie asked for a milkshake. Debbie returned with a tray of various slices and cake, with Millie behind her, carrying the drinks.

'Millie! Lovely to see you! This must be only your second day.' Harriet was pleased to see her. Debbie had messaged last night, to tell Harriet they'd made the right choice. Her exact words were *Millie is brilliant, fits right in.*

'Hello Harriet.' Millie looked directly at her. Harriet had noticed, in just two weeks of being a nursing mother, that many people, including women, were reluctant to make eye contact with a breast-feeding mother.

'Millie, this is Harriet's husband, Drum, and daughter Billie.' Debbie made the introductions. Billie looked up, waved hello, then turned back to the book she'd already opened on the table in front of her.

Placing the coffee down in front of them, Millie reached across to Billie, sliding her milkshake on to the table. 'Is that Anne of Green Gables? I loved those books so much that I made a trip to Prince Edward Island, the one and only time I went to Canada.' Harriet chuckled as Billie closed her book quickly and began asking Millie about her trip, finishing by saying 'Harri and I want to go to Canada, to visit Prince Edward Island.' She nodded her head firmly, her golden curls bouncing on her shoulders.

'That's something to look forward to Billie.' Millie leaned a bit closer. 'You should google Canada, there's a lot of other things to see and do there too. Did you know that in one part of the country French is their first language? Oh, and the skiing is wonderful in winter, but they also have enormous lakes.' Harriet could see Billie was taking all this in, her young face full of excitement.

'Thank you Millie!' Turning to her father, Billie held out her hand. 'Dad, may I have your phone? I need to google Canada.' Harriet winked at Millie as she straightened and was rewarded with a wink in return. Drum groaned and handed his phone to Billie.

———

CHAPTER 33

Returning from the bathroom, where she had changed Hamish, Harriet found Debbie sitting at their table, chatting with Drum. As she approached, Debbie held out her arms. 'May I hold him Harri?'

Laughing, Harriet placed Hamish in Debbie's arms. 'Oh, he's so handsome.' As Debbie spoke, Drum's chest seemed to inflate slightly. Debbie and Harriet caught his look of pride, and Harriet said drily, 'I have no idea where he gets his good looks.'

Debbie responded quickly. 'Total mystery. Yet here he is, the best-looking baby boy in town.'

Drum threw back his head and laughed. In an undertone he said, 'From my loins girls, from my loins!' and laughed again.

Billie piped up, 'what's loins Dad?' Debbie and Harriet giggled together as Drum tried to find the right words to explain. It ended up being something about breeding and bulls and progeny, and while Billie nodded, she still looked confused.

Debbie passed Hamish back to Harriet, saying in a whisper, 'it may be time for *the talk*, Harri. I vote Drum does it.'

34

MEGGIE

January – Barrington Book Club – Meeting 5
Present: Debbie, Rose and baby Harper, Harriet and baby
Hamish, Nicole, Laura, Meggie, Millie
Apologies: Frances, Melanie
Book: *Runt* by Craig Silvey

MEGGIE WALKED IN TO THE CAFÉ WITH HARRIET. SHE'D
driven them in Harriet's car, as it had the baby carrier apparatus in
the back. Harriet carried baby Hamish in her arms, but Meggie
had the baby bag, her handbag and their copies of the book.
Hamish was three weeks old and thriving, but Meggie knew
Harriet tended to do more than she should, so she'd dropped by
every day this week after work to help out. Helping out usually
meant hanging a load of washing, or bringing it in, then cuddling
Hamish while they had a chat. Meggie's desire for a baby of her
own hadn't receded. In fact, it was stronger than ever. Twice this
week, after leaving Harriet and Hamish, Meggie had cried on the

way home. Max hadn't said much, but he'd held her gently and told her he loved her.

Laura opened the door for them, the interior of the café was cool and a blessed relief from the late afternoon heat. 'Frances and Douglas are still in Sydney, with their son and his family. They're not back until next week. And Melanie's not coming, she's been struggling with the heat.'

Walking down to their table where Rose sat next to Debbie and Nicole, Harper asleep on her shoulder, Meggie glanced into the kitchen. Young Lucy was making coffee and she could see Millie in the kitchen.

Ensuring Harriet was comfortable, Meggie walked back to the kitchen to get some wine glasses. Laura had brought a bottle of something from Barrington Ridge Estate and Meggie was keen to try it.

With the glasses in hand, Meggie poked her head into the kitchen. 'Are you joining us for book club Millie?' She grinned and waved the glasses around. 'We have wine.'

Millie looked uncertain. 'Um. Thank you. I'm not sure. I stayed back to help Lucy with the coffee and snacks.' She looked past Meggie to Lucy at the coffee machine, then added quietly. 'Um. Debbie's feet are swollen. More than usual. And painful too, I think. I wanted to make sure she didn't do any work, and just enjoyed the company of her friends.'

'Swollen? Really? I'll check it out.' Meggie frowned. 'She's been wearing maxi skirts and wide leg pants the last few weeks. I can't say I've even *seen* her feet. And we've all been focussed on the babies. Harper and Hamish.'

'I hope I'm not speaking out of turn Meggie. But I know you

are all really close, and I've only been here a couple of weeks.' She hesitated.

'Thank you for mentioning it, Millie. And please. Stay for book club. I think you know everyone.' Meggie left the kitchen, grabbing another wine glass as she did. 'I'm pouring you a drink Millie. I know you don't have to drive home!'

Back at the table they all chatted while Lucy brought the other drinks. Meggie, Laura, Nicole and Millie drank wine. Meggie was impressed with the wine. She needed to make a time to catch up with Finn Anderson about the next few events she had booked. The talk flowed from babies to business, to the heat and the chance of fires and if anyone thought there'd be a cool change soon.

Lucy had been quiet, and cleared the table when they finished their snacks. Meggie saw Nicole watch her daughter as she returned to the kitchen. A pretty girl, but very shy, Meggie thought. She was about to comment when Millie leaned closer to Nicole. 'She's brilliant Nicole. In the kitchen especially, but great with the orders now too.'

'She isn't too quiet?' Nicole looked behind her. Lucy was still in the kitchen. 'Does she actually speak to the customers, or does she just wait for them to order? I'm not joking. I worry about her. All the time.'

Millie smiled then. Meggie suddenly thought how pretty she was with her straight white teeth, shoulder length wavy hair and high cheekbones. She didn't wear much makeup, and no wonder, her skin was youthful and smooth.

Speaking quietly, no doubt aware that Lucy wasn't far away, Millie reassured Nicole. 'Yes. She speaks to them. She has a whole other persona with the customers. She knows the regulars and even has fun with them. Just the other day Douglas Barlow came in to get takeaway coffee and said he'd have a friand while he waited. Lucy raised her eyebrows and said, 'the whole lot on the card Mr Barlow? Or cash for the friand?' He laughed, paid cash for the friand, and said 'just our little secret Lucy, don't tell Frances, will you?'

They all laughed, and Meggie made a mental note to try and catch up with Millie outside of work. Maybe dinner at the pub one night.

Lucy returned and Meggie placed her copy of *Runt* on the table. 'Runt, people. What did you think?'

'I bloody love it!' Laura was never one to mince words. 'Every school child should read this. It's just so *perfectly Australian.*'

'It really is. Billie adored it, despite saying it was a bit young for her. You know there's a movie coming out, I think Sam Neill is in it. We should take the kids. Billie, Tommy, Tiffany.' Harriet looked at Lucy. 'Would you come Lucy? I know you're way too old for the book, really, but I loved it too. I think it will be a lovely family movie.' Lucy nodded enthusiastically.

Talk turned then, from the merits of the book to the cinema and streaming channels. Debbie said she hadn't been to a movie at the cinema since she had Woz, and Rose said the same. Meggie mentioned that she and Harriet had caught a couple of movies when they'd been in Sydney for business.

'Once Harriet was pregnant, dinner and drinks was out of the question, so we changed to dinner and a movie.' Meggie grinned, then added. 'They have gold class in Sydney, so I had dinner and a movie *and* a drink.' She snorted.

Millie had been quiet. She hadn't read Runt, but said she was a big reader, generally, and read books on her iPad. But once they started talking about movies, she became quite animated. 'I always said I'd never live in a town without a movie cinema. I love the movies. Streaming on television just isn't the same. Some movies *need* the big screen. How long has it been since Barrington had a cinema? I see there's a building further up the main street that's now an arcade of sorts, that has the height. Was that a cinema at one time?'

'I can answer that.' Laura spoke up. 'The Majestic Theatre opened in the mid 1920's, but it closed about forty years ago. And you're right, it's got shops in it now. I don't think we have the population to support a cinema, sadly. And streaming services have taken some of the need away.'

'But Millie, there are good cinemas in Taree and Forster. We could drive over in a group, take two or even three cars, every now and then if something was playing that we'd enjoy.' Harriet passed Hamish to Nicole. 'I'm going to the bathroom, be back in a tic.'

Debbie was quiet. Meggie plucked the sleeping Harper from Rose's arms. 'I'll have my niece now, thank you Rose.' She sat with Debbie. The others were still discussing movie nights and Millie was googling forthcoming releases and reading the descriptions out loud.

Cuddling Harper in the crook of her right arm, Meggie raised her eyebrows at Debbie. 'Are you feeling alright Debbie? You've been quiet.'

'Oh yes. Well. Mostly.' She raised the hem of her skirt and wiggled one foot. 'My feet are swollen. More than usual.' She blinked back a couple of tears, then whispered. 'More than last time Meggie.' Meggie saw in an instant that she was right. Her feet were football shaped, and spongy looking.

'Have you been to the doctor about this Debbie? You're due in, what? Five weeks?' Meggie was concerned.

'Almost six weeks.' Debbie let her skirt slide back to the floor. 'I have an appointment next Monday.' Nibbling her bottom lip, she added, 'I'm worried. But I don't want to bother Rose with this.'

'And Jamie?'

'He knows I have an appointment, but Meggie, I don't want Jamie there. I want to hear from the doctor myself, first.' Debbie rushed on, 'Mum will come with me if I ask her to and Jamie can drop Woz at Day Care. My appointment is in Newcastle.'

'Can I help, Deb? I can take Warwick to day care and pick him up, if you want your mum with you.' Pausing then, Meggie touched Debbie on the arm. 'But I can come with you, to the doctor, if you want to keep it uncomplicated and digest any news you get before seeing Jamie or your mum.'

Debbie nodded then and seemed thoughtful. Harper began to squirm in Meggie's arms and she moved her to her shoulder. She heard Rose laugh. 'Aunty Meggie. Harper just spat up a whole heap of milk down your back. Here, take these wipes, I'll take Harper.'

'A little bit of milk spit won't hurt me.' Meggie took the wipes and turned her back to Debbie. 'Can you mop me up Deb? Here's a wipe.' Debbie mopped her up, then said quietly in Meggie's ear. 'Can you come with me Meggie, next week? Please?'

'Of course.' Meggie turned back to Debbie.

'What's our next book ladies?' Laura had her phone in her hand.

'I had a couple in mind.' Harriet pulled out her notepad. 'Has anyone read any Heather Reyburn books? She has a new series, about four books I think. Maybe only three are already out. I thought the first one – *A Stranger in Featherwood Falls*, might suit us. Rural romance slash mystery. But I'm open to ideas.'

Laura looked up from her phone. 'I've got it here.' She read the description aloud and they all nodded. 'Alright then, that's sorted.'

Everyone began packing up their things. Laura took the empty wine bottle and glasses to the kitchen and Lucy wiped their table down. Nicole, Lucy and Laura left, then Rose and Debbie. Meggie picked up Harriet's things, she was holding little Hamish, and they said good night to Millie, who followed them to the door.

'You go. I'm just going to do a last-minute check that everything is locked up.' Millie smiled at Meggie. 'Thank you for inviting me to join you. What a lovely group of friends you have.'

Meggie could see Harriet at the car, already placing Hamish in his baby seat. She turned to Millie. 'I spoke to Debbie. She has an appointment in the city next week. I'm going to drive her. Thank you Millie, for letting me know.'

35

DEBBIE

Meeting Meggie at the café was the plan, as Jamie was going to drop Warwick to day care at nine. Debbie breathed a sigh of relief as she parked the car. Her feet were already swollen. In fact, they hadn't subsided at all this week, even after elevating them in the evenings. Millie had insisted she go home straight after the morning rush on Monday, then called her that night and told her (very nicely) that she should stay home and rest. Debbie was grateful.

Millie had been there a month now and was confident in her role. She got on well with the staff and was getting to know the locals too. Just yesterday she had told Debbie that she'd joined a group of women who walked the river circuit each weekday morning. Debbie wondered if she might be induced to stay more than a year.

No longer worrying about the café, Debbie now had time to focus on life at home. It was also running smoothly and Jamie, used to juggling Woz on the days he didn't go to day car, had continued to take him out on the farm, giving Debbie time to rest. It also gave her time to worry. She'd been unable to sleep the night before and had been on doctor-google in the wee hours, reading up on her symptoms. She was convinced she had pre-eclampsia. Again. She worried for her baby more than herself. Then she thought about Warwick, and Jamie, and how they'd cope, without her.

As early as it was, Cathy's car was parked behind the building and Debbie didn't want to make her presence known. She just wanted to slide into Meggie's car and drive to the appointment at the John Hunter Hospital. Her obstetrician had rooms there.

Meggie pulled in. She drove a small SUV these days. Debbie waved, gathered her handbag from the other seat, and opened her door to step out. A wave of dizziness rolled over her. She stood for a moment, holding the open car door like a lifeline. *I feel sick.* She didn't know if she should lean over and vomit on the grass verge or try to clamber back in the car. Suddenly Meggie was beside her, one arm around her waist, holding her steady.

'Debbie? Debbie? Do you feel sick? You're very pale.' Meggie had helped her step back, until she was resting against the side of the car. Standing in front of her now, Meggie held her hands and looked intently into her eyes. Debbie blinked a couple of times. The nausea had cleared, but she still felt dizzy, and realised her head was aching too. She raised a hand to her temple.

'Debbie. You're not well. It's an hour and half to your Doctor. Maybe we should call at the local hospital first?' Rushing back to her own vehicle, Meggie returned with a water bottle. Removing the lid, she placed it in Debbie's hand. 'Have a sip Deb. We just need to assess the best course of action.'

Sipping the water slowly, Debbie closed her eyes for a

moment, taking two deep breaths. When she opened them she felt slightly better. No dizziness, but the headache remained and her vision seemed odd. *Blurry.*

'I'd like to stick with the plan Meggie. Go to my doctor in Newcastle. He was with me at Warwick's birth, knows about the pre-eclampsia.' Debbie tried to sound calm, but she was close to tears. She watched Meggie as she processed this.

Obviously coming to the same conclusion, Meggie nodded. 'Alright. Newcastle it is. We'll go straight there. But I want you to hold on to this water, okay?' Debbie nodded, relieved. She tried to smile.

Meggie settled Debbie into the passenger seat, then ran back to Debbie's car to ensure it was securely locked. Back in the driver's seat she started the car, then turned to Debbie. 'You have a line between your eyebrows Deb. Headache?'

Debbie nodded. 'Yes. It's not too bad. I have paracetamol.' She rummaged in her bag. Holding up the packet, she popped two into her hand and swallowed them with a swig from the water bottle. Attempting a smile, she nodded to Meggie. 'Let's go Meggs.'

———

They stopped in Raymond Terrace, briefly, for Debbie to use the bathroom. Her headache had subsided. Meggie bought more water.

And just like that, they were in the doctor's waiting room. Debbie was nervous, her feet were swollen and sore, especially the left one. She'd messaged Jamie to tell him they were here and she'd call him after the appointment.

There were two other women in the waiting room, both quite heavily pregnant. Debbie placed her hand on her own bump. She didn't think she was as big as she had been with Warwick, with about six weeks to go. *Has the baby stopped growing? He, or she, hasn't moved much today. Is the baby okay?* She was beginning to panic, shuffled forward in her seat, intending to stand but Meggie placed her hand over the one she held to her bump, squeezing gently.

'Debbie? Debbie.' Meggie lifted her hand to Debbie's cheek, stroking it once, gently. 'Look at me Deb. I can see you're internalising, over thinking. Just breathe Deb. In. Out. That's right.' Meggie's softly spoken words had a calming effect and Debbie slowed her breathing, eyes closed, and counted to ten under her breath. Meggie kept talking, quietly. About the waiting room, the road trip, their latest book club read. Debbie knew it was to distract her. It worked. And she was grateful. She wanted to tell Meggie that, but knew she'd cry if she tried to find the words, in that moment. *She'd tell her later.*

'Debbie Tait.' The doctor stood at the door, looking directly at her. He smiled. She tried to smile back, but her emotions were right at the surface and she felt tears welling again. He stepped closer.

'Hello Debbie. Lovely to see you.' His voice was calm, his tone kind. He turned to Meggie, still holding her hand. 'I'm Doctor Ross.'

Meggie smiled brightly and shook his hand. 'Meggie Hamilton.' Debbie was able to compose herself, in those few moments.

Standing, intending to follow Doctor Ross to his consulting room, she turned back to Meggie. 'Come with me Meggie. Please.' She looked at the kindly face of her doctor. He smiled and stood back, indicating with his arm for both women to walk ahead of him.

———

HALF AN HOUR LATER, DEBBIE WIPED HER EYES WITH A tissue from the box Doctor Ross had placed strategically on his desk.

'So it's not pre-eclampsia?' She was struggling to take in everything the doctor had said and was grateful Meggie had stayed through the whole consultation.

'Your blood pressure is elevated Debbie, we need to get that down. And although we won't have a full picture until the blood tests come back, it's likely you have developed gestational diabetes and are experiencing a slight loss of kidney function. All of this is contributing to the swelling in your feet and hands, and you mentioned some dizziness and blurred vision. Baby is slightly undersize, but healthy. It's you I'm concerned about.' He turned to his computer screen for a moment, making notes and Debbie let her hand creep across to Meggie's thigh. Meggie held it firmly. She hadn't said much during the consultation, but Debbie knew Meggie had taken in every word. Probably more than she had.

'I'd like to admit you Debbie, for a few days. We have a bed in maternity available. You can go home, and come back tomorrow if you wish, as I know you haven't come prepared. But if possible, I'd like to keep you here now. Today.' The doctor had leaned forward as he spoke, and while his tone was as kind as usual, she knew his words held a more serious intent. Debbie nodded, then turned to Meggie.

'I can stay. I'll call Jamie, he can bring what I need tomorrow.'

Looking back at the doctor she asked, 'could you speak with us. Together. If Jamie can come tomorrow?'

'Of course Debbie. I'll have my team take you up to the ward shortly, if you'd like to step back into the waiting room. There will be a form to complete.' He paused then. 'Debbie, this is a precaution. I'm hoping we'll only have you in for a few days while we get your blood pressure down and the diabetes under control. That should help with the swelling. Then you can safely return home. But not to work, Debbie. No café work until your baby is delivered.'

Breathing out, Debbie was relieved it wasn't pre-eclampsia. While the other conditions were serious, the doctor assured her they could be managed. And the gestational diabetes should go once she'd delivered.

'I'm sorry I won't be driving back with you Meggie, but I can't thank you enough for coming with me.' Back in the waiting room, Debbie leaned closer to Meggie until their shoulders touched.

Meggie grinned. 'I haven't heard anything bad Debbie. At least nothing that can't be treated. I'm happy I was here with you.' She picked up her handbag. 'I'm going to nip out, I have an errand to run. I can do that while you get settled in your room. I'll drop back in before I head home.'

Debbie was surprised but nodded. She hadn't thought Meggie might have things to do while she was in the city. 'Of course. Thank you.'

An hour later Debbie was in bed with her feet up wearing a hospital gown, but Jamie could bring her own things tomorrow. She wished she'd brought her phone charger, but maybe they could charge it at the nurse's station.

The door opened, and Meggie bustled in, carrying several shopping bags. Debbie laughed. 'Oh you made good use of your time Meggs. What have you bought?'

Perched on the side of the bed, Meggie opened the first bag. 'Peter Alexander pyjamas for you Deb. And fluffy slippers. Extra undies because, you know, Jamie will have no idea. These are a bit Bridget-Jones-ey, but I know they'll be comfy.' She rolled her eyes and Debbie laughed. From the other bag she pulled out deodorant, toothbrush and toothpaste, hairbrush and a good quality face wash and moisturiser.

'Oh Meggie,' Debbie was laughing-crying. 'You're the best. This is brilliant. Thank you so much.'

'Oh, I have one more thing.' Debbie watched her rummage around in her handbag.

Meggie pulled out a phone charger. 'You'll need this. To talk to Jamie. And give me and the posse regular updates.'

'The posse?' Debbie was still laughing. *Darling Meggie had thought of everything.*

'Book club. The posse.' Meggie sniggered. 'That's what I call you all, in my head.'

'Love it. The posse. Maybe we should rename book club?' Debbie felt lighter. The feeling of doom had receded and Meggie had replaced it with love and light. With her thoughtfulness. *Bless her.*

But Meggie hadn't finished. 'Now, hand me your phone.' She fiddled with Debbie's phone for a few moments, then turned it, so Debbie could see.

'I've loaded the Kindle app, it's free. And I've set up an

account, here, so you can download any books you like from Amazon and read them. I know it's a bit small, I almost bought you a Kindle, but I thought you could try this and see how you go. I know you generally read paperbacks. I've downloaded the current book club read.' She showed Debbie how to open it and how to download more books.

'Oh gosh. You're the best Meggie! Thank you.' Debbie felt better than she had in weeks, knowing she and her baby were in the best place, and soaking up the practical comfort offered by Meggie.

'I'd best go Debbie. I want to call in and let Rose know what's happened. I know you'll call Jamie, but do you want me to drop in and see him?' Meggie leaned over and kissed Debbie on the cheek.

'Bless you Meggs. I've already spoken to Jamie. But yes, see Rose. Once I know how long I'll be here, maybe *the Posse* can visit me if it's more than a couple of days.' Debbie grinned, leaning back.

36

MILLIE

IT WAS THURSDAY AFTERNOON, AND QUIETER THAN usual. The tennis ladies weren't in, competition didn't start again until school went back. Millie busied herself rearranging the café tables. They'd had a couple of family groups in, who had joined a few tables together.

Cathy appeared beside her. 'I have the canapes for the elopement event boxed up and ready to go. Are you sure you don't want Lucy to come with you?'

Millie shook her head. 'Thanks Cathy but I'll be fine. It's only thirty guests, and just canapes while they take the photos. The winery people are sending someone to manage the bar, so I don't have to worry about drinks and Meggie will be there too, running the show.'

Excited to visit Barrington Homestead for the first time, the home of Rose and Angus Hamilton, Millie had been looking forward to this small event. Rose was driving down to visit

Debbie, taking baby Harper with her. Her little boy would be at pre-school, then picked up by his dad. Millie had given a box of assorted slices and sweets to Rose to take to Debbie. Not so much for Debbie herself, but for the medical people looking after her. Rose had laughed, saying, 'you're so like Debbie, it's uncanny. This is exactly what she would do.'

Meggie had explained the house will be open for access to the kitchen, for refrigeration if needed, and plating up. The wedding ceremony would take place at the front steps to the homestead, then the canapes and drinks served on the back veranda, over-looking the gardens, orchard and green rolling paddocks studded with grazing cattle. Millie secretly hoped Meggie would show her the main part of the house, perhaps after the event was over. She understood the wedding party was relocating to the function room at the pub for their main dinner.

———

PARKING IN AN AREA JUST BEYOND THE HOUSE, NEXT TO a van with Barrington Ridge Estate on the side, Millie gazed at the homestead. *Majestic. Charming. And very grand.* She busied herself with her goods, then walked the short distance to the house. Meggie had told her to come in through the back veranda, as the arbour and chairs were already set up at the front.

Hearing voices from the front, Millie stepped through the back door from the veranda and made her way to where she assumed the kitchen was. High pressed-metal ceilings, polished floorboards and timber walls painted in heritage colours. *Stunning!* There was a man with his back to her, bent over a box of glasses. Millie cleared her throat and he stood, turning with a smile.

'Hello.' She smiled in return. Couldn't help it, he had such an open, friendly face. 'I'm Millie. With the catering.' She pointed to the black apron with the café logo on the bib she wore over black pants and short-sleeved white shirt.

'Hello. Oh good. I'm Finn. Barrington Ridge Estate.' He pointed to the logo on his own white shirt. 'Where do you want to set up? Am I in your way?'

Glancing through the kitchen window, Millie could see that several cars had arrived, and wedding guests were making their way to the front of the house. A white canvas pergola had been erected over the neatly set out chairs and she could see the arbour was shaded by the front veranda. It was a warm day, with little breeze.

'I need to get more boxes from the car, and I'll scope out the back veranda area, to see the set up. Have you had a look? Do you know where you want the bar?' Millie placed the boxes she carried on the bench, but now opened the fridge and found two completely empty shelves. *Thank you Rose.* She slid the box with the seafood blinis in there, but the other items didn't need refrigeration.

'I haven't done one of these before. Well, not at this venue. I'm happy to work it out with you.' Finn walked beside her as she returned to the car and helped carry the rest of her items inside. She was grateful.

'How long have you worked for Barrington Ridge?' They stood together on the back veranda, and Millie quickly worked out the best set up, in her head. 'Oh good. Meggie has two trestles, and white tablecloths. I think you'd be better at that end Finn, and I'll set up the smaller table closer to the door. That way I can nip in and out as needed.' She looked at him then, and saw he was studying her face as she spoke. *Was he looking at my mouth just then?* She blushed. Well, half blush, half hot flush. *Bloody peri menopause.* They symptoms were recent, and still took her by surprise.

'Barrington Ridge. A while.' He smiled warmly and Millie willed the heat to leave her face. 'Your set-up works for me. I'll move the tables.' Finn chuckled and Millie bristled. Was he laughing at her? She nodded, spun on her heel and walked back into the house. Peeking out the window, she saw the bride arrive. A woman in her forties, on the arm of an older gentleman. Probably her dad. A younger woman, maybe late teens, stepped out of the car too and followed the bride up the path. *That would be her daughter. They look alike.* Millie sniffled. She loved weddings. They radiated hope and happiness.

Meggie rushed in through the back. 'Hi Millie. You've met Finn?' She set down a basket of crisp white serviettes and small side plates. They matched the platters already on the bench.

'I have, thank you.' Finn strode in then, said Hi to Meggie, picked up a tray of glasses and left the room. 'We've worked out our set-up, for when the guests come around the back. It's a warm day but the back veranda is cool.'

'Good. You've got this.' Meggie opened her iPad and scanned a list that popped up. 'Okay, less than twenty minutes. The guests will come around to you and Finn, while I take the wedding party and photographer down to the stables for some shots, then we'll join you for canapes. We'll serve for about seventy-five minutes, then the wedding party will head back into town, and the guests can follow them.' She spun on her heel and was gone.

Millie set up the small table with a charcuterie board. She

planned to walk among the guests, once they appeared, carrying the platters. She glanced over to Finn. He had set up a water station, as well as wine and champagne glasses and he had an old-fashioned laundry tub filled with ice, beer and soft drink. Wine and champagne was in a separate, smaller antique-looking bucket, filled with ice. *Nice. Fits with the homestead. And theme.* She hoped once the guests had their first drink in hand, that he would walk among them too, topping them up.

Just minutes later, it seemed, the wedding group came around the side of the house, laughing and chatting. A couple of older ladies seemed ready to sit down and she was pleased when Finn directed them to a lovely wicker setting with several chairs. He was busy pouring drinks then, and Millie made up a smaller platter and took it to the older ladies, leaving it on the small table in the midst of their chairs. She carried one platter around, catching folks as they walked from the bar with their first drink.

The food went quickly, so she dashed to the kitchen to top up the platters and bring out the first seafood plate. With napkins in one hand, she walked through the small crowd again. Some were standing in the shade chatting, and a few others had settled in chairs on the lawn, close enough to still be shaded by the veranda as the sun was moving west. Finn seemed to be behind her, with each step, carrying white wine in one hand, and red in the other. The seafood blinis went quickly, and Millie rushed inside for more.

Most were on their second drink, and service had slowed. Finn sauntered over with a glass of red, only half full and a water in the other hand. 'We're almost done here. Want to try this one? It's a cab sav, bottled two years ago.' He handed her the glass. She was surprised but took it. 'And some water too, you've been working hard.' He set the water on the small table.

'Thank you. Um, just curious, but why the red? Not the white?' Millie swirled the wine, still keeping one eye on the guests, happily chatting together in small groups. She put the glass to her nose, inhaling the rich berry scent and something else. A little bit spicy. Aware he was gazing at her, she took a sip, rolling it around her mouth before swallowing. 'Silky. Soft in the mouth. It's good.' She grinned at him then and took another sip.

'Why the red? I just picked you for a red drinker. This one is, ah, full-bodied. My personal favourite.' His grin was cheeky. *Is he flirting with me? Full-bodied, huh? Like me I suppose.* Not sure whether to be affronted or pleased, she had no time to comment as the photographer came into view walking backwards, snapping the happy couple as they sashayed toward the laughing, clapping crowd. Family and friends gathered around and Finn quickly distributed champagne flutes, half-filled. Some looked like they had only water in them. The older ladies stood up from their seats, moving towards the group. One seemed a bit unsteady and Finn was by her side quickly, taking her elbow in his hand. *Nice man. A bit cheeky perhaps.*

Meggie was beside her. The groom was thanking everyone, toasting his bride and her daughter. Meggie whispered, 'how did you go? Enough food?' We're still here for about fifteen minutes.'

'It's gone down well. No seafood blinis left, a few of the chorizo and blue cheese mini tarts and one tray of three-cheese-polenta-balls left. Oh and a few crackers, dip and cured meats. I'll do another round with the platter, see if we have any takers. They're all starting to say they're saving themselves for dinner.' Millie was pleased, she'd had a few compliments on the food.

Millie walked the tray through the crowd again, but most seemed to have had enough. They had slowed their drinking too. A nice group of people, Meggie had said they were from Taree, looking for something a bit different for an intimate wedding. Millie loved the Barrington Elopements concept. She knew Meggie and Harriet ran it together and admired them. *This little town is full of smart women.*

Ten minutes later the bride and groom left, and within twenty minutes it was just Millie and Finn. Meggie had gone into town to ensure the next stage of the celebration was perfectly set up.

Millie carted the food platters and small plates into the kitchen, then came out and picked up the empty glasses. Finn was busy crating up the unused wine. She stepped out to deal with the tablecloths and napkins, but Finn had them bundled up and the trestles neatly folded.

'All this goes back to the storeroom at Meggie's office. I have the key.' Millie nodded at his words and returned to the kitchen. She washed up the platters and plates, then ran another sink and did the glassware. She was wiping them dry and placing them in the glass crates when Finn returned.

He stood in the doorway for a moment, then stepped in. 'Thank you Millie, you've saved me some time here.' From behind his back he pulled out an unopened bottle of the red she'd tasted earlier. 'Please, take this, with my thanks.'

He is flirting with me! Suddenly self-conscious, Millie straightened her shoulders. 'Thank you Finn, but I can't take this. I don't think it's yours to give. It either belongs to the owner of Barrington Ridge Estate, or to the bridal party.' She knew she sounded a bit snooty, but she wouldn't give away Debbie's food, without checking with her. Different when it's your own business.

'Oh. Of course. You're right. It belongs to the owner of the winery. The bridal party only pay for the opened bottles.' He smirked as he said it and Millie knew he was laughing at her old-fashioned ethics. *Maybe he hadn't been flirting.*

They finished up in the house, just as Angus returned with little Charlie. 'Hi Millie, Finn.' He had Charlie on his hip, his little face looked tired. Millie had wanted to ask for a tour of the house, but she could see Angus had his hands full. She'd have another opportunity, maybe one day when Rose was home.

They carried everything back to their vehicles, packing them quickly. Millie said goodbye and got into her car, starting the engine. She was about to back out when Finn knocked on her window. She rolled it down.

'Um, Millie. I'd like to catch up with you. When we're not working. Would you like to meet for dinner at the pub tonight? If you've no plans, of course.' He grinned and she was tempted.

She shook her head emphatically before she spoke. 'No! Thank you. But no. I can't.'

'Can't tonight? Or anytime?' Now he looked like he was making fun of her. She hadn't been on a date in twenty years. And why was he even asking? He was older than her by a few years, possibly, but nice looking. Fun too, if she was any guess. *And she was. Something. Not date-worthy? Not looking? Not attractive enough? Just. Not.*

'Alright. I get it.' He paused, then spoke quietly, his tone gentle. 'Millie, I've done my research. I know you're newly single. I've been separated myself, for almost two years. You haven't dated anyone, have you? Since your marriage?'

She shook her head, but smiled brightly, not wanting to get into *this* conversation. *No she hadn't dated. Not yet. Maybe not ever.* 'Thank you Finn, I'll see you around.' She backed out quickly, turned, and drove away from the beautiful old home. She looked in the rear-view mirror to see if he was leaving too, but he was still standing there, watching her car drive away. A butterfly flipped over in her tummy.

37

ROSE

Walking into the homestead, baby Harper in one arm and the baby bag and her handbag in the other, Rose dumped the bags on the floor in the hallway and headed for the kitchen. Angus was at the sink, his back to her. She could smell the casserole she'd put in the slow cooker before driving to Newcastle to visit Debbie, and looking around the kitchen, noted everything was clean and there were no signs at all there'd been a wedding there today.

Angus spun around, stepped over and took Harper from her arms. He leaned down, kissing Rose tenderly. She unconsciously squeezed her thighs together, then slid onto a chair at the kitchen bench. *What was that? The doctor said wait six weeks, but gosh, that kiss! Did something for me. Down there.* She waggled her eyebrows at her husband. 'Want to do that again.' She leaned forward, eyes closed.

'I'll kiss you again wife.' His voice was deep, with a sexy quality to it she hadn't heard in a while, his last word almost a growl. His mouth touched hers, then he deepened the kiss. Rose heard herself moan quietly. He moved around the bench, spun her to face him, and with the baby between them continued the kiss, only this time he sucked her bottom lip into his mouth, teasing it with his tongue.

Half standing, preparing to lead him to their bedroom, the baby woke and began to cry. Rose paused, breaking the kiss. Angus passed Harper to her. Rose moved off the chair, and kissed Angus once, quickly, hard on the lips. 'This conversation. Is not over.' Her words were breathy, sexy. She took a deep breath. 'Where is my son?' Harper continued to whimper.

'Fed, bathed and in bed asleep. A big day for the lad, he came with me to feed the horses after day care.' She saw Angus grin and she smiled back, grateful he'd taken care of Charlie this afternoon.

'I'll change Harper and feed her.' She sniffed the air. 'Dinner smells good. I vote we eat soon. And have an early night. I'll be up again at two to feed this one.' She walked from the room, the baby in her arms, but exaggerated the swing of her hips as she did. Once through the door she turned. He was still watching. Rose raised her eyebrows.

'I'm a bloke Rose. You move your hips like that and I'm ready.' He laughed then and she giggled. 'But sure. Change our baby and feed her. Then we'll eat. But Rose?'

Rose raised her eyebrows. 'Yes?'

'I'm all for going to bed early.'

38

LITTLE BEN

Ben reached for Melanie. She wasn't in the bed. He looked at his phone. After midnight. Patting her side of the bed, he found it stone cold. He threw the sheet off and stepped quietly into the hallway and peeked into Tiffany's room. She was asleep, the sheet half on the floor. He stepped in and pulled it up to her shoulders, but it was warm tonight, so he didn't tuck it in around her.

Back in the hallway he looked toward the bathroom. The light wasn't on. He headed for the kitchen. He found Melanie there, making a warm lemon and honey drink. Her favourite.

She smiled over her shoulder at him as he wrapped his arms around her, his hands finding her bump. He rubbed gently. 'Is my daughter keeping you awake?'

'Heartburn. Or maybe Braxton Hicks. I woke up feeling unsettled. I didn't want to disturb you, thought I'd come out here, make a drink, and read a little bit.' Melanie leant back against him and Ben held her more firmly. *He couldn't love this woman more.*

'Is there enough hot water for another one of those?' he pointed to the drink. 'Want some company".

'Yes. And yes.' Melanie lifted a cup down from the cupboard and made a second drink. Holding their cups, he led them to the sofa in the next room. He put his drink on the side table and made room for her to nestle in against him.

'Is there something on your mind Mel?' He rubbed his hand gently up and down her arm and felt her relax more fully into his side.

'Not really. I've been thinking about Debbie though, since I woke up. Gestational diabetes. And her kidney function suffered when Warwick was born. I just hope she's okay.' Melanie leaned her head back and smiled at him. 'Rose saw her today, she called me on her way home. She said Debbie's doing well and should be home next week. But she has to rest until the baby comes. But I know Rose is concerned too.'

'We're lucky you've been well Melanie.' He chuckled. 'I'm really excited to meet little Bronte next week. Hopefully you won't go over, I don't think I can bear waiting.'

Melanie sat up then, turned toward him, placing her hands on either side of his face. He could see her eyes were tear filled. 'Ben. I love you so much. This baby will be born into a happy, safe home where both parents adore her. And her big sister.' She closed her eyes for a moment. 'I was terrified when Tiffany was due. Didn't know if Greg would be there or not. Didn't know if I even *wanted* him there. But I was so frightened. In the end he wasn't there. But mum was.' Tears leaked from her eyes and Ben's heart broke for her, knowing what she'd endured, for years, with her ex. 'But this time. With you Ben. It's perfect. So perfect. Too perfect and I sometimes wake up with a terrible feeling of doom, like it's all too good to be true.' He pulled her to him again, murmuring words of love against her hair. Rewarded when her body relaxed, and she seemed to drift off to sleep.

To himself he promised that no harm would come to her, or his baby daughter. Or Tiffany. He had been to see Douglas Barlow earlier in the week, asking about the process to officially adopt Tiffany as his daughter. He wanted her to have the same security her baby sister would have. That was his commitment. To Melanie, Tiffany and baby Bronte.

BEN WOKE. THEY WERE STILL ON THE SOFA AND HIS LEFT arm was numb where Melanie still slept against him. He tried to move it without waking her, but she stretched and sat up. She looked at her fit watch. 'It's two. We should go to bed.'

He stood, then helped Melanie to her feet. She whispered that she would use the bathroom, then come to bed. Ben put the bedside lamp on, so she could see when she came back, and stretched out on his back. Strangely, he felt hyper-vigilant and thought he'd get up and check Tiffany again. Maybe tuck her in this time. He'd barely put his feet on the floor when he heard Melanie call his name.

He strode to the bathroom, she was standing by the toilet, a puddle at her feet. She looked up at him, smiling yet fearful. 'My water just broke.'

Grinning, he leapt into action. They had a plan. He'd call Melanie's mum and she would come to be with Tiffany. Melanie's bag was packed for hospital, he just had to get dressed and drive her. He rushed from the room and called Margaret Mitchell. She answered after only two rings. She'd been on high alert for days, she said.

Back in the bathroom, Melanie had shed her nightie and was standing in the shower. He held the towel when she stepped out and helped her dry off, handing her the loose top and yoga pants she had put aside for the hospital trip. 'Any contractions? How do you feel?

'Two. Close together. Ben, this baby is coming. Quickly I think. How long will mum be?' Melanie looked flushed and flustered.

'She said fifteen minutes. It's only been five. But we have time, don't we, to get to the hospital? Babies aren't born this quickly.' He tried to sound certain but could feel his heart pushing the blood around his arteries, a shushing sound in his ears. *The baby is coming!*

'Call mum again and get the car out. Tiffany will be alright if we leave now, mum won't be long.' Melanie stopped, holding the edge of the bathroom sink. She looked up at Ben, smiling through tears. 'I have to push Ben. Hurry, get the car. Or you will be delivering your daughter yourself!'

Ben ran to their room, pulled on shorts and a tee and slipped his feet into canvas shoes. Grabbing his wallet and keys he ran through to the garage and backed the car out. Leaving the engine running, he pelted back inside, to find Tiffany standing at her bedroom door, rubbing her eyes.

'What's happening? I heard voices.' Her hair was messy and one side of her face pink, where she's had her head on the pillow.

He knelt down, taking her in his arms. 'The baby is coming Tiffany. Quickly. I've called Nanna and she's on her way, but I need to take Mummy straight to the hospital. Can you stay up and let Nanna in? She won't be more than a few minutes now.'

Tiffany nodded, looking wistful. 'I wish I could come to the hospital.'

Ben squeezed her. 'We talked about this Tiff. But I'll come back for you as soon as the baby is born. For you and Nanna.'

'Even if it's the middle of the night?'

Ben nodded. 'Go and sit on the sofa, wait for her to come.' He kissed the top of her head. 'Love you Tiff.'

Racing back to Melanie, he helped her walk down the hall, then outside to the car. As he backed out she whispered, her face anguished. 'I can feel her head, Ben.'

39

———

HARRIET

HARRIET WOKE IN A POOL OF SWEAT, HER BREASTS aching and rolled onto her back. The room was in darkness and Drum was asleep beside her, his breathing loud and rhythmic. Not quite snoring. She touched her right breast, felt a damp patch on her pyjama top, and her breast was rock hard. *What time is it?* She felt disoriented. She'd fed Hamish at nine, so it must be close to one now. She was surprised he hadn't cried. Squinting at the bedside clock, she saw it was almost four am. *What?* She looked again. Three fifty-six. She frowned, touching her other breast. Rock hard. And sore.

Paralysed by fear, knowing she needed to check the baby, she just lay there. Putting both hands to her face, she moaned quietly. 'No. Not Hamish. No.' She couldn't bear to get out of bed. *Couldn't get out of bed.*

As if sensing her distress, Drum's breathing changed. He was waking up. He reached over, patting her shoulder. 'Harri?' His question was murmured, his mouth close to her ear.

184

Harriet began to cry quietly and Drum was instantly fully awake. He turned on a side lamp. She saw the concern on his face and shook her head, crying more. Trying to speak, while still sobbing, she hiccupped between words. 'It's Hamish. (hiccup) He hasn't. (hiccup) Woken for his feed.' Turning into Drum's arms, she cried harder. 'It's four. And he hasn't woken up. I can't go in there.'

Moving her gently out of his arms, Drum wasted no time. He was on his feet and already out the door before she could finish her thought. Holding her breath she waited. She heard the baby's room door open. Nothing. Then Drum's footsteps, returning to their room. He sat on the edge of the bed and gathered her into his arms.

'Harriet, you need to get up now.' Drum's words were firm, but she shook her head. Scooping her into his arms as if she weighed nothing at all, he carried her to the next room. Placing her on her feet beside the cot, he steadied her with his arm. The room was filled with a soft yellow glow from the nightlight. Still crying, she turned her head to look at Hamish. His little face angelic, he lay on his back, eyes closed and a tiny stuffed bunny in one hand.

Looking at him, laying there so peacefully, she almost thought he was only sleeping. Lifting her arm, she reached in to touch him, gently, on the cheek. She drew her hand back in shock and turned to Drum, who was grinning. 'He's warm. He's still warm.'

As she spoke the words, Hamish's eyelids fluttered, then opened. Before she could acknowledge her joy, he opened his mouth and let out a loud wail. Drum nudged her. 'Our son is hungry. He's been asleep for seven hours.' He picked Hamish up and placed him to his shoulder, patting his back, which quietened his crying momentarily. 'You do know what day it is today, don't you Harriet?' Drum moved to the change table, expertly undoing the onesie while Harriet gaped, relief now flooding her body.

'Day?' She frowned, tried to recall the date.

'Today's Hamish's due date. If he'd gone full term.' The baby now changed, Drum led Harriet to the big comfy chair by the cot they'd dubbed the feeding chair. Hamish cries increased when Drum placed him in her arms. The baby could smell her milk. She opened her top and unclipped the maternity bra, settling the baby into the nook of her arm. He latched on and sucked hard and Harriet winced, then relaxed as her milk began to flow.

'Four weeks premature and he slept seven hours.' Eyes shining she looked at Drum in wonder.

Drum's face was a mixture of love and pride. 'He's a Murray.' And he shrugged then, before leaning down and kissing the top of her head. 'He's thriving Harriet. He's gaining weight and feeding well. He may sleep longer at night now, for a while, but when he has another growth spurt he'll wake more often.'

Tears ran down her face again. Happiness replaced her earlier despair. Delivering Hamish safely had been almost too good to be true and she realised she had been waiting for something bad to happen. Smiling through her tears, she whispered, 'I love you Drum Murray.'

40

MEGGIE

NOT SURE WHAT HAD WOKEN HER, MEGGIE STRETCHED, then opened her eyes. It had been a warm night and she hadn't put her nightwear back on after making love with Max earlier. *Max.* A smile played around her mouth. *It was early, maybe she'd wake him up.*

Rolling over she came face to face with him. An already-wide-awake Max. He was on his side, propped up on one elbow gazing at her, his eyes full of love. She blinked. Love. *And lust.*

Revelling in her nakedness, she lazily draped one long leg over his hip, eyebrows raised in invitation. Leaning down, he nipped her mouth, then moved lower to kiss her breasts. She pushed him away, onto his back, and straddled him in one swift movement. No foreplay, no tenderness. Meggie lowered herself onto him and began moving. He moaned.

Last night they had taken their time. Their lovemaking had been gentle at first, then more demanding until Max had slowed everything down, making it last. She had come before him, and he had teased her to a second orgasm before reaching his own. But this morning it was her way. And she wanted it hard and fast. Riding him like this made her feel powerful.

Leaning forward she pinned his hands above his hand and increased her pace. His eyes never left hers. He was so intense, he *smouldered.* If he kept looking at her like that she'd lose control. She growled, deep in her throat. His expression changed and he somehow managed to half sit up with her still on top. He buried his face in her breasts and she threw her head back and let go. He took control now, slowed a little and kissed her throat gently. Then his eyes darkened and he tipped her over, onto her back, and settled between her legs, grinding hard. She raised her hips to meet his powerful thrusts. Once. Twice. Then he shuddered and collapsed, rolling to one side with Meggie in his arms.

He kissed her gently. 'Good morning.'

'Good morning Max.' Her smile was lazy, her eyelids half closed. They relaxed together as dawn light crept into the room. She was drifting off when Max's phone beeped. He was the on-call Vet, he and Angus took it in turns. Meggie rolled away to let him reach his phone but turned back when he chuckled.

'What is it?' She tried to focus on the message on the small screen that Max held out to her. Too close, she couldn't read it. Taking the phone from him, she looked at it again. The message was from Ben.

Bronte born at 1:15am. 3.2kg. Both well.

'Oh.' Meggie handed the phone back to Max, slightly bemused. 'That's lovely. She's a bit early. A week maybe. I'll drop by the hospital today.' She sighed. 'I'll get up.'

'Wait.' Max was tapping a reply in the phone now, and Meggie waited. He put the phone down and reached for her again, hugging her tightly. His face was serious. 'I love you Meggie Hamilton. I'm so happy. With you. Here in Barrington. Tommy loves it here.' His mouth quirked up at the edges. 'And he loves you. And Meggie, I really want to have a baby with you. But I also want you to know that you're enough. Just like this. If it doesn't happen for us, I'm still so bloody happy.' He squeezed her hard, and she saw the truth of his words in his eyes and simply just nodded.

Quietly, her head resting on his shoulder, she looked up at him. 'I think so too Max. I love our life together. Yes, I still want a baby. But if it doesn't happen, my life with you, here, *is enough*. I don't think even a baby could make me feel any happier than I do right now.'

41

MILLIE

Debbie called in to the café on her return from hospital with Jamie carrying Warwick in his arms. It was just on closing time on Saturday and the staff had left. Millie was restocking the drinks cabinet when they walked in and couldn't hide her delight and relief at seeing Debbie. In three steps Millie was in front of her, and without forethought, threw her arms around the younger woman, hugging her tightly for a moment. Debbie hugged her back, whispering 'thank you' as she did.

They sat at the table closest to the counter and chatted while Millie made drinks and packed up a fresh lasagne for them to take home for dinner.

Watching Debbie's movements as she tended to Warwick when he spilled some of his milkshake, Millie thought she seemed more comfortable. She tried to surreptitiously get a peek at Debbie's feet, but the maxi dress she wore kept them hidden.

Debbie caught on and laughingly pulled her skirt up a bit. 'Just regular-size-feet now Millie. And my blood pressure and sugar levels are back within normal range.' She raised her eyebrows then. 'For a diabetic, that is.' Her tone and expression was happy and relaxed, and although Jamie didn't say much, Millie loved the way he handled his young son, showing open affection and sharing a laugh.

As they were leaving, Debbie held back while Jamie carried Warwick out to the car. She turned to Millie, hugging her quickly. 'I'm so grateful you're here Millie. Cathy called me two days ago to tell me again how well you've settled in and that she loves working with you. Knowing this has definitely helped my recovery. I want to thank you. But also need to ask you if *you're okay?* Are you happy here Millie? Is there anything *you* need?'

Millie blinked. *Debbie was asking about her?* The thoughtfulness of this young woman, her boss, amazed Millie. Despite what Debbie was dealing with herself, she cared enough to check in with her staff. Grinning, Millie answered. 'It's me who should thank you Debbie. Giving me this chance. I adore the café, the staff and this town. And you. There's nothing I need, except to see you doing well and to deliver your baby safely.' Another quick hug and Debbie was gone, waving from the car as Jamie pulled away from the kerb.

Millie tidied up the table they had used and walked to the front door. Turning the sign from OPEN to CLOSED, a movement outside caught her eye. Finn, the wine guy from the event a few days earlier, was approaching. Millie opened the door, smiled and said, 'Hello Finn.'

'Millie, hello. Just closing up I see?' His grin was friendly, and Millie thought how perfect he was for the hospitality industry. 'I've just dropped off some wine stock to Meggie up the road, and

I'm officially off duty. Would you like to catch up for a drink? We could walk down to the pub if you've no plans.'

Hesitating, Millie's brain was racing. *He's asking me out. Again. Me?* She couldn't help glancing down at herself, still wearing the café apron over her customary black pants and white shirt. While Finn may be a couple of years older, he was nice looking and pleasant, and Millie couldn't understand his interest in *her*.

Starting to shake her head, Millie tried to find the right words to refuse his invitation. But what she really wanted to ask was *why? Why her?*

'Millie.' His voice was softer, his tone sincere. 'I'd like to catch up over a drink or coffee and get to know you. We can just talk. We're in the same industry and we'll be doing some of Meggie's events together.' He hesitated then. 'But I won't ask again if it makes you uncomfortable.'

He took a half step back with his last words, and Millie realised she didn't want him to walk away. Not like that. Without thinking, she blurted out. 'Why?' She blushed then, or maybe it was another hot flush. There was never any warning and now she was embarrassed, knowing her face was flaming red. And not just her face. Her chest and neck too.

Finn looked away for a moment, a slight frown on his face, then he returned his gaze to Millie. 'Honestly?"

She nodded. *Ok. Here it is. It's about business, or the café.*

His next words surprised her. 'This will probably scare you off, but I can't lie to you. I like you Millie. No, that's not right, I don't know you well enough to really say that.' He grinned again, then, and his face lit up. 'In for a penny.' He drew in a deep breath. 'I'm attracted to you Millie. You're very pretty. There. I said it.' He crossed his arms over his chest, still smiling, but his stance was defensive.

He's nervous. He does like me! She laughed aloud, thrilled to be called pretty when she generally thought of herself as frumpy and, frankly, *past it.* Lifting her chin, her mouth curved upwards, she nodded. 'I can't very well say no now, can I?' Her sense of humour intact, she added, 'I wouldn't like to be responsible for your actions, you know, if I knocked back such a smooth invitation.'

He roared with laughter at that, and she giggled too. 'Well, that's settled. Now, let's have that drink. To the pub?'

Thinking of her outfit, Millie looked down. She was still in her work gear and there was a splodge of something on one sleeve. 'I live across the road, above the post office. Would you mind if I met you at the pub in about twenty minutes? I'd like to get changed.'

'I'll be there. I'll order drinks. Red wine?' Finn stepped away as he spoke.

'Yes please. Something light. A pinot perhaps?' Millie watched Finn stride away, then raced through to the back of the café, ensuring everything was locked up, before letting herself out and hurrying home to get changed. There was a spring in her step as she raced upstairs to her apartment.

It was closer to thirty minutes when Millie walked in, wearing chocolate coloured wide leg pants and a loose shirt with three quarter sleeves. It was an outfit she'd had for a while, made from bamboo material. She'd worn it to a wedding several years ago, but it was good quality and hadn't dated. In fact it was almost too big now, where it had been snug when she wore it last. She'd washed her face quickly and put fresh mascara and lipstick on. She rarely wore much make up and thought one of her few attractive qualities was her light olive complexion, which didn't require coverage.

Finn waved from a corner seat in the bistro area. She could see a few men out in the main bar, but this area was quiet. A staff member was setting a long table for dinner across the room. She slid into the booth across from Finn. She hadn't noticed earlier, but he wore a collared short-sleeve shirt, light blue, with dark blue jeans.

'Your wine madam.' Finn slid a glass across to her. She noticed he was sipping on a beer.

'Thank you.' She nodded at the beer in front of him. 'You don't drink the wares you sell?'

'Funny! Yes I do, but it's three in the afternoon and I need to drive home after this.' He picked up his glass. 'It's light beer. Not my favourite. But needs must.'

She smiled at that. 'Tell me about yourself Finn? You work at the winery. It's not large, I heard. Is that full time for you? Are you mostly in charge of distribution?'

'Full time. Yes. Actually I do a bit of everything. From tending the vines through to bottling and marketing. It's a varied job. Long hours sometimes, but right now it's quiet enough. It's, ah, a fairly new business. This is only the second season. ' Finn took another sip of his beer and Millie thought again how pleasant he was to look at, with his straight white teeth and short dark wavy hair. She could see a few strands of grey here and there. Taller than her with broad shoulders and a solid build, he looked fit and strong. She wondered if he had been a football player in his youth.

'What about you Millie. Just to be upfront, I've heard you're

here for Debbie's maternity leave and that you recently separated.'
He smiled his encouragement and Millie told him a little bit about
the breakdown of her marriage, which led to the sale of the business. She didn't elaborate and didn't want to whinge about Rudy,
her ex.

He told her he'd been separated for about two years, that he
had three kids, all a bit older than hers. He'd married young, he
said. It had been good for a long time. But then it wasn't. in the
end, she left him and it had taken him by surprise. One of his boys
worked with him at the winery. That surprised her, but maybe he
was friends with the owner. He didn't say much about his boss, so
she didn't ask.

Talking to Finn was easy, and she found herself laughing at
what her kids would call 'dad jokes' but somehow he pulled them
off. Looking down, her wine glass was empty and so was his beer.
Smiling now, she said, 'we seem to be on a roll. Would you like
another drink? My shout.'

'Yes, but I'll get it. I asked you out, remember.' He was out of
his seat and heading to the bar before she could comment further.

Returning, he grinned again. 'Bob behind the bar was asking
about you. I think he's a fan.'

Millie glanced over at the bar. Bob was about fifty. He caught
her looking and winked. Millie blushed. 'Oh goodness. I've been
in here a couple of times with Meggie. Now I'm embarrassed.

They chatted then about travel and holidays. He'd been on
several overseas trips, some with his wife when they were married
and others for business. Millie had travelled too. Her ex-husband
was German and there had been several trips to visit his family and
they'd taken the children for a white Christmas a couple of times.
She laughed then. 'They were several generations in hotels and

café's, my ex is a Pastry Chef. When they first met me,' she laughed, pointing to her wavy brown hair, brown eyes and olive complexion, 'they acted like I was wearing shoes for the first time.' Laughing harder, she added, 'I should have realised. Then.'

'Oh that's too funny. I bet you have stories.' Finn was laughing with her and Millie felt young, carefree and fun. She couldn't remember the last time she'd felt like that.

He sipped his beer, then leaned forward. 'So Millie Tucker. Is this your first date. Post marriage? How am I doing?'

'You're funny. And I'm relaxed. And yes, Finn, 'she paused, ' what is your last name?'

'Anderson.'

'Yes Finn Anderson, it is my first date. Honestly, I didn't think I'd ever date again. I thought, you know, *that* time had passed for me. But you've given me a new lease, you really have.' More quietly, she added, 'thank you.' Then chuckling, she raised her eyebrows. 'What about you Finn? I don't think this is *your* first date. Post marriage.'

'You're right about that. In fact, I moped for a while. Not because I was heart-broken, but because my vision of what my life was changed so dramatically. We were married at twenty and I just thought we'd be together, always. There were times I would have left, but you know, the kids and the vows I made held me back. Then the choice was taken from me. That hurt. My pride more than my heart perhaps.' He finished the beer in his glass. 'But Lucas, the son that works with me, got me on one of these dating apps. You know, swipe left, swipe right. It was good for me, it got me out. So yes, I've been on a few dates. More than a few. But I stopped before Christmas. The dates were all much the same. And I felt like I was always *trying* to be what they were looking for. But now, meeting you organically, feels easier. I'm just me. You're good company Millie.'

She raised her eyebrows again, giggled, and said, 'so you're just a boy, sitting in front of a girl ...' She didn't finish the movie quote, and blushed, because she wasn't sure if he'd *get* it.

'Asking her to love him.' He finished the line and threw back his head, laughing loudly. 'So you like movies Millie? We haven't discussed that. Or music. So I think we need a second date.'

'I love the movies. It's my one disappointment with Barrington. No cinema. But I'm told there's a couple on the coast and another in Taree.' Millie finished her wine. 'Are you a movie lover yourself Finn?'

'Movies, yes. I admit I haven't been to the cinema for a long time but love the streaming channels we get now. I'm a big fan of the classics, but I'm up for anything.' He looked at his watch. 'I shouldn't drink any more if I'm driving home.' He winked at Millie. 'Am I driving home Millie?'

Frowning, it took her a moment to process this. *Was he asking if he could stay the night? It wasn't even dinner time yet.* 'Yes. You are driving home Finn.' She spoke the words firmly, trying to hide her surprise at his question.

'I thought so. But a man can try.' The way he said it made her laugh, and she held her hand to her mouth in mock shock.

'Stop it!'

'Wait one moment, Millie, I'll walk you across the street.' He stood and walked through the side door towards the bathroom. She should have done that too but didn't want him to think she'd left when he asked her to wait. Bob, from behind the bar came over and picked up their empty glasses.

'Millie. We haven't met officially. I'm Bob.' She took the hand he offered and shook it. He continued, leaning closer to her. 'If it doesn't work out with Finn, you let me know. I'll take you out.' She saw Finn returning and Bob gave her a wink and ambled back to the bar. She had one hand over her mouth, again, not sure if she should laugh. Too funny!

Walking outside with Finn, she turned and mock-punched his upper arm. *Rock hard biceps.* 'Did you set Bob up?'

'What do you mean? I saw him speaking to you just then.' Finn frowned.

'Bob just told me that if it doesn't work out with you I should let him know, he'll take me out.' Millie snort-laughed as she spoke, then wiped the tears from her eyes mumbling, 'sorry. It was too funny.'

'The bastard! Trying to cut my grass the minute my back is turned.' Finn's words seemed a little too loud to be in jest, but that made her laugh more. He laughed too then, but Millie had the impression he wasn't happy about Bob's remarks. That such a small thing should give her confidence. Yet it did.

At the downstairs door to her flat, on the main street, they stopped. 'Thank you Finn. I've had the best afternoon. You're a lot of fun.' She stood on tiptoe and kissed his cheek.

'Good. That was the plan. How about dinner and a movie next time? I'm away next weekend, but the one after? The Saturday night?'

'Yes. Yes Finn, I'd like that.' She opened the door, then turned back to him. 'But I'm picking the movie.'

He laughed as he strode away. 'Alright. You pick the movie, I'll pick the restaurant.'

42

FRANCES

Frances stepped on to the street, closing the door to the old bank building behind her. She walked briskly into the café and was greeted by the new manager. Frances smiled but couldn't remember her name. Then she heard another customer say 'Millie' and she smiled to herself. *Millie. That's right, while Debbie is on maternity leave.*

Paying the woman. *Millie.* Frances took the paper bag with their sandwiches. She'd make a pot of tea for them at the office. Humming to herself, she walked along the main street. At the door to the Vet clinic she paused, then turned, suddenly confused. Walking back on the pavement, until she was almost in the roadway, she looked up. Vet Clinic? Shaking her head she looked back the way she'd come, to the café. Then she looked the other way. Her shoulders slumped. *Where was the office? It should be right here.* Head spinning, she felt a bit dizzy. *Why was nothing where it should be?*

Glancing at the front of the real estate office just a couple of doors further on, Frances decided to drop in there for a moment. *She could sit with Rosemary Evans until her head cleared, then she'd go back to the office.*

Opening the door, she peered around her. It looked different. There was a young woman sitting at Rosemary's desk. Frances didn't know her.

'Hello Frances.' The woman stood up, smiling. 'What are you doing here? Are you after one of the Ben's?' The woman hesitated. 'Frances? Frances are you unwell?'

'I think I am. Yes. My head.' Frances put a hand to her head and let the other woman lead her to the chair in front of Rosemary's desk.

'I'll get you some water. Won't be a tic.' She walked smartly from the room, returning a moment later with a glass of water and Ben Evans senior. He was frowning. And he looked different too. She couldn't put her finger on it.

Frances took a sip of water and set the glass down carefully on the desk. Beginning to stand, she said, 'I just popped in to see Rosemary for a moment, but I can see she's not here.' Looking at the paper bag in her hand, she brightened. 'I've got to get back, Douglas will be waiting for his lunch.'

Ben laid a gentle hand on her shoulder. 'Sit for a moment Frances.' He perched on the edge of the desk and took one of her hands in his. 'Rosemary passed away Frances. Several years ago. You were at her funeral.'

It came rushing back to her then. *The coffin, the funeral. It was a very large turnout.* Frances whispered, 'it rained that day, didn't it?'

Ben nodded sadly. 'Yes it did Frances.'

She didn't know how to respond. *How had she forgotten that?* Rosemary had been one of her best friends.

The door opened and Douglas appeared. 'There you are Frances, love.' He took the lunch bag from her hand. 'Oh good, I see you have our lunch. Let's head back to the office and make a pot of tea.'

43

DEBBIE

February – Barrington Book Club – Meeting 6
Present: Debbie, Rose and baby Harper, Harriet and baby
Hamish, Melanie and baby Bronte, Laura, Meggie, Frances and
Millie
Apologies: Nicole
Book: *A Stranger in Featherwood Falls* by Heather Reyburn

DEBBIE ARRIVED WITH ROSE AND HARPER AS SHE wasn't driving. While her symptoms were under control, she sometimes felt light-headed and decided it was safer not to drive until after she gave birth.

Millie had their table set up and everyone was already there. Even Melanie with baby Bronte, only a couple of weeks old and as cute as a button. Laura was pouring wine and Debbie noticed Meggie didn't have any. She looked across at Meggie and met her eye. Meggie half smiled and Debbie grinned back. Frances also turned the wine down, but Millie had a glass.

They chatted generally while eating the snacks Millie had put out for them. Debbie held Hamish, marvelling at his alertness, while Harriet enjoyed her latte.

Laura asked to hold Bronte and Melanie looked pleased to hand her across the table. 'So Melanie, if your husband is to be believed, he practically delivered the baby in the car.' Laura chuckled and Debbie looked at Melanie with interest. This was the first time she'd seen her since Bronte was born and she was curious to hear her story.

'Not quite Laura. But Bronte *was* in a hurry. I'd gotten up around midnight, feeling *something*. Just unsettled. No strong contractions. Ben heard me and got up too, and we had tea and sat together on the couch for a while. But then my water broke, I had two contractions and the need to push was really strong. We were at the hospital in under twenty minutes.' She pulled a face. 'We even left Tiffany alone, but mum was on her way and wouldn't have been more than five minutes. I still feel guilty about that.'

'Go on.' Laura encouraged .

'As we got into the car I could feel her head. Like. Right there!' she pointed to her nether regions and Debbie squeezed her legs in sympathy and made an *ouch* face.

'Really? That quickly?' This was Rose, leaning forward. 'Was Tiffany a quick birth?'

'No. Tiff took ages. It felt like days, but I think it was twenty hours or so. I was in agony with her.' Melanie shook her head ruefully. 'But Bronte, I could feel her coming out as Ben parked the car.' She giggled then. 'In the ambulance bay. He said some choice words when a medic came out telling him he couldn't park there. But when they opened the car door and saw me. Well, all hell broke loose.' Bronte began to cry, softly, and Melanie took her from Laura. opened her shirt and juggled the baby into place to feed. Rose had Harper on her breast, while Hamish slept in Debbie's arms.

'And then?' Debbie prodded Melanie gently.

'Oh yes. Well, they put me on a stretcher and we were barely inside the building, in the emergency room, when she just sort of, *slithered out*. And Ben, well, he caught her. Literally.' Melanie touched her baby's cheek. 'And she's such a good girl, too.'

Debbie sighed. 'My new birth goal. Two contractions and the baby *slithers* out'. They laughed uproariously at that, then talked some more about their individual birth experiences before turning to their chosen book.

Debbie noticed Frances was quiet. 'How are you Frances? Did you enjoy the book.'

Frances seemed to take a deep breath, then shook her head. 'I'm dealing with a health issue at the moment, and if you don't mind, I'd like to share it here.' She looked at Meggie then. 'Have you not said anything Meggie?'

Meggie smiled warmly at Frances. 'Of course not Frances. But I'm pleased you're sharing with us. With your friends.'

Debbie had no idea where this was going, but it seemed serious, and she saw everyone had quietened so Frances could speak.

'I've been forgetting things. Not all the time. Just here and there. Douglas reminds me about appointments. A lot.' Tears welled in her eyes, and Laura reached across and touched her arm. In comfort or solidarity, Debbie wasn't sure. 'Then last week I got lost. I picked up my lunch. From Millie. And I walked up the street, looking for our office.' She turned to Laura then. 'It used to be where the Vet clinic is now. And it upset me that it wasn't there, so I went into Evans Real Estate, expecting to see Rosemary.'

Debbie gasped. She wasn't the only one. Rosemary had passed away several years before.

'Go on Frances.' Laura spoke kindly.

'I saw Meggie, but I didn't recognise her. And when Ben appeared, he looked different too. He sat with me and I think Meggie called Douglas.' Frances looked across at Meggie who nodded.

'When Douglas arrived, I remembered. Who Meggie was. Where I was.' Tears trickled down her face and Debbie felt like crying herself. She wasn't the only one. Rose looked upset too. Taking another deep breath Frances added, 'I've got Dementia. Douglas has suspected for a while. I've had moments where I've wondered too, but I didn't want to say anything. Just thought it was part of aging. I've seen a specialist and I have more appointments in the coming weeks, to assess the level of damage and the speed,' she sobbed then, 'of my cognitive decline.'

'But you're good right now Frances.' Debbie looked around. 'You know all of us. Our names. Where we fit in.'

'It's a strange disease and yes, I'm feeling good tonight. But I've been practicing too. I've started making up folders on the computer and printing them out. Who people are. Where they fit. Adding a picture if I can. And I studied it this afternoon.' She smiled sadly.

'We'll know more in the next few weeks. But it will get worse. There's no escaping this. Douglas and I have talked about it a lot since, well, *the incident,* and we might retire or take some time off at least. There are a couple of trips we'd like to make, here in Australia. We'll do them soon.' Frances picked up her coffee, taking a small sip. 'I want to thank you, all of you, for including me in your book club. I don't know if I'll be able to read the books from now on, but I want you to know how much being here with you has meant to me.'

'Oh Frances.' Debbie passed Hamish back to Harriet and walked around to Frances. Leaning down she hugged her thin shoulders. 'We love you. We love you being here. Please keep coming. We'll pick you up and take you home after. We'll look after you.' Debbie looked around the table. 'Won't we?'

'Absolutely.' Laura spoke firmly and they all chimed in saying yes, and please stay. Frances nodded her thanks and wiped her eyes with a handkerchief. This signalled for a change of subject, and Harriet began to talk about the book and how much she enjoyed the author's writing style. Debbie was pleased. It gave Frances time to compose herself.

'This one touched me deeply.' Laura put her hand to her heart. 'A woman alone on a cattle property after the death of her husband. I *felt* that.'

'I like the women in this story. Strong women. Capable.' Rose nodded to Laura. 'And I can see parallels with your life Laura. But not just that. For me it was the writing, and the way the mystery unfolded. It may be a cliché to say this, but I couldn't put it down from about the halfway point.' Rose rolled her eyes then. 'To the detriment of my own work-in-progress.'

They laughed then and the evening rolled on. Debbie had to get up twice to use the bathroom, the little one was pressing on her bladder. *Not long to go now.* In fact, anytime, would suit her.

They talked about their next book, and Meggie mentioned a debut novel by an Australian author called Julie Bennett. '*The Understudy*. It's brilliant, I've read it. A modern historical set when the Sydney Opera House opened in 1973. Brilliantly researched and a fascinating story. Her new one is coming out very soon and I'd love to read it with the group in a couple of months. What do you say?'

'I'm keen. I've seen reviews for the first one.' Rose gave a thumbs-up and they all agreed.

Debbie spoke up then, suddenly feeling excited. 'Perhaps I'll have *my* baby by next month.' She turned to Melanie. 'If only it will *slither* out!' They stayed and chatted. No one seemed keen to leave and Debbie watched as they all ensured Frances was included in the conversation. She sighed. *Small towns. So much love.*

44

ROSE

Two days after book club, Rose and Angus walked upstairs to see Douglas Barlow. Angus carried Harper in his arms while Rose juggled the baby bag.

Frances greeted them, as usual, and offered tea.

'No thank you Frances, we're going to have a coffee at the café after this.' Angus stepped aside as Rose hugged Frances quickly. The older woman moved closer to Angus then, gazing at Harper, who was asleep, her mouth slightly open.

'She really is lovely.' Frances looked from Angus to Rose. 'I can see both of you in her features, but I have to say, she really is a mini-Meggie.'

Rose laughed. 'I think so too Frances. And her Auntie Meggie is already besotted. She was at her birth and has seen her almost every day since.' Douglas appeared at the door of his office and greeted them warmly. Rose turned back to Frances. 'Are you busy Frances? Do you want to join us, and hold Harper while we read through and sign our wills?'

Frances clapped her hands with pleasure, then held them out to take the baby. She snuggled her expertly against her shoulder and followed them into the office, where Douglas returned to his side of the desk.

Douglas handed a copy of their wills to each of them and waited while they read them. Angus asked a couple of questions regarding insurance and superannuation, but largely all seemed to be in order.

'We have everything covered in here, if something should happen to either of you, and how the other will move forward.' Douglas hesitated. 'We haven't discussed your wishes if something should happen to *both* of you. It's my oversight, but can we discuss this for a moment please?'

'Both of us?' Rose frowned. 'If we, er, had a car accident, for example?'

'Yes.' Douglas nodded. 'It's extremely unlikely, of course. But what would you want for your children if they were minors and this eventuated?'

'Oh.' Angus frowned slightly, shaking his head. The thought was untenable to Rose too. But then she looked at Angus and said firmly. 'Meggie. And Max. I'd choose Meggie and Max.'

Angus looked relieved. 'Agreed. Meggie and Max. They already adore wee Charlie and Harper. Max is my business partner and Meggie is my sister. It should be them.'

'I thought of Debbie and Jamie first, but just for a second. Debbie and I have been friends forever.' Rose gazed at Angus for a moment. 'But Meggie is family.'

'Good.' Douglas sat back and lay his pen down. 'We'll add them in as guardians until the children are eighteen. But Rose, Angus, you need to confirm this with them. Meggie and Max.

CHAPTER 44

And let me know. I'd be reluctant to add this to the wills without their knowledge.'

'You're right Douglas, of course. We'll talk to them and confirm back with you. This week.' Angus sighed, then looked at Rose. 'This makes me think of Charlie, Rose. Your grandfather, not our wayward son.'

Rose raised her eyebrows in question and waited. Angus continued, 'The conversations he must have had. With Douglas certainly, but in his own mind, to make his will out the way he did. I'm only just realising that it's not a simple matter.'

'Charlie. Bless him.' Rose was hit by a rush of emotion for her grandfather. Love, certainly, but gratitude too for writing his will in a way that protected her from making hasty decisions. Angus reached across and took her hand in his, squeezing it gently.

45

MEGGIE

Grabbing her phone from the bedside table, Meggie read the message then called out to Max, who had just walked out of the room to wake Tommy up. 'Rose just messaged, they want us to come for a barbecue tonight.'

Max reappeared. 'Sure. But it's Thursday night, and I'm on call. And Tommy has school tomorrow. Friday would be better.'

'Okay.' Meggie messaged back. Within moments her phone pinged with a reply from Rose. 'No. she wants us tonight. Says it won't be late, they're keeping baby-hours themselves.'

Max shrugged. 'All good. What can we take?'

Meggie waved him away. 'Go. Wake Tommy. I'll sort it out with Rose.'

In the end, Meggie made a salad and bought fresh bread rolls from the bakery. Rose said they were keeping it simple.

CHAPTER 45

Tommy happily played farms on the loungeroom floor with Charlie after they'd eaten an early dinner. He built a complex farm ecosystem out of blocks and plastic animals, and Charlie was having fun trying to insert dinosaurs and sharks into enclosures that held cows, horses and pigs. Meggie noticed Tommy was patient with him. *He'll be a good big brother one day.*

The dinner conversation had been warm, and fun, but Meggie wondered if there was something Angus and Rose wanted to discuss. There seemed to be an undercurrent to the evening.

Angus cleared his throat. 'Meggie, Max, there's something we'd like to ask you.' Rose moved her chair closer to Angus and Meggie was suddenly on high alert. *Was something wrong? Was one of them sick?*

Max slung his arm over the back of Meggie's chair, his hand gently rubbing her shoulder. Meggie knew it was his way of telling her to relax. 'What is it Angus?'

'We've already asked you to be godparents to Harper.' Rose smiled at Meggie. 'We'll have the christening in a few months. I'm hoping you'll organise the celebration after. Something small. Just our close friends.'

Meggie breathed out. *Is that all?* 'Of course. Easily done. If you have a date, I'll put some ideas together and we can go from there.' She relaxed.

'There's more Meggie.' Angus looked directly at her, then at Max. 'We've just redone our wills. With Douglas. It all changes once you have children.'

'Indeed.' Max nodded his agreement. His body seemed to tense slightly.

'We want to ask you. Both of you. If we can name you in our wills as the children's guardians, should anything happen to both of us.' Rose said the last bit quickly, and Meggie breathed in sharply, sneaking a look at Max, who seemed surprised.

Rose stood, then walked around to Meggie, pulling a chair up on her other side. She took Meggie's hand in hers. 'It's very, very, unlikely that anything would happen to *both* of us. But not impossible. We love you. Wee Charlie loves you and I know Harper will too. Would you take care of them if we needed you to?'

Meggie saw Rose was close to tears and couldn't stop her own. The thought of losing her brother and Rose was devastating. Meggie nodded, hugging Rose tightly. 'Of course. May it never come to pass, but yes, absolutely, yes.' They held each other, for what seemed like minutes.

When she let Rose go, Angus was there. He took her in his arms. 'Love you Meggs. Thank you.' Rose had embraced Max too and the four of them stood for a moment, by the table.

Angus looked at Max. 'Mate?'

Meggie could see how close to the surface Max's emotions were. He and Angus weren't just business partners, but brothers-in-law. Max nodded. 'Yes, mate. No question.'

'Good man.' Angus slapped Max on the back, just as Tommy ran in, with little Charlie right behind him. 'Is it time for dessert?' His happy young face warmed Meggie's heart. She held out her arms and he walked into them. Kissing the top of his Meggie said, laughing, 'it's always time for dessert Tommy. Come with me, Rose told me she has mini-sticky-date-puddings hidden away. Let's see if we can find them.'

Charlie, now in Max's arms, clapped his hands. 'Dicky-date, dicky-date!' Meggie laughed and walked with Tommy to the kitchen.

46

———

MILLIE

It was date night. Her first with Finn. Millie hadn't had a *first date* in more than twenty years. To say she was nervous was an understatement. She knew that dating had changed in the last two decades. For a start, there were all the phone apps. The *swiping*. Left or right. She didn't really know. What she *did* know, was that people *hooked-up*. Often on a first date. They made *booty-calls*. Millie shivered then. She couldn't imagine taking her gear off for someone she barely knew. And really, did people *her age* even do that? Surely not. Finn seemed like an easy going, respectable kind of person. But did he have *expectations?*

'Not this little black duck.' Millie murmured to herself. She dressed in pale blue capri pants. She'd bought them in Europe a decade ago and wondered if they would fit her now. Not only did they fit her, but they were slightly loose around the waist. She *had* lost weight. Her early morning walks were working. And she enjoyed the exercise, the routine. More than that, while she admitted to herself no one would call her skinny, she was now *fit*. She teamed the pants with a loose linen top in navy and white canvas shoes. She felt good, and stopped herself from looking in the mirror, knowing she'd overthink the outfit and change.

Finn was picking her up. They were driving across to the coast and he knew a little seafood café near the Tuncurry cinema where, he said, the service was quick and the food fresh. She was looking forward to it. The meal, the movie, and seeing Finn. She'd chosen a drama, a dual-timeline-world-war-two-movie. She'd wanted to see it for ages, and it was inspired by true events. There was a romantic comedy she was keen to see too, but she wasn't sure if Finn would like it.

Not comfortable having him come right upstairs to her apartment, she chose to wait outside the door to the building, on the main street. A light breeze ruffled her wavy hair, and she put her hand up, in an attempt to brush it out of her eyes. *Maybe she should change her hair, get a smarter cut.* Her daughter had suggested that last time she'd been home. She'd told Millie that her hairstyle had been the same for twenty years. This was probably true, but in her defence, her hair was wavy and she quite liked the shoulder length style.

A white car pulled in to the kerb and Millie didn't give it more than a cursory glance. It was a small Mercedes and Finn drove the Barrington Ridge Estate van. The car door opened and Finn stepped out. 'Hi Millie.' He closed the door and walked to where she stood. He wore a pale blue open-neck short-sleeve linen shirt, tan coloured chinos and navy canvas shoes. Without socks. Very cool. And he looked younger. *Younger than her?* His smile was broad and confident when he stepped close, took her hand in his and kissed her on the cheek. 'Ready?'

Nodding, Millie felt a bit self-conscious. Settling into the car, all leather seats and polished dash, Millie knew it was a few years old, but well-maintained. She'd had the same model herself, before her life turned to crap. 'Nice car.' She smiled across at him.

Pulling away from the kerb, he grinned at her. 'You expected the van, didn't you?'

Laughing, she agreed. 'I did. You're full of surprises.'

'The van is owned by the business. This car is mine.' He accelerated as they left the outskirts of town. 'How are you settling into Barrington? Not too small for you?'

'Not at all.' Millie was enthusiastic, this was a subject close to her heart. 'The job was advertised as a three-to-six-month maternity leave position, and I'll be honest, I needed the work. And the change. But I wasn't sure about the small-town bit. I wondered if it would be, you know, *too small*.' She glanced at him, hoping she hadn't offended him. 'But Debbie extended the offer to twelve months, and I'm loving it.'

'I know what you mean. But Barrington has a little *something*, don't you think? I've started to get to know some of the locals. Working on events with Meggie Hamilton and Harriet Murray has really helped lift the profile of our wines, locally at least. This town has a real sense of community. I haven't experienced that before.'

Millie looked at Finn as he spoke. His eyes remained on the road and she had a chance to study him. He had a lovely speaking voice, his tone deep. *Not too deep.* And expressive. She wondered if he'd ever done any public speaking, she was sure he could project *that voice* to the back of a large room.

Her gaze wandered further. He had both hands on the wheel

and she couldn't help noticing his biceps. He glanced at her quickly and she blushed. *He saw me checking him out.*

'Um, Millie, there's something I need to tell you.' And now *he* sounded uncertain. *What?* 'You'll find out soon enough, so it's best I tell you now. From the start.' He sounded more than uncertain, he was nervous. Her mind was racing. *I'm not really divorced. I have a sexually transmitted disease. I'm wanted in two states. What??*

'Um, what Finn?' Now she sounded uncertain. But her mind had already connected the rest of his sentence. *From the start. Is this the start of something?*

'I have, um.' He paused. Her mind screamed *what? Just tell me???*

But all she said was, 'um, take your time.'

'I have. A. Tattoo.' His face was serious and he stared straight ahead, concentrating on his driving.

Millie giggled. *Not wanted in two states then.* 'A tattoo? Where?' She was relieved. *Was that all.*

Finn seemed to relax when she laughed, and he chuckled. 'More than one, actually. On my.'

He stopped and she snort-laughed. 'Where?!' She had no idea what he was going to say about the location of his body art, but in her heart she was already okay with it.

Finn laughed then. 'Arms. On my arms.'

Still giggling, Millie reached across and raised the elbow-length sleeve of his shirt with one finger. A set of legs came into view, wearing high heels. She tugged the sleeve higher and saw the torso of a woman wearing a bathing suit. Old-fashioned. A bit like the women painted on the sides of world war two fighter planes. She pressed the shirt against his arm and could just make out the top half of the woman through the fabric. But she saw another tattoo, beside it.

She let his sleeve drop, grinning. 'Cute. How many? Really?'

'You don't mind?' He glanced at her quickly. 'I have five. All done in my late teens. My son, Lucas, tells me they're awful. Actually, he says they're *daggy*.' Finn grinned and Millie laughed with him. 'Millie, you're lovely, and I, well, my youth was spent on the wrong side of the tracks. I wasn't sure, if you'd, um, like the tattoos.'

'I can't say I like them or dislike them. But I would never have known you had them, they're hidden when you wear a short-sleeve shirt.' She chuckled again. The whole conversation had relaxed her, or maybe it had given her confidence. 'But I will tell you, that if I'd brought you home to meet my parents when I was a teenager, I would not have been allowed to date you.' She laughed loudly then, and loved it when he joined in.

'And your parents Millie? Are they, um, still with us?' Finn's tone was light.

'Oh yes. They are. They live interstate, but they've promised to visit.' Still giggling, she added, 'I look forward to introducing you.'

———

THE CAFÉ WAS LOVELY AND FINN WAS RIGHT, THE FOOD was fresh. She enjoyed an Asian-inspired calamari salad and he chose prawn skewers with a peanut sauce on a bed of fragrant rice. She drank a glass of wine. A cabernet sauvignon to accompany her salad, and Finn enjoyed a pinot noir. One glass seemed to be enough and the cinema, when they finished their meal, was only a short walk from the restaurant.

Millie insisted on buying the movie tickets, as it was her choice. Finn started to object, but saw she wanted it to be her treat and agreed. They took bottled water into the cinema and found seats in the middle. They had the row to themselves, the cinema was only half full. They were chatting quietly when the previews of upcoming movies commenced and she was thrilled when Finn stopped the conversation while they watched. Leaning closer to him, she whispered, 'thank you. I love the previews. It helps me choose my next cinema visit.'

The preview for the romantic comedy Millie had almost chosen for this trip came on, and she loved it, telling herself she'd drive over and see it before it finished its run. What surprised her was that Finn seemed to enjoy it too, laughing loudly in all the right places. She wanted to ask him then if he'd like to see it with her, but the main feature began and they both settled back in their seats. Millie had to use a tissue a couple of times.

The sad scenes always affected her more deeply when she knew the story was based on real life events. When the lights came up at the end, she hoped her mascara hadn't smudged. Finn reached over and took her hand. 'Thank you Millie. What a beautifully filmed and moving story. I had no idea about the history of this one.' He squeezed her hand and let it go, moving to stand up.

The trip home was fun, they chatted easily. Firstly about the movie and that particular aspect of the second world war, then about favourite movies and books. She learned that Finn was a reader, although mostly biographies and true crime stories. It helped her warm to him even more. She had already decided she liked him, but apart from the kiss on her cheek when he picked her up and the quick hand hold at the end of the movie, he'd given no indication of the level of his interest.

Finn parked in front of her building, got out of the car quickly, and came around to her side. Millie had already opened the door, but he held it for her while she stepped out. She wasn't sure what to do next. She was reluctant to invite him up to her apartment in case it signalled *something more*. But she wanted to say or do something to let him know she'd like to go out with him again. Hiding her uncertainty, she rummaged in her handbag for her keys.

With the keys in her hand she braved a glance. His expression was warm and friendly, much as it had been all night. In fact, she couldn't remember when she'd been in such easy company. They had shared more than a few laughs during the course of their date. Part of her hoped he'd kiss her goodnight. But she'd never make the first move.

'Millie.' His voice drew her focus back to him. She had been staring at him while her mind galloped away.

She blushed. 'Finn. Er, thank you. I've had a lovely time.' She had no idea what to do next, so turned to the door and inserted her key in the lock.

'Millie. Wait.' *Gosh she loved his voice. He could narrate romantic novels, she'd never put them down.* She spun to face him. Reaching up, he tilted her chin upwards, stepped close and kissed her gently. Not fully on her lips, more like the side of her mouth. It tingled. *She* tingled. Her eyes met his, and without thinking it through, she leaned forward and kissed him back. Right on the mouth. Her lips moved against his for the briefest of moments, and she was about to draw back when he reached around her, drawing her closer, and kissed her. *Really kissed her.* She'd often scoffed when women in the novels she read went weak at the knees, but for a moment her own legs turned to jelly as he deepened the kiss. Instead of pulling back, she wound her arms around his neck, aware that her breasts were pushed into his chest, almost breathless when the tip of his tongue met hers.

Millie had no idea how long they kissed. It could have been five minutes or thirty. She couldn't remember the last time she'd felt so sexy. Finally the kiss ended and she found herself backed against her front door, Finn's arms around her. One held the back of her head and the other was somewhere lower than her waist but not quite on her bum. Drawing in a breath, she looked at him. His eyes were dark, his desire evident. She could feel the rise and fall of her chest against his, her breathing still heavy.

'Millie.' His voice was lower now, almost a growl. *Damn. That voice. So sexy.* 'I want you to invite me in.' He kissed her mouth again, gently. 'But I don't think you're ready. So I'll walk away. This time.' He stepped back. Millie hadn't spoken. Couldn't speak. She raised a trembling hand to her lips. They felt swollen. He moved back into her orbit. 'Don't look at me like that.' He lowered his head and kissed her mouth, then her cheek, then nibbled his way down to her collarbone. She let her head fall back and if the door hadn't been behind her, she would have fallen. He stopped, took the keys from her hand and opened the front door. With one hand on her elbow, he helped her step inside. She looked at the stairs, up to the next floor to her apartment.

Finn stepped away but was still holding the door. 'I'm leaving Millie. Lock this when I close it. I'll call you.' She nodded. The door closed and she locked it, then leaned against it, whispering, 'goodnight Finn.'

47

HARRIET

'I'M FINE DRUM. HAMISH IS THRIVING.' HARRIET DREW in a sharp breath. Drum was leaning on the doorjamb of the bathroom, arms and legs crossed, as she stared into the mirror applying mascara. She put the cap on the mascara tube and returned it to the drawer. Turning, she faced him. 'What exactly are you worried about?' She knew her chin had lifted. She hadn't expected this from Drum.

He spoke quietly and although he was trying to look nonchalant, Harriet knew him too well to be fooled by that. He was tense. And annoyed. 'Harriet. You're recovering from surgery. It's only been eight weeks. Don't you think it's too soon to go back to work? And Laura is there now. Ben told me last week she's doing really well.'

'Drum.' Her tone held a warning. 'I'm going to a meeting. With the Bens, Meggie and Laura. We are doing some forward planning. That's all.' She looked at Hamish, asleep in his cot. She'd only just fed him, he'd sleep for a while. 'The meeting is at ten and we should be done by twelve. Then Meggie and I will have lunch and talk about our own business and the forward bookings.'

Drum sighed then and straightened. 'Harriet. I'm not trying to stop you from going back to work. But you're still healing.' He shuffled his feet. 'I don't want you overdoing it, that's all.'

'Drum Murray. I know we're married, but I am an independent, capable woman and I *need* to work. I love my business and what Meggie and I are building. And it's good for Barrington, you know that.' Harriet relented then and walked to him. She wrapped her arms around his waist. 'It will be easy to take Hamish to work now, while he's small. Once he becomes mobile I'll have to re-think how I work.'

Drum nodded, then gave a sheepish grin. 'I'm sorry Harri. I've grown used to you being at home during the day. I'm being selfish. I'll miss you.' He hugged her then and she melted against him.

Leaning back, she pursed her lips and he laughed, then kissed her. 'Drum, I already know I only want to work school hours. And maybe not every day. But perhaps three days a week I can take Billie to school, have Hamish with me, and bring her home from school too. It's important to me that she feels loved and supported.' She chuckled then. 'But I didn't factor *you* into the equation Drum.'

'Oh, now you're just rubbing salt into my wounds. But Harri? He cocked an eyebrow and she nodded for him to continue. 'You hadn't told me your plans, that you weren't thinking full time. If you had, I'd not have said anything.'

Now she cocked an eyebrow. 'Really Drum Murray? I'll keep that in mind for future reference.'

———

THE MEETING WENT WELL. BIG BEN HAD OFFERED HIS office to Harriet. It was the largest and would fit a portable cot for Hamish. Laura was using the main reception desk and Big Ben seemed to spend most of the time at the other desk in the front office anyway. The meeting room was available if he needed privacy for contract negotiations with clients. Meggie had an office and so did Little Ben, and it left Harriet's old office free. Harriet had another plan for this room but wanted to talk to Meggie at lunch first.

Harriet was delighted with how quickly Laura had picked up the property management work and she was almost qualified for sales too. She was organised and hardworking and they had increased the rental portfolio by fifteen percent in the short time she'd been with them. This left more time for Harriet and Meggie to concentrate on the elopement and events business, and Harriet's core business - bringing new people to the region.

The other topic of conversation, at the end of their meeting, was about the Council elections. Candidate nominations were due to open on the first of next month, with the election in the middle of April. The local Council operated with a Mayor and eight councillors. During the current four-year term there were only two female councillors. One was staying on, she was brilliant at engaging with the smaller communities in the region. The other, a younger woman, had been studying and was leaving to move into the medical field. Council positions were part-time, yet quite well paid.

'You know as well as I do Ben Evans, that there are at least four male councillors, now, who are just there because they've *bought themselves a job*. They don't represent us well. In fact, their decision *not* to take on board the options raised through community consultation, with respect to the saleyards redevelopment, is tantamount to gross negligence.' Laura never minced words and Harriet was pleased. Laura sometimes said what others were thinking but were too afraid to articulate.

'We need more candidates. You're right Laura.' Big Ben looked at his son. 'I think Drum Murray will renominate. He represents the farmers interests well. And you, son. I'm counting on you standing in my stead this time.'

'I've discussed it with Melanie and yes, I'll stand.' He grinned at Laura. 'With you here Laura, we've got a bit more of dad too. And with Meggie and Harriet helping out, we'll be fine here.' He looked at Laura then. 'Do you have someone in mind Laura, to nominate this year? Women perhaps.'

'Yes I do. I've gotten to know Meggie, Harriet, Rose and Debbie well in the last couple of years. Meggie probably doesn't have the profile yet to get votes, and I'm not sure Rose would be keen. But Meggie, in another four years, it's something you should consider.' Laura turned to Harriet then, who had tried not to chuckle at the surprised look on Meggie's face.

'Harriet. You're well known now and you've been good for the region. With the right campaign I think you'd pull enough votes. The danger is that some folks might think you and Ben, working out of the same office, are interchangeable and having you nominate could split Ben's votes. And you're married to Drum, which is problematic from a political point of view. It's still worth thinking about. But Debbie is my first-choice candidate. Everyone knows her, the café has been great for the town. And she's on maternity leave. She might consider it. She's a long term local, she knows the region well and her husband is a local farmer. What do you think?' Laura leaned back, looking pleased with herself.

'Debbie would be good.' Harriet looked at Meggie for a moment. 'Although she's never mentioned any interest in local politics to me. But we can canvas her.' Harriet frowned then. 'I could be interested. Maybe for next time. But I would worry that my candidacy would split Drum's votes. 'But what about you Laura? You're obviously politically minded. Would you be interested?'

'No. People love me or hate me. But possibly next time too, when I've had more time in this role, to help me build a better profile.' Laura looked at Big Ben, who winked at her. Harriet could see they'd talked about this previously.

'There's someone else. Not a woman. But a good candidate I think.' Harriet leaned forward. 'Angus Hamilton. He was here through the drought, he's married to Rose Gordon. Old Charlie Gordon 'anointed him' for want of a better term. He's been here long enough. He knows the townsfolk and the rural community and he's well respected.' She looked at Little Ben. 'Have you ever discussed this with Angus?'

'We were in drought for the last election. He was struggling. We all were. And he hadn't been here long enough then. But you're right Harri, I think Angus would be a shoe-in.' Big Ben gave her a pleased nod and his father murmured, 'good thinking Harriet.'

Hamish gave a little cry at that moment. He'd been sound asleep in her arms since the meeting began. She stood up. 'I'll just feed Master Murray here, then Meggie and I might go for lunch.' She looked at Laura. 'Want to join us Laura? Girls lunch?'

'I'd love to Harri, but I've got new tenants coming in shortly. If I finish inside an hour, I'll drop down for a coffee.' Laura stood too, and the meeting wrapped up as Harriet left the room.

48

MEGGIE

Harriet relaxed on the couch in her office to feed Hamish, with Meggie sitting at the desk. 'I wasn't expecting that. The discussion about local council. But I guess it's something we have to talk about, being in business here. I've heard enough about the saleyards debacle from Ben and Drum to know the current council hasn't been as cohesive as it could be. She screwed up her nose. 'I'm not sure I'd like to do it. From what I've seen you lose your privacy, to a degree, when you take public office.'

'My thoughts too. Billie already gets teased at school because Drum's on council. Not often, but it happens. I don't know if Debbie's ever given it much thought. But we should ask her. I think we need another catch up, all of us, but Debbie is almost to her due date and I don't want to stress her out. I think the timing might not be right for her.'

Once down at the café with Hamish now asleep in his stroller, they ordered lunch. Millie served them.

CHAPTER 48

'You're looking well Millie. Are you still enjoying our little town?' Meggie smiled as she spoke.

Millie seemed to pause for a moment, then she grinned. 'I love it here. I absolutely love this town, the café, my work.' She looked at both of them then. 'And book club. I adore book club. Getting to know you all. I think it's really helped me settle in here.'

'Ha ha. Book club. Yes.' Meggie nudged Harriet. 'It came about because Harri read a book I'd loaned her, which she had forgotten was mine, I might add, and she had questions.' She laughed then, Harriet chuckled and Millie smiled, slightly bemused but she nodded at them. 'Brilliant. That sounds like a story. I'd love to hear it.'

'Maybe next book club Millie.' Harriet looked over her shoulder, squinting at the specials board. 'What's nice today? I feel like chicken.'

'We have an Asian-inspired chicken salad with ginger, garlic, chilli and peanuts. Or an avocado and chicken salad wrap. And all our usual lunch deals.' Millie glanced at the counter where Meggie could see a queue forming.

'Go Millie. I'll come and order for us when that line clears.' Meggie turned back to Harriet as Millie rushed away. 'The chicken salad sounds good.'

Harriet nodded. 'Yes. The salad. And coffee please.'

'Harriet, there's something I want to tell you. And ask you.' Meggie paused.

Harriet gave Meggie her full attention, then said quietly, 'you're pregnant, aren't you?'

Meggie nodded. 'Five weeks. I haven't wanted to jinx it. I wondered if you'd worked it out. Debbie did, at last book club. But she promised not to say anything.'

'I'm so happy for you Meggie.' Harriet beamed and Meggie felt her own smile in response. 'So how can I help? You wanted to ask me something?' Harriet placed a hand over Meggie's.

'I've got a referral to the specialist obstetrician Debbie sees in Newcastle. He's really lovely. I have an appointment next week. It's on book club day, in the morning. I know it may be a big ask, with Hamish and everything, but could you come with me?'

Meggie loved that Harriet didn't hesitate. 'Of course. We can make that work. No problem.' She hesitated. 'Max?'

'He knows. Of course he knows. And he would come with me. And I could ask Rose too, and I know she'd come. But Harriet, forgive me if I'm overstepping, but we've been through a lot together. With your own pregnancy. And, well, it's you I'd like with me. Good news or bad. And if it's bad, if I'm told I can't carry a baby past the first trimester, I'd rather process that on the way home before I tell Max.' Meggie wiped a tear from the corner of her eye. 'Harri, my expectations aren't high. Max is way more confident than I am.'

'It's no problem Meggie. Can I tell Drum? You know, why I'm going with you,' Harriet patted Meggie's hand.

'Yes. Tell Drum. I know he won't say anything.' Meggie leaned forward and hugged Harriet. 'Thank you.'

Harriet laughed. 'Go order for us Meggs, my tummy is rumbling.'

49

ROSE

'STAND FOR COUNCIL? REALLY?' ROSE FROWNED. 'You've never mentioned an interest in local government, Angus.' She handed Angus the salad, and followed him to the dining table, carrying two serves of pistachio-crumbed veal. It was late and Rose wondered if the veal was overdone. It had taken ages to settle Charlie in his bed, and Harper had drifted off mid-feed so Rose was sure she'd wake again. Probably in the middle of their dinner.

'I'm not that interested Rose. I'm not politically geared. At all. Not like Ben. And Drum has been here so long, I think his father was on Council in his day and probably his grandfather too. So he's all over it.' Angus sighed, cutting a piece of the veal. He chewed silently for a moment, then served himself some salad. 'The veal is really tasty Rose. I don't think it's overdone.'

Taking a bite herself, Rose nodded. 'You're right. I was worried that taking it off the heat to sort Charlie out, then putting it back on may have dried it out a bit.' She filled her water glass, thinking for a moment. 'Don't do it if you're not keen. I understand Ben's argument, that they need better people to stand for Council. I agree. And yes, I think you'd get the votes. But Angus, don't take something on that doesn't hold your interest. It will be a struggle.'

Angus breathed out, then spoke quietly. 'Thank you. I needed to hear that. I think I'd get the votes too, but how well will I represent those voters if my heart isn't in it? And if I'm not a good councillor, will the practice suffer? And that affects not just us, but Max and Meggie too.'

They ate in silence for a few minutes. 'Who else is there? Did Ben say they were approaching others?' Rose picked a couple of cherry tomatoes out of the salad, popping them straight into her mouth. 'These are so good, I picked them this morning.'

'Ben's hoping for more women. Says they're under-represented.' Angus gave Rose a look then, that she'd call calculated. 'Would you be interested?' He seemed to warm to his idea. 'You're well-known, a generational local. You're smart and you speak well. You understand rural issues but also business. You know marketing too.'

'I've never considered it either. But you know that my grandfather was on Council when I was young. He wanted Dad to stand, but I think that was the year Mum got sick.' Taking a deep breath, Rose gazed down at her plate. 'Wow! That just brought a memory back. Dad didn't want to. I remember him saying he didn't have the time. But I think he just didn't want to do it. They had an argument at the dinner table about it. Not a bad one, but Charlie said something like *don't complain afterwards if your interests aren't represented, you had your chance.*'

'Do you want to think about it Rose? Wee Charlie is in day care and if there's anything on at night, I can be here with the kids.

CHAPTER 49

It may be hard having someone look after Harper for Council meetings, they're twice a month I think, and for a whole day.' Angus scooped up the last of his salad.

His words caught her off-guard, and an idea was already forming. 'Look after Harper? I'm still breast-feeding and expect to continue until she's at least nine months. Longer if I can. I'd take her with me to the meetings. And once she's weaned I would make other arrangements.' She could hear the obstinacy in her own voice. Then doubt crept in. 'But I don't have the profile you have Angus. I don't get out into the community nearly as much.'

'Ben said we'd run as a bloc. With him and Drum and he also wants to talk to Debbie. He said Harriet would manage the campaign. Maybe we should have a get-together to talk about it?' Angus stood, clearing the table as he spoke.

'Debbie? She'd be great, but I think the timing isn't good for her. It depends how well she is after the birth. But I'd like to see more women on Council too.' Rose gathered up the remaining items from the table and followed Angus back to the kitchen. The dirty dishes were piled up on the sink, but he had the fridge door open. Rose laughed. 'Still hungry? There's some leftover apple pie. I can warm it up, add some ice cream.' She pointed to the covered dish and he withdrew it from the fridge, then kissed the top of her head.

'Apple pie and ice-cream, perfect.' He cocked his head on one side. 'Is that Harper? Did you hear anything?'

Pausing, Rose stopped. She shook her head. 'I can't hear her. Can you creep down and have a look?' She laughed as he started down the hall, arms held in front in an exaggerated creeping stance. 'Bring her back if she's awake.'

Angus returned with Harper in his arms. She had her thumb

in her mouth, but her eyes were wide open. 'What's with the thumb?' Angus took her into the living area and waited while Rose settled in a lounge chair, then handed her over. 'I changed her, so if she falls asleep I can just put her back to bed.'

'Thank you. The thumb? It's new. I think she's only just found it and she's using it to self-soothe.' Rose smiled up at Angus, who was hovering. 'Your pie should be warm enough. Just put some ice cream on it and you're set.'

'Aren't you having any?' He was already at the door when he asked.

'No. I'm full, that veal was more than enough for me.' Rose kissed the top of Harper's head, inhaling her warm baby-smells. She couldn't get enough of her.

50

MILLIE

March – Barrington Book Club – Meeting 7
Present: Rose and baby Harper, Harriet and baby Hamish,
Laura, Meggie, Nicole, Frances and Millie
Apologies: Debbie, Melanie
Book: *The Understudy* by Julie Bennett

'DEBBIE CALLED JUST AFTER LUNCH TO SAY SHE WON'T come in tonight.' Millie held the door open for Rose as she wheeled the stroller in, with Harper sleeping soundly.

'And Melanie's away for a few days with Ben and the girls.' Rose smiled at Millie, then waved to Laura, who was at the table holding a bottle of wine. 'No wine for me Laura. I'm running late because Harper threw up after her feed and we both needed a complete change.'

Millie liked the way these women were with each other, supportive but still fun. Laura called back to Rose, 'it's me, Millie and Nic for wine tonight. The others have opted for coffee.'

Locking the front door, Millie moved to the coffee machine. Harriet had already started the drinks and Meggie and Frances were organising plates and napkins.

They'd all settled at the table when Millie carried over a plate of still-warm mini quiches she'd baked before they arrived, plus finger sandwiches and an assortment of slices and cakes. 'The hot weather seems to have left us, so I thought some warm food might be the ticket tonight.'

'Good thinking Millie.' Laura picked one up and popped the whole thing into her mouth. 'Mmm. Good. Did Cathy make these?'

'Um. No. I did after Cathy left.' Millie blushed. She loved book club and these women, but she still felt a little bit like *café staff* rather than book club attendee. And that wasn't because the others weren't welcoming, but she was still a newcomer and didn't want to overstep.

Rose ate one then, closing her eyes briefly while she chewed. 'Tasty.' She opened her eyes, quickly counted the quiches, then took another. 'I count three each, so be quick ladies.' They laughed and Millie relaxed, chuckling with them. She picked up a couple of finger sandwiches.

Meggie gathered some food for her plate. 'Millie? About Debbie? Is she okay? I messaged earlier today and she said she'd be here.'

Shaking her head, Millie frowned. 'She didn't say why she wasn't coming. But she's almost to her due date, so maybe she just needs to rest.'

'Probably.' Rose looked thoughtful. 'I'll message her when we finish, it won't be late. Just to check in with her.' She turned to Frances then, who was sitting beside her. 'And how are you

Frances?'

'Good today, Rose. Some days are harder than others.' Frances sounded good tonight. Confident, Millie thought. 'And we've made plans for our first trip. We're going to drive down to Victoria, spend a couple of nights in Melbourne and then on Phillip Island. I've always wanted to see the fairy penguins. Then a few days in Gippsland and make our way back up the east coast.'

'Sounds lovely Frances. I love Melbourne but I've never been to Phillip Island either.' Laura smiled warmly.

'Douglas has arranged for a temporary Solicitor to handle the office. But he's talking about retiring later this year, so we can travel more.' Frances looked away for a moment and Millie saw her swallow before she spoke again. 'I'm doing everything recommended to slow the process. The dementia. But really, we don't know. How long we have to do things together.'

Rose put her arm around the older woman's shoulders for a moment. 'None of us really know Frances, life as we know it can change in a heartbeat.' The others nodded and murmured 'yes' in response to Rose, but Millie felt a cold finger of fear run up her spine. She shuddered imperceptibly.

Baby Hamish cried loudly and the mood of the room changed quickly. Harriet lifted him out of his carrier and settled him, then passed him over to Laura when she held her arms out for him. The others chatted and laughed and enjoyed the snacks on the table. Except Meggie. Millie noticed Meggie was sipping water and hadn't touched any of the food. She thought Rose noticed too, but she didn't comment.

With Hamish happy in Laura's arms, Harriet brought out her notebook and copy of The Understudy. 'I'm starting. I loved this one so much, I've pre-ordered her new book already. I lived in Sydney and know the areas described in the book. But the story! What a page turner, great characters, intrigue and a whole lot of living history around the opening of the opera house.'

'Oh me too. My new favourite.' Laura was nodding. 'I know little about opera, but this story intrigued me. I've finished two other books since this one. I devoured it so quickly.'

Rose now had Harper on her lap and patted her little back a couple of times. 'Books like this.' She paused. 'The characters, the setting, the whole-bloody-awesomeness.' Rose stopped and shaking her head slightly, she kissed the top of Harper's head.

'Rose!' They all turned to Frances, who looked indignant. 'If this is about your own writing. Doubting your writing ability. Then just don't!' Frances shook her head sadly. 'I'm sure this is a wonderful book, but it was too much for me. Too big. I read a couple of chapters but had to re-read them the next day.' She rolled her eyes. 'Of course, that's not because of the book, as you all know.' She turned to Rose then. 'But I love reading. And I *have* been reading. Or rather, re-reading. Rose, I picked up your first book and re-read it and I fell in love with your story all over again. So that's what I'm doing now. Reading books I've loved, again. And it's easier for me. And enjoyable.' She grinned. 'So I'm still a reader.'

Millie couldn't help herself, she clapped her hands at that. How wonderful! And brave. Everyone seemed to speak at once then, while Rose and Harriet settled their babies for a feed. Meggie excused herself for the bathroom and Laura poured the last of the wine into Millie's glass, having topped Frances up first.

'I'm driving tonight, taking Frances home, so no more for me.' Laura placed the empty bottle on the next table.

"Nice wine Laura. What's the label?' Millie savoured the light red.

'It's from Barrington Ridge. Ben and I did a cellar door visit and bought a whole case. Six of these and six whites.' Laura smacked her lips together and Millie giggled.

'I haven't been out there yet. But it's on my to-do list.' Millie was hoping Finn might invite her at the weekend. As she spoke, her phone vibrated beside her copy of The Understudy on the table. 'Excuse me.' Millie picked it up, expecting a text from one of the kids.

'Oh! It's from Debbie.' Millie opened the text message as the others stopped their conversations in expectation. 'Oh! Oh!' Millie looked across the table to Rose. 'They're on their way to Newcastle. Debbie's in labour. She asked me to let you all know.' Another text popped through and Millie read it aloud. 'Tell them not to worry. Jamie and Mum with me. I'll group message when we have news.'

'Brilliant!' Rose moved Harper to her other breast. 'Now we know why Debbie didn't come tonight. She must have realised labour was starting.'

'Thank you Millie.' Harriet looked at the others round the table as she spoke, including them in her words. 'Thank you for looking after us tonight. And fingers crossed all goes well for Debbie.'

'Yes. Wishing her a safe delivery.' Meggie looked at Harriet as she spoke, eyebrows raised. Millie wondered what that was about, Meggie seemed a bit pale. Whatever it was, Harriet knew, because she smiled and nodded in what looked to be encouragement.

Meggie cleared her throat then. 'I have news.' She looked at

Rose. 'Harriet knows, and I called Rose and Angus this afternoon. 'I'm pregnant. Again. Six weeks.'

'That's wonderful Meggie.' Laura spoke quietly but Millie could see Meggie had more to say.

'I've been to see Debbie's obstetrician in Newcastle this morning. Harriet came with me.' Her face brightened then. 'There's no reason to expect I won't carry this baby to full term.' She glanced at Harriet before continuing. 'But I am low in magnesium and selenium, which sometimes triggers miscarriage. So I'm on supplements and need to eat more tuna and salmon and foods rich in selenium.' She smiled then and Millie felt relief. *She was becoming invested in the lives of these women.*

'And I've got morning sickness except it's all-day-sickness. But I'm even grateful for that.' Meggie had tears in her eyes and Millie could see some of the others did too. But before the emotion in the room could take over Rose jumped to her feet, walked around the table and hugged her sister-in-law tightly. The room erupted then, into happy chatter. Millie sat back, surveying it all. She noticed Frances was quiet and now looked tired. Laura seemed to notice at the same moment and spoke up quite loudly.

'Next book? Suggestions?' Laura asked as Harriet helped Millie clear the table.

'I'd like to suggest one. I'm friends with an independent author from Brisbane, Leanne Lovegrove. She has a new one out called *Buried in Between*. Small town romance and a hint of mystery.' Rose pulled a copy of the book from her bag and handed it around. 'It's available from all retailers. Mine came directly from Leanne, it arrived yesterday. If anyone wants a paperback I can order them directly from her.'

Millie handed the book back to Rose. 'Love the cover. Yes,

order me a paperback please.' They chatted about who else needed a copy, then Laura stood. 'Okay Frances, I'll take you home now if you're ready.'

Millie thought Frances looked momentarily confused.

Laura added, 'Douglas will be waiting for you Frances.' Frances stood then, gathering her things and nodded. 'Yes. Yes of course. Douglas. Thank you.'

The group broke up and Millie stacked their plates in the dishwasher out in the kitchen. Rose was the last to leave, Harper had fallen asleep in the stroller after her feed. She stood in the kitchen with Millie while she checked the back entrance was locked up.

'Millie. I know Debbie has told you how happy she is that you're here, running the café. But I want to thank you too. You've taken a lot of stress from her shoulders and her health has benefited.'

Pleased and a bit embarrassed, Millie murmured, 'you don't have to thank me Rose. I love it here. I love being part of book club too. Getting to know you all has been a highlight for me.'

'Ha ha.' Rose nudged her shoulder. 'You're part of the girl-posse now. There's no escaping!'

Millie laughed. 'Girl-posse?'

'Apparently that's the name Angus, Max, Drum and Ben have given book club. They don't think we know.' Rose laughed loudly, then put her hand over her mouth when Harper gave a quiet cry.

Giggling, Millie walked to the front door with Rose as she pushed the stroller. 'Love it. I won't tell them I know!'

———

THE SUN WAS JUST BEGINNING TO RISE WHEN MILLIE'S phone pinged in her pocket. She was heading home from her dawn walk and slowed to read the message. It was a group message from Debbie to all the book club friends.

> Scarlett born at 3:50AM. She's perfect and we should be home tomorrow. I'm well too. XX

A photo of the baby wrapped in a pale pink blanket followed. Scarlett had a sweet little face, her cheeks tinged pink and no hair at all on her head. Millie let out a sigh of relief and began to send a message in return. As she did the phone buzzed several times with messages sent by the others. Millie sped up, there'd be lots of questions at the café today by locals wishing Debbie well. *Small town news travels quickly.*

51

———

HARRIET

'I KNOW DEBBIE'S ONLY BEEN HOME A WEEK, BUT nominations for Council are open now. I'd really like to have a chat with everyone. And because it's political, we can't really do it at the pub over dinner. Do you think we could have them all here? Are you okay with that Harri?' Drum was laying on his side, propped up on his elbow. Harriet was sitting up, her back resting against pillows and the bed head while little Hamish snuffled and snorted at her breast.

Frowning, Harriet disengaged the baby from her chest and handed him to Drum. 'He's just fussing, not drinking. I don't think he's really hungry.' She glanced at her watch. 'Billie will be up soon, I'd better have a shower. Can you undress Hamish once I'm in and hand him to me? It will save me running a bath and I want to drop Billie at school then go to the office. Just for the morning.' She stepped out of bed and stretched. 'But in answer to your question, lunch or afternoon tea here on the weekend might be easier than dinner. Out on the veranda and the bigger kids can play in the garden.'

'Afternoon tea sounds good. It's not a big commitment and we can pick up the food from the café.' Drum was out of bed now, tickling Hamish on the tummy as he undressed him.

'No need to pick anything up. Billie and I can do some cooking. If we have it on Saturday afternoon, we can cook in the morning. Two types of cake, a batch of scones and a caramel slice. Oh, and maybe some mini sausage rolls for the bigger kids. Want me to ask when I go in if everyone's available? Say two-thirty until five?'

Drum carried Hamish into the ensuite. Harriet was under the shower now and he waited while she washed and rinsed her hair, before handing their son in. 'It's quite a lot Harri. Both Bens and Laura, then another five couples including us plus little Charlie and Warwick and the bigger kids.'

'It will be fine. Actually, I can ask them each to bring a plate. Some savoury and some sweet. You sort the drinks out with the men. And Billie and I will cook too.' She'd soaped Hamish up and rinsed him off while she spoke, then held him out to Drum, who wrapped him in a towel.

Ten minutes later Harriet walked into the kitchen, dressed in navy wide-leg pants, a white shirt and white sneakers. She hadn't worn heels since Hamish was born, but now the days were cooling she'd have to dig her boots out and give them a polish and pull jumpers and scarves out of her winter wardrobe.

Billie flew into the room behind her and rushed straight to Hamish, laying on a thick rug on the floor. She lay down beside him, said good morning and pulled several colourful toys within his reach.

CHAPTER 51

Harriet rolled her eyes at Drum, then smiled at Billie. 'Good morning Billie.'

Billie jumped to her feet and quickly hugged Harriet, then her father. 'Morning! I'm making orange juice.' She grabbed several oranges from the fridge and disappeared into the pantry. Billie was growing up and Harriet was grateful she adored her new little brother. Drum grinned at her, then walked over and kissed her gently, saying 'love you.'

Billie set three glasses of orange juice on the breakfast table and Harriet stirred the scrambled eggs over the heat. 'Can you put some bread in the toaster please? The eggs won't be long.'

'I've got it.' Drum busied himself on the other side of the kitchen. Billie set three plates on the table.

'Billie, we might have a few people over for afternoon tea on Saturday. Want to help me cook that morning? Cakes, scones and slice.' Harriet watched as Billie nodded.

'Who's coming? Tiffany? Tommy?' Billie stepped back as Drum put a slice of buttered toast on each plate and Harriet carried the pan over and served the eggs.

'Yes. And wee Charlie and Warwick. Harri thought the afternoon would be best, you can all play outside while we chat on the back veranda.' Drum ruffled his daughter's hair, but she pushed his hand away. 'Daa-ad! I've just done my hair.'

'Sorry.' Drum winked at her. 'Looks gorgeous.'

Harriet glanced at Billie. She had her hair up in a pony tail. It wasn't perfect, her riotous curls were always hard to tame. But she had been trying to do more things herself since Hamish arrived. 'I can help with your hair before we leave. I'm driving in, so you don't need to catch the bus today and we have an extra ten minutes. If you want, I can do that French braid you like.'

'The ponytail is fine.' Billie took a bite of toast, then grinned at Harriet. 'But I do like that French braid. Only if you have time Harri.'

'I have time. And it looks very pretty.' Harriet watched Billie smile at this, then nod vigorously.

52

DEBBIE

DEBBIE STROLLED INTO THE CAFÉ WITH BABY SCARLETT in her arms. Her mum Rachel was with her, holding little Warwick's hand. Getting to the table at the back took almost ten minutes. Customers and staff waved, said hello and many wanted to have a peek at the baby. Debbie didn't mind, she actually felt better just a few days after birth than she had for the six weeks prior. And she was besotted by Scarlett.

Millie bustled over, her delight at seeing Debbie evident. 'Hi Debbie, Rachel.' Handing some crayons and paper to Warwick she bent down, so she was on his level. 'What can you draw for me to today Warwick?'

'I'm Woz.' He blinked his eyes as he said it and Debbie shared an amused look with her mum.

'Woz. Of course.' Millie put her hand to her face in mock-shock. 'I know that!' Warwick giggled and Millie turned to Debbie, who moved Scarlett in her arms so Millie could see her face. She was sleeping.

'She's gorgeous Debbie and she looks like you!' Millie touched the baby lightly on her cheek. 'And how are you?'

'Honestly? A bit euphoric. I think I have the opposite of the baby blues.' Debbie knew she was gushing, but it was true. She did feel fabulous. 'And it's likely the diabetes will disappear quickly too. My sugar levels have already come down considerably.'

'Just don't overdo it Deb. You need to rest when Scarlett sleeps.' Rachel spoke quickly and Debbie shared a look with Millie. Her mum was wonderful, but sometimes Debbie wished she wasn't so free with her advice.

'What would you like? I'll get it ready for you.' Millie seemed to sense Debbie's discomfort and pulled a notebook from her pocket.

'Chai for me and a small chocolate milkshake for Woz.' Debbie looked at her mum, eyebrows raised.

'Oh, thanks Millie. Flat white for me.' Rachel glanced towards the counter and cake display. Leaning in, she said to Debbie. 'Want to share something? A muffin?'

Laughing, Debbie shook her head. 'I'm good Mum, but order one. You can cut a bit off for Woz.'

'Okay. A chocolate chip muffin. With a plate and knife please Millie.'

They spoke quietly for a while and Debbie watched Millie and her team in the café. She could see it was running well under Millie's leadership and she relaxed. She was in no hurry to go back to work.

Harriet arrived with Hamish in his stroller, joining them at the table. 'Hi Deb, Hi Rachel.' She looked at Scarlett, then held out her arms. 'May I?'

'Of course. She's just beginning to wake up, so don't be

surprised if she cries.' Debbie handed Scarlett to Harriet, who snuggled her against her shoulder. Her little eyes fluttered open, then closed again. 'Well she's happy there Harri.'

Warwick began to fuss, having finished his milkshake and the shared muffin. Rachel stood up. 'Want to come to the park for a swing Warwick? With Nanna?' He nodded his head and Rachel strolled out of the café, holding his hand.

'How's he been with the baby?' Harriet patted Scarlett's back gently when she made a small sound, a bit like a kitten. 'You're a pretty girl, aren't you?' Harriet spoke to Scarlett, her voice gentle. Debbie glowed. *Scarlet is a pretty baby.*

'He's been good. Mostly.' Debbie giggled. 'Although he's been asking when she'll be able to play outside with him. At the moment he finds her a bit, um boring, I think.' Harriet laughed with her. Warwick had been gentle when she'd placed Scarlett in his arms. Jamie had been sitting on the couch with him, prepared to grab her if he was a rough.

'Deb, I know it's soon for you, but we're having a get-together at our house on Saturday. The gang. We thought afternoon tea might be easier than dinner. Do you think you and Jamie, and the kids of course, can come?' Harriet's tone was persuasive and Debbie sensed an undercurrent but couldn't put her finger on it.

'Sure. We've got no plans. I could ask mum to have Warwick.' As she spoke, Hamish let out a loud wail from his stroller. Harriet laughed and handed Scarlett to Debbie, then extracted her son. She rocked him in her arms for a moment, but he continued to cry.

Sighing, Harriet moved her chair slightly, so her back was to the room, and opened her shirt. 'Master Hamish does not like to wait for his food. He gets really loud.' She seemed relaxed about it and Debbie shared a smile of acknowledgement with her.

'We'll bring something, of course. Anything in particular?' Debbie poured a glass of water from the jug on the table and pushed it closer to Harriet.

'Thanks. Everyone's bringing a plate. Billie and I will make scones, carrot cake and some mini sausage rolls. For the kids. Bring whatever is easy for you Deb.' Harriet drank the water. Debbie knew it was important to stay hydrated when breast-feeding.

'Okay. How about a tray of savoury treats for the adults?'

'Perfect. Thank you. I'm so pleased you can come.' Harriet's words were warm.

53

FRANCES

Frances frowned. 'Afternoon tea sounds lovely, Douglas. But can you explain to me again who Harriet is?' She knew Montrose Homestead. Murrays had built it and lived there forever.

Douglas patted her hand. 'Drum Murray's wife. She's lovely. She goes to book club, so you know her quite well.'

Frances knew he was being patient with her. She had good days and bad days. Today was not a good day. She'd woken early and called her mother for a chat, but the call wouldn't connect. She'd cried when Douglas had found her, in the hallway, the telephone still in her hand, and told her that her mother had died, years ago. Frances knew he was right. He'd explained it all. But in her heart it felt like she'd spoken to her only yesterday.

The Drum Murray she remembered was away at boarding school in Sydney. And try as she might, she just couldn't conjure up an image of his wife, who Douglas said she knew quite well.

She clearly recalled speaking to Drum's mother about how well he was doing at school.

Like it was just last week.

But it wasn't.

Douglas explained that Drum was a grown man, his parents had passed on, and he was married. With children. Frances shook her head sadly. Time no longer seemed linear to her. It jumped around all over the place and was very confusing.

'What were you asking me Douglas?' Now the thread of the conversation was lost to her. She hated this feeling. *Of not knowing.*

'Afternoon tea at the Murray's on Saturday. The young ones will be there, and some of their children. We can stay for a little while but come home if you're struggling.' Douglas put his arms around her. She loved the familiarity of his embrace. 'I think you'll enjoy it love.'

'Alright.'

54

LITTLE BEN

Melanie sniffled, looking up at him with her wide blue eyes. Ben's heart broke for her. 'I feel like I've failed her. I fed Tiffany for six months.' Her tears began in earnest and Ben drew her into his arms, the baby between them.

'It doesn't matter Mel. It's more important that *you* feel well. And you fed her for the first few weeks. A lot of babies don't get that.' He kissed the top of her head. 'Bronte is thriving on the formula, and she's putting on weight. You're not a failure Mel, you're the best mum in the world.'

They stood like that for ages, until Bronte began to wriggle. Ben scooped the baby into his arms and kissed Melanie. 'I'll make her bottle and a pot of tea for us. Curl up on the couch Mel, I'll bring it in.'

Watching her face relax as she nodded and retreated to the living room, warmed his heart. He'd been so worried about her. Bronte hadn't fed well from the start, but Melanie hadn't told him. He had no experience, but worried when Melanie was getting up to the baby every two hours. He'd felt powerless to help. When he mentioned giving her a bottle, at first he'd meant for her to express her breast milk and use that to bottle feed. But as he watched her struggle to express, he began to wonder if *that* was the problem. Then at four weeks, Melanie had become ill. Like she had the flu. But it wasn't the flu, it mas mastitis and it really knocked both of them around.

The doctor had prescribed antibiotics for Melanie and recommended supplementing feeds with baby formula for Bronte. He'd told them the baby was underweight and this would help.

The formula had made a big change to their lives. Bronte was sleeping longer, which meant Melanie was getting more sleep. And he was able to get up and do a night feed himself. He admitted he loved the night-time feed when the rest of the household was asleep. Just him and Bronte. He chuckled. She had this cute little way of wrapping her hand around his little finger as he held the bottle. *He couldn't love her more.* Or Mel and Tiffany.

Melanie had picked up quickly, the mastitis had cleared up and she'd let her breast milk dry up. What she hadn't mentioned is that she hadn't told her friends she'd stopped breast-feeding, and she was nervous to do so. He snorted at that. He knew her friends would support the decision she'd made. It was Melanie's own guilt that was the problem. He'd tried to tell her there was nothing to be guilty about, but he knew bottle feeding contravened the way she'd planned to mother Bronte. But things didn't always go to plan.

Then, when the last book club was on, she'd talked him into a long weekend away in Sydney. They'd gone to Taronga Zoo and ridden the Manly Ferry and Tiffany had loved it. Mel had put some colour back into her cheeks and Bronte was growing. But she still hadn't told the *girl-posse*. And now, when he'd talked about the get together at Drum and Harriet's she'd become upset.

Ben took Bronte and the bottle into Mel, then poured their tea. He took Bronte from Melanie's arms and held the bottle in place until she'd drained it. Her eyes were closing and he moved her up to his shoulder, rubbing her back gently until she burped.

Melanie giggled. 'See, she does take after her father.' He laughed quietly, happy to see Mel make a joke.

With Bronte tucked up in her cot, he returned to the living room. 'You know it doesn't matter, don't you Mel? And Rose, Debbie and the others won't give it a second thought. Please say you'll come with me on Saturday. Billie has already told Tiffany and they're plotting for Tif to go home with Billie on Friday night. To help cook and set up.' He laughed at that. But the girls, although not quite ten, were both good little cooks and he knew they *would* help Harriet set up.

'You're right. I know you're right. But I'm embarrassed. More now, that I've been feeding her the bottle for weeks and I haven't said.' Melanie hung her head.

'You're making more out of it than it deserves. And your mothering decisions, *our* child-raising decisions, are no-one's business but our own. You don't have to tell them anything. When Bronte needs a feed, we'll make up a bottle and feed her.' Ben hoped his words didn't sound as exasperated as he felt. He used his trump card, saying quietly. 'It's not about what anyone else thinks. It's about what's best for Bronte, and you. End of story.'

Melanie sipped her tea and he saw her eyes were filled with tears again. He'd been trying hard to be supportive but sometimes the right words escaped him. 'Ben.' She reached for his hand. 'I love you. So much.' She breathed in through her nose, then wiped a tear from her cheek. 'I couldn't do it without you. I know I've been, um, all over the place since Bronte arrived. Everything just seems harder than I remembered with Tiffany.' She brought his hand to her mouth and kissed his knuckles lightly. 'I am doing better and I'm being silly about telling the girls. But the longer I let it go, the more it became an issue in my own mind.'

'Do you want me to say something? You know, on the quiet? I could just mention it to Harriet and let her know you feel a bit anxious about it all.' He would if he had to, but he personally thought that was also making it more of a *thing* than it needed to be.

Melanie shook her head. 'No. I'm being silly. I'll tell them on Saturday.' Smiling then, she turned to him. 'What shall we take? Did Harriet give any suggestions?'

'Cheese and crackers? Keep it simple. Something we can graze on while we chat.' Ben had already mentioned this to Harriet and she'd told him that was perfect.

THE AFTERNOON WAS WARM BUT NOT HOT AND THEY relaxed on the back deck of Melrose, chatting and snacking as the children played a rowdy game of hide and seek in the garden. Tiffany, Billie and Tommy included little Charlie and Warwick and their laughing and calling out to each other cut across the adults' conversation, but no one seemed to mind. Rose and Harriet had nursed their babies, but Bronte and Debbie's Scarlett hadn't woken. Ben had seen Melanie sharing a joke with the girls earlier, and she'd accepted a glass of wine from Laura, which no one commented on. He wondered if Melanie had already worked it into the conversation.

Douglas had kept Frances close to him in the beginning, but she'd gone into the kitchen with Harriet and Meggie to help bring food out and seemed to be managing. Douglas had confided in him that Frances was experiencing more short-term memory loss and they were working with her doctors to tweak her medication in the hope that will help.

Finally, all together at last, Ben began the conversation about the forthcoming local government elections.

Then Laura spoke up, her voice firm. 'Women are under-represented on local Council. We all know that. We need younger people to nominate, and more women.' Ben was pleased it was coming from Laura. She was always direct and nobody could misinterpret her meaning, but he almost choked on his beer when she continued. 'The current Council are mostly a bunch of old dicks.' She grinned at his father, then winked at Drum. 'Present company excepted, of course.'

Drum roared with laughter. 'Thank you Laura. I've already filled out the paperwork.' He turned to Angus. 'Have you given it any more thought Angus?'

'I have.' Angus spoke clearly and Ben looked at him. Angus was well known and respected. He'd get the votes. 'I've discussed it with Rose and she supports my decision.' Ben was thrilled, but only for a moment. Angus continued, 'I'm not going to nominate. I'm not keen. At all. And if I'm not invested, I'd make a poor councillor.' Angus looked at Max, and then Meggie. 'If I did a half-assed job, it would affect business. And that impacts Max and Meggie too. I'm sorry Drum, but it's a no from me.' Ben winced. Darn. He'd thought Angus would do it.

'I support Angus and I think it is the right decision for him. For us.' Rose had moved to sit with Laura as she spoke. 'If I have the support of all of you here, I will nominate.' Ben didn't think he'd heard her properly. *Rose? Really?* 'I grew up here, but I've worked in Sydney. I have farming, business and communication skills. I'm passionate about the region and I think I have something to offer.' She'd raised her chin a little bit. 'My grandfather was on Council, when I was young, but my father refused to consider it when he was asked. My only concern is that I don't have the profile Angus has, I'm not out and about as much in the community.' She looked directly at Ben then. 'But if I campaign with you and Drum, I believe I have a chance.'

Harriet clapped her hands. 'Brilliant! Well done Rose. You will be fabulous. I'm your campaign manager and you are more well-known than you think. You're Charlie Gordon's grand-daughter, which in itself will guarantee votes from some of the older ones, but your stand against Rosewood Beef buying up land during the drought here a few years ago also gives you local credibility. And you're a best-selling author.'

Rose blushed at Harriet's words amid resounding murmurs of approval from the group. Ben was pleased. He'd be happy to work with Rose on Council.

Laura looked at Debbie. She was sitting beside Melanie. Jamie had dashed out into the garden when Billie cried out that something was rustling in the undergrowth by the side of the house. It was still warm enough for snakes to be out. Jamie returned, laughing. 'A blue tongue lizard. It took one look at the kids and dived under the house.'

'Debbie?' She looked up, laughter still on her lips. 'I know Scarlett is not even two weeks old, but would you be interested? In standing for Council?' Laura, as usual, had gotten straight to the point.

'Me?' Debbie looked at Jamie, then back to Laura. 'Why me?'

'Debbie. Your business has had more of an impact on this town since it opened than any other in recent history. You've created a destination, and your work with the Chamber of Commerce hasn't gone unnoticed. You'd get the votes Debbie, there's not a person in the region who doesn't know who you are. You're married to a local farmer and your father was the bank manager here for many years. You have Millie managing the café and you're on maternity leave. Council is part time, two meetings per month. Have you never thought about it?' when Laura finished they all looked at Debbie, waiting for her response. She glanced at Jamie, then at Rose.

'I'd better let the cat out of the bag. In fact a conversation like this came up the day before Scarlett was born. With my father.' Debbie chuckled. 'He's been playing his cards close to his chest. But Steve Webb is going to stand for Mayor. He's not happy with the current disharmony at Council meetings. The way they are run, the decisions they are making and the way they're spending ratepayers money. Everyone knows dad. He's going to announce next week.' Debbie stopped then. 'But I think that rules me out standing as a councillor. I don't think it's a good look for us both to run. And I've taken time off from the café to be at home with Jamie and our children. That's my priority.'

Douglas cleared his throat. 'Steve mentioned he was nominating for Mayor a few days ago and I believe he's a good candidate.' He turned to Debbie. 'In four years you will have Warwick at school and little Scarlett in day care. Your time will come.' He looked at Harriet then. 'I also think Harriet should consider it next time, and you too Laura.' He smiled warmly at them all. 'The future of the region is in good hands.'

They all started speaking at once then, but Ben frowned. Steve as Mayor. Tick. Then him, Drum and Rose. Good. But there were eight council positions and it would be good to have another who was progressive. He'd give it some thought. Melanie walked across to him, Bronte in her arms. She leant down, her words quiet. 'I'm going in to make a bottle for Bronte. Will you hold her for a minute?' He nodded, and watched as she picked up the bag of baby stuff and walked inside. Harriet followed her in. He saw that Frances was holding baby Hamish. She hadn't said much all day, but she'd been happy and relaxed.

55

MEGGIE

Strolling into the kitchen after using the bathroom, Meggie leaned against the counter. Melanie was making up a bottle of formula, chatting to Harriet as she did. Harriet turned to her. 'How are you feeling Meggie? Much morning sickness?'

'A bit. Not always in the morning. But I really don't mind.' She patted her tummy. Max said it was still flat, but she thought she detected a little bulge.

Rose appeared and hugged Meggie spontaneously. 'So happy for you Meggs. I've got a good feeling.'

Meggie laughed. 'I do too Rose. I'm taking the supplements.' She chuckled. 'Max won't let me do anything at home. He and Tommy do all the lifting and carrying. They even hang the washing out for me.'

'I've just caught the end of this conversation, but don't stop them from doing that Meggie. Ever.' Debbie laughed as she walked to the sink and washed a cloth under the tap. 'Scarlett threw up. Ugh, I hate the smell of baby vomit.' She mopped at her shoulder.

Melanie turned then, a bottle in her hand. Meggie thought she looked stressed. And tired. 'Melanie. Are you okay?'

'Yes. Yes I am. Now.' She paused, the bottle still in her hand.

Rose moved closer to her. 'What do you mean Mel? *Now?* Have you been unwell?'

'Yes. Sort of.' She held the bottle up and Meggie could see she was close to tears. 'I had to wean Scarlett. Weeks ago. I had mastitis.' She sobbed then and Rose put an arm around her shoulders. 'It's okay Mel. Were you very sick? I had it once with Charlie. So painful.'

Melanie shook her head. 'It's not that. Really. Before the mastitis, Bronte wasn't putting on weight. She was waking every couple of hours to feed and wouldn't stop crying. It turns out, she wasn't getting enough.' She waved a hand across her chest. 'Milk. She wasn't getting enough milk.' She seemed to gather herself then. 'But once we started with the formula. Well. She started sleeping better, and she's put on the right amount of weight. And. And I'm not so tired.'

'Oh. Well that's good then.' Rose shook her head. 'I know there's an expectation to breast feed as long as you can. And I've been lucky. But Melanie, I wouldn't hesitate to change to formula if it was the best thing for baby and me. Don't ever feel guilty about that.'

'Same.' Harriet patted Melanie on the back. 'I've committed to breast feed Hamish for three months. And I will go a bit longer if it feels right. But I'll probably wean at six months at the latest.' She shrugged her shoulders. 'it's different for every mother, Melanie.'

'Have you been worrying about this Mel? Surely seeing Bronte put on weight and sleep longer at night has put you at ease?' Debbie glanced outside. 'Harriet I think the kids are back on the veranda, looking for food. Should we heat up the last of the sausage rolls?

Meggie glanced at Melanie. Her face had brightened and she looked relieved. *Note to self. We have a girl-posse and they always have our back.*

MILLIE

Saturday. Millie was driving out to Barrington Ridge Estate to have lunch with Finn. She was excited to see the operation and looking forward to seeing Finn. But she was nervous about meeting his son Lucas. She'd offered to bring a picnic to share, but Finn said he had lunch sorted. She'd also asked if his boss wouldn't mind her being there, but he told her they weren't open this weekend, so it was no problem.

Not sure what to wear, she'd finally settled on navy capri pants she hadn't worn in years, and she'd splashed out on a linen shirt in palest peach. It was the first piece of clothing she'd bought since her marriage ended. It was a quality piece that she'd found on a discount rack. She'd thought it would be too small, but the shop assistant insisted it would fit. She was right. Millie wore it out over the pants, the three-quarter sleeves ending in a loose cuff that she adored.

Millie had been to the local hairdresser too. The one Meggie had recommended who worked from her home. She had a trim and blow dry, and the hairdresser had talked her out of putting a colour through, saying her hair had a lot of natural warmth.

Setting off in her little old car, Millie checked her phone for about the hundredth time. Only fifteen minutes out of town and an easy drive. She patted the basket on the seat beside her. She'd made individual sticky date puddings the night before. They just needed to be warmed, and she would pour the butterscotch sauce over them, for dessert.

The road wound around rolling hills covered in lush grass and grazing cattle, horses and sheep. She hadn't been out this side of town and she marvelled at how pretty it was, with farm entrances graced by trees covered in autumn finery.

The entrance to the winery was well marked, but she had slowed already when vineyards came into view, the vines marching over the hillside in neat green rows. Suddenly nervous, she came to a complete stop at the entrance. The driveway was lined with agapanthus, a mixture of purple and white flowers nodding gently in the breeze. Taking a nervous deep breath, Millie drove slowly towards the timber lined building she guessed to be the cellar door.

She'd barely stopped the car when Finn appeared, opening the car door for her. She stepped out and he kissed her cheek, making her flush with pleasure.

'Welcome to Barrington Ridge Estate, Millie. May I show you around?' He took her hand and began to lead her to the entrance but she stopped, remembering the desserts on her front seat.

'Yes, thank you, but, um, I brought something. Sweet. For later. Needs to be in the fridge.' She waved her arm back at the car.

'You didn't have to.' He winked. 'But I never say no to something sweet. For later.'

His words made her blush again, although she could see he was teasing her. She lifted the basket out and handed it to Finn. He slid open the large barn-style door and led her into the cool interior of the tasting area. The ceilings were high with huge rough-cut beams and cleverly hidden lighting spanning the room. The floor was polished cement with a sort of pebbly finish and there was a long tasting bar - the counter was polished timber slabs, with timber and steel bar stools set along one side.

He walked behind the bar and disappeared through a door with the basket, returning moments later with a younger version of himself. Slightly taller than Finn but with the same broad shoulders, he had dark hair and an easy smile.

'This is Lucas. Lucas, this is Millie.' A few years older than her own son, without forethought, she stepped over and gave him a quick hug, at the same time saying 'lovely to meet you.' He seemed momentarily surprised but hugged her back before retreating behind the bar.

'Lucas is heading into town to pick up supplies that have been delivered to the transport depot, so we're on our own for lunch.' Finn's words were delivered lightly, but Millie felt a small thrill of anticipation run through her. She wondered if he'd arranged for them to be alone.

'Oh. I brought dessert. Maybe you can join us for that when you get back?' Millie smiled warmly at Finn's son, who now seemed eager to leave.

Finn took her hand and led her to a larger shed behind the cellar door. It was a machinery she and laughed out loud when he opened the door to a beaten-up old jeep with no roof.

'It's a Mini Moke, older than me. My first car. It's no longer registered for the road but I use it around the farm and taught my kids to drive in it. It's safe, if you're game?' Finn looked at her, eyes twinkling.

'Oh I'm game!' Millie slid in. 'Too cute. And funny!' They drove all the way around the farm, mostly covered in vineyards, but there were a couple of paddocks with horses of various breeds and sizes.

'The horses? Do you ride Finn?' Millie looked at him quizzically. He'd told her previously that he grew up in the southern suburbs of Sydney.

'They're all rescue horses.' He shrugged. 'The paddocks weren't in use and Wendy from the tourism office told me a local animal welfare group needed somewhere to keep them. It saves slashing the paddocks and we're not ready to cultivate them for vines just yet.'

His nonchalance surprised Millie. Then it hit her.

Cheeks flaming, she looked at him. 'You don't just work here, do you Finn? You own Barrington Ridge Estate.' She was embarrassed. And annoyed. Her eyes narrowed. 'Why didn't you tell me? Correct my assumption?'

He looked sheepish. 'At first, at the wedding at Barrington Homestead, I was a bit miffed that you assumed I was just the 'distribution guy' and you wouldn't take the bottle of wine I offered.' Finn reached across and held her hand. They were at the top of the hill when he stopped the vehicle. 'Then I was trying to find the right time to tell you. I really didn't want you to be embarrassed, and I also didn't want to ruin the rapport we'd developed. So I said nothing. I'm sorry. And I knew it would become obvious when you came out here today.'

'Actually, I should be apologising.' She touched her cheeks. They were still warm. 'I should never have assumed. I'm sorry.'

'Don't be. To be honest, I've been having so much fun I didn't want to burst the bubble. But I'm glad you know now. I'm not one for keeping secrets.' Finn pointed to the entrance to the property in the distance. 'We have just over one hundred acres. Fifteen in vines, not all mature, and twenty in the paddocks where the horses are. The rest is over the other side of the hill there. A little bit of old forest and a lot of scrub. I'm not planning to cultivate that area, it's a fabulous habitat for native flora and fauna.'

'It's really pretty, and I love the cellar door design. She looked down at the buildings. She could see the visitor car park where her car sat, the cellar door building and a larger production shed behind it. Then the machinery shed beyond that. There was another building, similar to the cellar door, set away from the other buildings. Millie pointed to it. 'Is that your house?'

Finn laughed. 'It is. We built it in the same barn-style as the cellar door. It's basically three apartments. I have a three-bedroom loft apartment and there are a couple of two-bedroom apartments on the ground floor. Lucas uses one and the other is for staff, when we're picking. It's modern inside, a bit like a Sydney warehouse conversion.'

Millie nodded, taking it all in. Finn was an entrepreneur, like her ex-husband Rudy. Except Rudy had been flashy, always trying to impress. Finn was the opposite. She could see he liked to fly under the radar.

'And in case you're wondering, despite my tattoos and wrong-side-of-the-tracks upbringing, I haven't developed this with, er, ill-gotten gains.' He laughed and Millie blanched. The thought had crossed her mind, for the briefest of moments. He continued. 'I've been in the industry for a long time. I worked with one of the biggest producers in South Australia for more than twenty years. I invested well, mostly in property. The divorce knocked me around a bit, but the property portfolio did well. I cashed in everything for the settlement and built this with my share. It's been a bit of a slog but this year we've actually seen some returns and I think the future looks good.'

'It's beautiful. What an achievement.' Millie was impressed. With the place and his attitude.

'I don't live high, Millie.' His grin was infectious. 'But I live well. Good food, wine, the company of family and friends. And a business I'm passionate about.'

Millie thought he was going to say something else, but he released the brake and they drove back down to the outbuildings.

'Lunch? I'm keeping it simple. Eye fillet steak on the barbie and a fresh salad. And wine, of course.' They parked the car and walked back to the cellar door.

'We'll use the barbecue over here.' He motioned to a high bar chair. 'Perch up here and I'll get everything ready.'

'Can I help? Make the salad?' Millie sipped the glass of water he'd given her, saying they'd have wine when the food was ready.

'No. it's all done. We'll eat in here.' He stood on the other side of the bar now, and she could smell the steak cooking. 'I thought about doing this in my apartment.'

Millie cocked her head on one side. 'Why didn't you?'

'I like you. A lot. And if I cooked for you in my apartment, it would be too easy to, um, romance you.' The way he said 'romance' made her squeeze her legs together involuntarily. He was right, there was chemistry between them. But she wasn't ready. And he knew that. It just made her like him more.

'Good call.' She grinned then, relaxing. He wasn't going to put any pressure on her. The ball was in her court.

———

THE AFTERNOON WAS WANING WHEN LUCAS RETURNED. Millie asked Finn to warm the sticky date puddings and sauce and they enjoyed then sitting at a picnic table outside the main building. When they finished, Lucas seemed in no hurry to leave, speaking generally about the town, the forthcoming footy-tipping competition at the pub and the next two wedding events they had booked for Barrington Elopements.

Millie looked at her watch and stood. 'It's getting late, I need to head off.' Finn didn't try to talk her into staying a bit longer, and she was surprised at how disappointed she felt. He walked her to her car, the basket in his hands. She opened he car door and he reached past her to place the basket on the passenger seat. She suddenly felt awkward and began to thank him again for a lovely afternoon.

Finn moved closer and drew her to him in a hug. She liked the feel of his arms around her. *Big, strong arms.* He murmured in her ear, his voice low and gravelly. 'We will do this again Millie.' She melted against him at the sound of his voice, 'very soon.'

Millie straightened and looked into his eyes. Then leaned forward and kissed him, gently, on the mouth. 'I look forward to that.' She murmured.

He sucked in a breath, crushed her to him and kissed her back, hard and fast. The look in his eyes almost undid her. But Lucas called out to him then, and he released her. He shaded his eyes with his hand and waved to Lucas. Something about locking the machinery shed up for the night.

Once in the car, Millie wound her window down. 'Dinner at my place next time. I'll cook for you. Next weekend?' She hoped she was reading his signals correctly. She really wanted to see more of him.

'Yes. And no.' He had one arm on the roof of the car, leaning down with his face at the open window.

Millie frowned. 'Yes and no?'

'Yes to dinner at your place. No to next weekend.' He grinned then and she relaxed. 'Millie, I can't wait that long. How about Tuesday night?' She nodded mutely. She couldn't wait either. Gosh. *Does this mean she's dating?* Giggling to herself, she drove away.

57

Humming to herself, she carefully placed the little one in the capsule, ensuring the seatbelt was firmly fastened. It was book club night and she'd been looking forward to it for days.

With her favourite country rock station turned down low, she drove slowly along the driveway, entering the road carefully. It was just on dusk, with the sun setting in the west, spreading red-gold tentacles across the mountain tops. *Nothing beats the magnificent Barrington Tops at sunset on a warm autumn evening.*

She sped up a little, glancing several times in the mirror, strategically placed to see her angelic baby, arms waving while making sweet little cooing noises. Bubbling over with happiness, she sang along to the radio, laughing at herself when she got ahead of the artist. *Keep up Keith.*

Coming into the last corner, before the bridge, she slowed. Another quick glance in the mirror to check the baby and she accidentally veered onto the edge of road, one wheel spinning in loose sand and gravel. She jerked the steering wheel, over-correcting, and that's when she saw them.

Cows. Three of them. Two by the side of the road, and one ambling across the middle.

Crying out, her heart thumping out of her chest, she braked hard while trying to turn to check on the baby. They hit the one on the road, jarring her hands on the wheel and throwing her forward against the seat belt, and then back, as the airbag activated. The windscreen shattered and the car spun to one side, the engine revving furiously.

In slow motion the car tipped over, seeming to hover on two wheels for a moment, then rolled onto the roof, and she gasped in pain. It rolled twice more down the embankment.

She heard the baby scream. Once. Then nothing.

58

MILLIE

April – Barrington Book Club – Meeting 8
Present: All
Apologies: None
Book: *Buried in Between* by Leanne Lovegrove

MILLIE HAD JUST SET A CHEESE BOARD, PLATES AND napkins on the table when Meggie walked in.

'Hi Millie. What can I do to help?' Meggie grinned and walked to the table, slung her bag over the back of a chair and slid her copy of the book onto the table. 'I loved this one. The element of mystery really pulled me in.'

'All good here. Maybe grab a few wine glasses.' Millie chuckled. 'You know. Laura.'

Meggie laughed out loud. 'Laura. Love her to bits.'

Millie strolled back to the counter, taking two of the glasses Meggie handed to her. 'But this book really got me in the feels. Custody issues from the father's point of view.' She shook her head sadly. 'I don't think we, as a society, give that enough air-time.'

'You're right. Did you know that Max lost his first wife in a car accident? He and Tommy and his older daughter Indiana really struggled with that for a long time. And not in the ways you would think.' Meggie followed Millie to the table with the rest of the glasses. 'There's always more to a story, don't you think?'

Millie nodded. 'Always. Here come the others.' She giggled then. 'Will we tell them we've already discussed the book and they can just start on the food and wine?'

Meggie snort-laughed, then tapped Millie on the shoulder. 'Stop it! Too funny!'

Exactly at six Nicole strolled in with Laura and Frances behind her. Laura held a bottle of wine aloft, grinning as she walked through the door. Millie and Meggie exchanged a look, trying not to laugh out loud.

Meggie shook her head, trying to look sad. 'Not for me tonight, Laura. I'm over ten weeks now.' She stood side-on and pushed her belly out. 'I'm getting a bump.'

'Oh yeah,' Nicole nudged her with her shoulder. 'you're huge Meggie.' They laughed at her, and Millie thought, not for the first time, what a lovely fun group of women they were.

Melanie arrived with Bronte in her arms and the baby bag over her shoulder.

'Let me help you Melanie.' Millie stepped forward and lifted the bag from Melanie's shoulder. As she did, a siren wailed. She looked at the others. 'Is that police, fire or ambulance? I can never tell.'

Laura walked to the door and opened it. An ambulance raced

past. Then a fire engine. More sirens could be heard in the distance.

Laura frowned. 'They're heading out past the general store.' She sniffed the air. 'I can't smell smoke. Not a fire then.' She looked at the others. 'It's ten past. Rose, Debbie and Harriet should be here by now. They said they were coming.'

Millie froze. Meggie sat down on the nearest chair. 'You don't think?' She whispered.

Nicole knelt beside her. 'It may be an accident and they can't get through, or they've been diverted. And we can't call them if they're driving. Let's wait a few more minutes.'

They huddled together, not speaking much. Millie offered to make coffee but they all shook their heads. Even Laura set the wine aside, unopened. Bronte began to cry and Melanie asked Millie if she could warm a bottle for her.

Another ten minutes went by and the others hadn't arrived. Millie shivered. This did not bode well.

Meggie was pale. She pulled her phone from her pocket. 'I'm calling Max, he might know something.' He didn't answer, and she began to cry. 'Why won't he pick up? Where's Max?' Nicole and Melanie comforted her, while Laura sat with Frances who was agitated and confused. Melanie sent a text to Ben.

The door swung open then, and Max appeared, with Tommy behind him. He strode to Meggie and gathered her in his arms. Tommy looked shaken so Millie put an arm around him, holding him by her side.

Max looked at the women, watching him in anticipation. He cleared his throat. 'There's been an accident.' He stopped, wiped his arm roughly across his face. 'It seems that. It's.' He looked at the ceiling, then held out his arm for Tommy, who walked across and nestled in beside him, Meggie still on his other side. 'It seems that her car hit a cow, just before the bridge.' He drew in his breath deeply. 'It rolled. Several times. Down the embankment.' He shook his head sadly, looking down, then lifted his face. He was crying. 'It's Debbie's car.'

There was silence for a moment. Melanie cried out, 'no!'

Laura whispered, 'but she's alright? She'll be alright?'

Millie drew in a breath. *Debbie. No. It can't be.*

Rose appeared with Harper in her arms. Angus was behind her, carrying Charlie. Max pulled a chair out for Rose and she sat. Millie had never seen her so pale.

Millie went behind the counter and began to make coffee. *Flat white. Most people will drink flat white. Maybe some chai lattes too.* She needed to be busy. She couldn't process what she'd heard. Billie burst through the door and ran straight to Tommy, who hugged her. She was crying. Harriet and Drum were behind her. Drum had Hamish in his arms.

Rose blew her nose, then looked at Angus. He cleared his throat and the room was silent. 'Rose wasn't far behind Debbie. Saw the whole thing. Called triple zero. Harriet arrived then too, seeing Rose's car with the hazard lights on. Rose sent me a text.' He placed his hand on his wife's shoulder. 'I got there at the same time as the police. And ambulance.' His next words seemed to catch in his throat. 'And Jamie.' Millie heard someone gasp. Melanie, she thought. Angus hoisted Charlie on to his other hip. 'It took me a few minutes to get there. I had to get Charlie in the car, couldn't leave him in the house. Alone.'

Millie knew she was crying. All of them were.

Meggie's voice quivered. 'Will she be alright? Debbie?' Reaching for Tommy, she held him close. 'And Scarlett?' The pain etched on Angus's face said it all. He shook his head. He couldn't say the words, but they all knew.

Rose tried to stand, but Millie could see her legs were visibly shaking. Angus knelt by her chair. Harriet sat beside Rose then, and Nicole took Hamish from her arms. They pulled their chairs into a rough circle, no one saying much.

Ben and Tiffany arrived, then Big Ben and Douglas, who spoke quietly to a few people, before putting his arm around Frances. 'It's best I get Frances home.' He looked around the room. 'I'll be in touch with you. All of you. In the morning.'

Millie set sandwiches, cakes and some savoury snacks on a side table and was relieved when the kids ate something, although most of the adults didn't. Wee Charlie didn't understand what was happening, and the bigger children fed him, then moved to another table and played some games quietly.

Laura opened the wine, offering small glasses to anyone who wanted it.

'We probably should all get home. There's nothing we can do right now.' Angus held his hand out to Rose.

'Jamie? Who's with Jamie?' Rose was crying again.

'His parents. And Debbie's. They've all gone back to the farm.' Angus looked at Drum, who nodded.

'And Debbie? And Scarlett? Where are they now?' Rose's voice had risen, she sounded almost hysterical. Meggie stepped across and put her arms around Rose.

Big Ben cleared his throat. 'They've taken them. To the hospital.' *To the morgue* Millie thought.

And then it was over. They began leaving, one by one. Laura and Nicole helped Millie clear up, even though she said she was fine.

As she was leaving, Laura put a steadying hand on Millie's shoulder. 'This place will be busy tomorrow. The news will be out by then. Will you be alright?' Big Ben was hovering in the doorway.

Millie nodded. 'Busy is good. Less time. To think.' She put her hand to her mouth then and squeezed her eyes closed for a moment. Opening them, she whispered, 'I need to call Cathy. The other staff. It's best it comes from me.'

Laura nodded. 'Yes. Go home Millie. Make some calls. Will you be alright? You can come home with me if you'd rather?'

Laura's offer warmed Millie's heart, but she shook her head.

Walking across the road by herself a short while later, Millie dug out her door key, and paused. *This town. The way they all came together tonight in their grief. The way they rallied.* An idea was forming in her mind, and she rushed inside. But first she needed to make those calls.

59

ROSE

Dawn's pale fingers crept through the shutters and Rose rolled towards Angus. He was on his back, arms behind his head. She wasn't sure if he'd slept at all. She hadn't thought she would, but after feeding Harper around two, she'd drifted off.

Angus held his arm out and Rose slid closer and snuggled against his side, his large hand on her back was comforting.

'Debbie. And Scarlett.' Rose gazed at him, the deep sadness in his eyes mirroring her own. She had replayed the scene in her mind dozens of times overnight. *She'd seen the cattle, lit up by Debbie's headlights, and slowed. By the time she pulled up, Debbie's car was on its roof down the embankment, the engine still running. Rose had left her car in the middle of the road, hazard lights on and raced down the embankment as she called triple zero. Rose had lay down on the damp earth, scrabbling at Debbie's door. It wouldn't open, but she could see Debbie clearly through the window. Her eyes were open. And lifeless. She'd crawled around to the other side. For Scarlett. Harriet was beside her then, pulling her back, crying and shaking her head. By the time Harriet helped her back up to her own car, Angus had arrived, then Drum. Jamie and his Dad were there too, with the police and ambulance. They'd huddled together in Drum's car, Harper in her lap, until the police told them they could leave.*

Angus shook his head. 'And Jamie. And Woz.' He turned towards Rose, gathering her to him and held her tightly. His next words were anguished. 'It could have been you, Rose. If you'd left a minute earlier, it could have been you. And Harper.'

Holding him tightly, she nodded. 'Or Harriet. We were all on that road, heading to book club, only a minute apart.' She shook her head then. 'Debbie's a good driver, she knows the road like the back of her hand. And that corner before the bridge. There's often cows there, we all slow down.' Rose swiped tears from her face. She felt unaccountably angry. 'Was she going too fast? Was she distracted by Scarlett? Did the cows just appear and she had no time to slow down?'

Breathing in sharply through his nose, Angus rocked her in his arms for a moment. 'There are no answers Rose. We may never know. Don't try to make sense of it. Of how it happened.' He moved away slightly, looking into her eyes. 'What we need to do now is support Jamie and Woz and their family.'

'Yes. I know. We will.' She buried her face in his neck and wept while he stroked her hair. Noise in the hall changed her focus. 'Charlie is up,' Rose whispered.

'I'll see to Charlie. Have a shower Rose and get dressed. We'll close the clinic today and Max will take emergency call outs, anything else can wait. I think we should go over to Jamie's. We can take the children, Charlie will play with Woz and we can talk to Jamie, see what he needs. Work out what we can do for him. Today. This week. Whenever and whatever.' He paused. 'And we'll go into the police station after that. They want you and Harriet to make statements.'

Angus's words kicked Rose into action and her mind raced as she stripped off and stepped into the shower. *Stop wallowing. You've lost your best friend, but Jamie has lost his wife and baby daughter. Be there for him.*

60

MELANIE

'The clinic is closed today. Do you think Tiffany should have the day off school?' Melanie passed the bottle to Ben, who popped it into Bronte's mouth. She began sucking in earnest and Ben's quick smile was replaced by a look of sadness.

'Should we go over to Jamie's? This morning? What do you want to do Mel?' Ben's gaze swung to the doorway. Tiffany stood there in her pyjamas. Her hair was tousled and she looked tired, although she'd slept half an hour longer than usual.

'I don't want to go to school today mum.' Tiffany walked across to Melanie, who opened her arms, then held her close.

'You can stay with us today.' Melanie looked at Ben over Tiffany's head and he nodded.

'I want to see Nanna and Poppy Tait. And Uncle Jamie. And Woz. Can we go there after breakfast?' Tiffany sniffled, then looked up at Melanie. 'Is it really true? Auntie Debbie and baby Scarlett?' She shook her head, not able to find the words.

Kissing the top of her head, Melanie held her own emotion in check. 'It is Tiff. They will all be sad and upset and we must try to help them, alright? Yes, we'll go out to the farm after breakfast and perhaps you can play with little Warwick. That will be a big help.' She was relieved when Tiffany nodded eagerly. 'Go and get dressed Tiff, we'll just have toast this morning, then we'll go out to the farm.'

Bronte had finished the bottle, so Melanie took her from Ben just as his phone vibrated. He looked at it briefly, then at Melanie. 'Laura and dad are at the office now, they've put a closed sign on the door and have diverted the office phone. Dad will field calls. They're going to drop by Debbie's parents, see if they can offer support there.'

'Okay. I'll get Bronte ready and check on Tiff. Can you start breakfast?' Melanie walked into his arms, the simple act comforting her.

61

———

HARRIET

'Ben has closed the office. Angus has too. Meggie wants to know if Max and Tommy can come out here?' Harriet lay her phone down for a moment, to pour the orange juice. Billie hovered beside her. 'They're not sending Tommy to school today.'

'No problem, I already thought we'd keep Billie home too.' Drum turned to Billie. 'Run and get dressed, you can take Tommy riding today, if you like.' Billie's face brightened and she shot from the room.

Drum turned back to Harriet, saying quietly. 'There's more to this, isn't there?'

Harriet nodded. 'You remember Tommy's mum was killed in a car accident? He barely spoke for months. Max wants to keep him close, but also offer some distraction. Meggie suggested they come here.'

'Of course! I had forgotten that. Yes, they can all come here, absolutely.' Drum stirred the porridge as he spoke.

'Um, well. You will have to entertain them on your own.'

Harriet gave him a sheepish grin. 'I'm going in to the café to help Millie. I think they'll be inundated. And there's a chance some of her team may not come in. Cathy has worked with Debbie since the beginning.' She lifted her chin. 'Millie messaged me earlier. She thought about closing today, out of respect, but then decided it would be the place locals would come to. For news. Share their grief. And I know the business Drum. I can help. In fact, Meggie said she'd meet me there.'

Harriet watched Drum's face as he processed this. After a few moments he asked just one question. 'And Hamish? Will you take him with you?'

'No.' her voice was firm. 'I've expressed. There are three bottles made up. He's yours today.' Harriet hoped this wasn't too much for Drum, or too soon. He had fed Hamish a number of times with the bottle, but she'd always been around.

Drum laughed then. 'You don't think I can do it, do you?' He quirked an eyebrow.

Chuckling, Harriet glanced at Billie as she rushed back into the room on his last words. 'Of course you can look after Hamish without me.' She saw the surprise on Billie's face, followed by pleasure when she added, 'you have Billie here, she's all over it.'

'I am Dad, I know exactly what to do.' Her curls bounced on her shoulders as she turned away, calling over her shoulder, 'I can hear him now. He's awake. I'll get him!'

62

MEGGIE

THERE WASN'T AN EMPTY SEAT IN THE CAFÉ WHEN Meggie arrived. She waved to Harriet, standing at the coffee machine and young Lucy delivering a tray of drinks to a table near the back. Making her way inside, she slid behind the counter and peeked into the kitchen. Cathy was there, and Nicole.

Millie popped out from a storeroom, a box of takeaway coffee cups in her arms. She set it down near Harriet then turned and gave Meggie a quick hug.

Meggie reached for an apron she spied under the counter and tied it on. 'What can I do Millie? How can I help?'

'I don't want *you* doing any lifting or carrying Meggie.' Millie raised her eyes towards the ceiling and grimaced. 'Cathy arrived at five to do the baking, and Nicole and Lucy shortly after. We usually open at seven but a crowd was outside by six, I saw them from my window. So I came over and opened. We've been flat out ever since. Having Harriet on the coffee machine is a great help, but what is slowing us down is the locals turning up, asking questions, wanting to help. Would it be too much for you Meggie, to deal with that?'

'Not at all. I'll stand near the front, talk to anyone I know is local as they arrive.' She turned to Millie, 'there are flowers being laid outside, beside the doors, and cards.' She drew in a breath. 'And soft toys.' She shook her head then, willing herself to remain dry-eyed.

'I know. I honestly don't know what to do about that. I'll bring them inside when we close. Keep the cards for Jamie and the family.' Millie shook her head sadly. 'I wondered though, and I'd like your opinion. A lot of people are here just to pay their respects. They're buying coffee, but not many are eating. I thought, we could set up a table over by the side wall there, and maybe keep it stocked with sandwiches, slices and finger food. Those that want to.' Millie glanced at Harriet, then back to Meggie. 'Those that want to just come in and share their grief. We can feed them, at least. I don't want anyone rushed, you know to provide an empty table. I think it's important anyone who knew Debbie feels welcome here and can stay as long as they.' She hesitated again. 'As long as they *need* to.'

Meggie clapped her hands. 'Brilliant! Let's do that. And why don't we make some large pots of tea and put out milk and sugar on that table too? Those that want to can help themselves. It will take pressure off the coffee machine.'

'I wondered if I should have closed to the public today. But after last night, the way everyone came here. I thought it better to open.' Millie seemed to be seeking approval, but Meggie simply touched her arm gently.

CHAPTER 62

'Your instincts are good Millie, no need to second guess yourself today.' Meggie pointed across the room. 'Let's move those two tables, where the people are just leaving, and we'll set them against the side.'

Millie nodded. 'I'll ask Nicole to help me.' She looked at Meggie fiercely for a moment. 'Don't you lift anything.'

63

FRANCES

The church had never been so full. People were standing in the side aisles and along the back wall. Douglas guided her to a row near the front, and Ben Evans made room for them.

The coffin at the front was covered in flower bouquets and wreaths. Frances peered again. And a number of little stuffed animals, mostly pink. She furrowed her brow. *Who died? A child?* She couldn't recall the details but knew Douglas had told her in the car. She clutched her pearl necklace for a moment, trying to remember.

The service was not long. Frances stood with the rest of the congregation when the minister recited The Lord is My Shepherd. She knew it by heart and murmured the words, along with everyone else.

It wasn't until Rose Gordon went to the pulpit for the eulogy that Frances thought she knew. It was Rose's mother, Helen. Breast cancer. Terrible disease. But when Rose began to speak, Frances remembered. *Debbie. Debbie Webb. No Tait. And her little baby girl. Car accident.* Frances gasped. *No! Not Debbie. Too young. Too soon. They must be together in the coffin.* Douglas reached for her hand then and gave it a squeeze. Frances pulled a crisp white handkerchief from her sleeve and dabbed at her eyes, her heart heavy, the grief or Debbie's loss rolling over her.

The sermon ended and the front two rows stood. And that's when she saw Jamie. *Jamie Tait. Debbie's handsome young husband.* He had their son Warwick in his arms, and his parents on either side of him. She saw his grief-ravaged face as he walked past them, out of the church and she thought her heart would break for him. Debbie's parents followed, Frances had known them all her adult life. Steve had his arm around Rachael, who was crying noisily, a tissue held to her eyes. She seemed to stagger for a moment and Ben Evans stepped out, to her other side, and helped Steve walk her outside. Frances shook her head and leaned her shoulder against Douglas. He helped her stand then, and they followed the procession down the aisle and outside.

She blinked in the bright autumn sunshine.

64

MILLIE

It was Tuesday night. Finn was coming to dinner, a week later than planned. He and Lucas had attended the funeral yesterday and stood with Millie in the back. Meggie had waved from closer to the front, beckoning them to join her, but she could see Cathy standing with her husband and daughter and waved back, indicating she'd stay where she was.

Millie had cooked a lamb backstrap with Moroccan flavours and carrot couscous. She wanted to serve something she didn't think he'd make himself. And it was best served warm, rather than hot. For dessert she had mini chocolate berry trifles in small glass jars. She'd made them the night before and they looked delicious. About a trillion calories in each one, but the *new Millie* wasn't focussed on weight. She was focussed on *life*. Even more so after recent events. *Life is short.*

Wearing navy blue capri pants that she'd worn before, white canvas runners and a white linen shirt. Millie felt perfectly dressed for dinner-at-home. The only jewellery she wore was her engagement ring, on her other hand, because it was an antique and she loved it, and small pearls at her ears. She'd put on lacy underwear at first, but it was a set she'd bought when her marriage was happy and she took it off, throwing it in the wash basket. *I'll never wear that set again.* She changed to full brief knickers in palest pink, they'd not show under her pants and a white bra with a little bit of lace on it. More mumsy-than-sexy. But she wasn't planning to let Finn see her underwear. *Not tonight, anyway.*

Finn rang the bell outside the downstairs door and Millie ran lightly down to let him in. She had been excited all day and opened the door with a broad smile. He stepped inside and she closed the door and locked it, then turned to lead him upstairs.

'Wait.' From behind his back Finn produced a bouquet of flowers, mostly Australian natives, tied up with a big hessian bow, and a bottle of red wine. The one she'd enjoyed the very first time they'd met. She took them, then reached up to kiss him on the cheek. 'These are gorgeous Finn, thank you.' She quickly ran up the stairs, the flowers and wine in her hand, calling back to him, 'come on up.'

When she got to the top she looked behind her, to find him standing stock still on the very first step.

'Problem?' she called down, eyebrows raised.

'No problem, just recovering from watching you, er, running up the stairs.' His grin was cheeky as he took the steps two at a time, reaching her in moments. 'The view was good. Really good. From down there.'

'Stop it!' Millie put her hand to her mouth and giggled. She knew her bum wasn't tiny, but she had to admit, all the walking and running up and down the stairs may have made it more *shapely* than it used to be.

Millie led him inside. She'd already set the table and the lamb was in the oven, still warm. 'Shall we open the wine? Or can I offer you a beer?' She'd bought a six pack of the light beer he'd had at the pub that time.

'Dinner smells delicious and a beer before dinner would be lovely. Thank you.' He walked to the window and looked out. 'Quite a view. You can see the Bucketts Mountains, and everything that's happening down in the main street.'

'I'm really enjoying it here.' Millie fetched the beer, and a cider for herself, and stood beside him at the window. 'Because the apartment is old, the rooms are large and the walls are thick, so it's surprisingly quiet.'

She turned then and led him to the sofa. They settled side by side and he placed his drink on the side table, moving a coaster under it. *So he's house-trained.* She put her drink down too, and turned sideways, one leg tucked under her.

'How is it going for you at the café? It's been a week. Any news?' Finn was watching her closely.

Millie smiled and shook her head. 'The first two days we had so many helpers, and the place was full, as people,' she frowned, 'Not *people*. Locals, friends, came in to pay their respects, and grieve together I think. By the end of the week we were back to normal. Normal staff, normal customer numbers. Business as usual. But I haven't seen or heard from Jamie, or the family. Rose and Angus Hamilton picked up all the flowers, gifts and cards. Some of them were on the coffin yesterday. Douglas Barlow popped in on Friday and said he'd make enquiries after the funeral.'

Finn reached across and took her hand in his. 'How are you feeling Millie? Such a terrible loss. But also the uncertainty must be difficult for you? And the staff? Cathy, is it? How is she doing?'

The warmth of his words, his kindness, almost made her cry. She sucked in a breath. 'Cathy told me today that she wants to retire. She doesn't want to work there now Debbie has gone. I don't think it's personal, I think it's something she's been thinking about. I hope that's what it is. But she'll wait until we see what Jamie wants to do with the business.'

Taking a sip of his beer, Finn looked thoughtful. 'He's a farmer, isn't he?' She nodded. 'It's unlikely he'll want to keep it long term, even with a manager, I expect.'

'You're right. Douglas Barlow owns the building, and most of the fit out. But the business is Debbie's.' The fear Millie had been keeping at bay surfaced. 'I'm not sure if he'll try to sell it, or even just close it down.' She shook her head and tears pricked at her eyes. 'If you're ready, I'll serve our dinner.' She stood quickly, before he had answered, and rushed to the kitchen. Leaning against the sink for a moment, she counted to ten in an effort to calm herself.

Finn, as if sensing her need to compose herself, was standing at the window again. Millie walked in with the meal on a platter so they could serve themselves. 'Take a seat Finn. And open the wine please.'

He poured the wine and she lifted her glass. 'Thank you Finn, I've been looking forward to this.' She flushed then, wondering if she sounded a bit too eager.

'Oh me too.' He grinned, and picked up the servers she offered him. Instead of lifting some of the lamb to his own plate, he served her. 'So now you know I'm not a complete neanderthal.' His voice was light and she laughed.

'I've never thought that Finn.' She watched him add a healthy serving to his own plate.

'Smells wonderful. I can see it's lamb, but the flavour is something else. Something exotic.' He leaned close to his plate and breathed in.

'You'll inhale the couscous if you do that.' Millie laughed. She felt relaxed for the first time since the accident. 'It's Moroccan lamb. Best served warm, not hot. On a carrot and herb couscous. And just a heads-up, there's garlic and chilli involved.' She sipped the wine then and raised her glass slightly. 'I do adore this red and it's perfect with our meal.'

———

'Aah Millie. A man could get used to this.' Finn leaned back in his chair, his plate now empty and only a few scraps of couscous left on the platter. They'd talked about books, movies and music. Then their children and failed marriages. Not in great detail, but in a lets-share-our-back-story kind of way.

Millie hadn't put any music on, and now wished she had. She simply hadn't thought about it. She began to clear their plates, and he immediately helped. She didn't try to tell him not to. In her old life she would have insisted he sit while she did it. But she wasn't starting that way with Finn. His help was welcome.

Back in the kitchen she rinsed their plates and packed them in the dishwasher. Then she brought the little trifles out of the fridge and he gave a low whistle. 'Wow! They're cute. It's all about presentation in the food business.' He followed her back to the table and she handed him a small spoon. 'Before I dig in, what exactly am I having here?' He turned the glass jar around. 'I see berries, maybe three kinds, and cream or custard. Something chocolate too.'

His words lightened her mood another notch. 'Individual chocolate berry trifle. You nailed it.' She dug her spoon in and took a bite, closing her eyes while she explored the flavours on her tongue. *Delicious. Sweet. Maybe too sweet.* She opened her eyes and found him watching her, a strange expression on his face.

Finn set his jar down, wiped his mouth with the napkin and looked into her eyes. 'Delicious. And sweet. And I'm going to finish the whole thing. But first Millie, I need to kiss you.'

'Oh.' Millie had no words. She didn't speak or nod. She just gazed into his eyes. Her mind was screaming, *kiss me, kiss me, kiss me.* And then she was on her feet, in his arms and they were kissing. Really kissing. His arms were strong and his kisses gentle, then more demanding. She sighed and melted against him, kissing him back. His hand was on her back, and when he slid it lower, to her derriere, she didn't stop him. He walked her backwards, and they were somehow tangled up on the couch.

'Millie.' He almost growled her name and Millie couldn't remember ever feeling this excited. She pulled his shirt from his jeans, tried to unbutton it. Now his hand was under her shirt, on her breast and she let her head loll back. He kissed her neck, her collar bone and then down her chest. He tugged at the bottom of her shirt and she raised her arms, helping him remove it.

Finn paused, one hand still on her breast. 'I want to make love to you Millie.' It was a statement, but also a question.

Millie nodded. 'Yes.' Was all she could say. He stood then, and taking her hand led her to her bedroom. He lay her gently on the bed and continued to kiss and explore her body. His jeans were unbuttoned and Millie tentatively reached a hand inside. 'Oh.' She blushed. *Big. I think it's big.*

He chuckled, stood for a moment and removed his jeans, returning to kiss her mouth, teasing her tongue with his. She quivered, her whole body shaking. She was just so. *So ready.* He'd somehow flicked her bra undone, and now she was laying there, her breasts exposed. They were large and no longer as firm as they'd been before children, and weight, and gravity had changed them. She felt a flicker of nerves, but Finn didn't seem to notice. He'd moved down to flick her nipple with his tongue. She wanted to lift him back up, have him come back to her mouth. Wanted to tell him her nipples were no longer sensitive and sexy, but his arousal changed her mind. His arousal made her aroused.

Millie was nervous then, as he stopped for a moment, to tug on her pants. She hadn't expected this. Tonight. She hadn't land-scaped. She put her hand to her mouth. *What would he think? He's probably dated all those cougars with barely-there-landing strips. Oh no!* She wanted to stop him then, wanted to scream *wait, I'm not ready.*

And then he laughed. She was horrified and looked down. He had her capri pants half off, but her underwear was still on. With one hand on the waistband, he looked at her. Like he couldn't get enough, but he was grinning too. 'Millie. These underpants. Very bridget-jonesy.' He removed his hand from the waistband and replaced it with his teeth, yanking the knickers all the way down while growling like a tiger. His eyes were on hers though, and the merriment in them made her laugh. All the tension left her and she slapped him away.

'I didn't dress with this in mind Finn Anderson.' She used her prim and proper voice, trying to inject a slight English accent.

'Ah, Millie my love. But now that we're here.' He tugged again and her knickers and pants were off and she was naked. For the first time in two decades a man was seeing her, all of her, *for the first time.*

Finn moved up, covering her with his body, his chest broad with a slight covering of hair and now she could see the tattoos on his arms. 'You're beautiful, so beautiful. I want to make love to you Millie. Tell me you want me too.'

Millie held his face with her hands and kissed him gently, slowly. 'Yes. I want you too Finn.'

———

LATER, THEY LAY TOGETHER AND SHE MADE LAZY circles with her hand on his chest. 'Hmmm. Good work Finn Anderson.' She felt light and loved. Although he hadn't said it, may never say it, she felt it. It was more than sex. He really did *make-love* to her. And that sent her mind into overdrive. All those years with Rudy, sex had been perfunctory, quick and with little or no foreplay. *She'd faked* it. Many times. Sighing she lay back. *Not with Finn though.* No faking it with Finn. She was barely aware of foreplay stopping and sex starting. The whole thing had been a dizzying experience of exploding desire, then settling into a rhythm, then another explosion. She wondered if she'd ever truly had an orgasm with her ex-husband. Now she doubted everything she ever knew about sex.

Finn tapped her head. 'Earth to Millie. Where did you go just now?'

'I'm not telling you, you'll become obnoxiously conceited.' Millie sighed. 'You've turned me into a jelly-person, I no longer have bones.'

'Ah, my work here is done.' He sat up. 'Stay right here.' He got up, naked, and padded from the room.

Millie murmured, 'couldn't move if I wanted to.'

Finn returned with the half-eaten trifles, a spoon in the top of each little glass jar. 'Dessert madam. It's too good not to eat.'

65

ROSE

'Thank you Angus. For supporting me these last two weeks.' Rose sighed. 'I almost pulled out of the race. But if Steve can still stand for Mayor, I can run for Council. We'd best get going.' *Debbie's dear sweet face, smiling at her, ran through her mind.* She picked up her bag, about to walk by him but Angus placed his arm across the doorway. She turned to him.

With his arms wrapped around her, he whispered in her ear. 'We're doing it for Debbie. Steve is doing it for Debbie. She wanted you to run, Rose. And I know you'll get the votes today.' He kissed her gently. 'I love you Rose.'

Kissing him back she laughed. 'You tell me that every single day Angus Hamilton.'

'That's my promise to you Rose. Every. Single. Day.' They stood together for a moment, then Rose looked at her watch.

'We need to get going. Your mum is watching Charlie and Harper, she'll bring them down later. And I'm grateful you and Max are cooking the barbecue at the polling booth at the school.'

'The democracy-sausage. Only in Australia.' Angus chuckled.

———

Everyone was there, helping. Melanie gave out how-to-vote flyers and Laura manned a cold drink station. Angus and Max cooked sausages and Meggie and Harriet served them to locals as they came to cast their votes.

Debbie's dad, Steve, was there with Rose, Ben and Drum. And Jill Tait. The biggest surprise, after Debbie's accident, was her mother-in-law nominating for Council. Jill was well known in the farming community, like Drum, but she was also a long-time member of the CWA, and that organisation stretched the width and breadth of the country.

Rose wondered if Jamie would come by. They hadn't seen much of him since the first few days. She supposed he would, he'd have to vote. He stayed in touch, answered their calls and messages, but explained he and Warwick were just learning to cope together. He had his parents, and Debbie's, helping but he needed to stay close to home. They understood, but Rose worried for him.

Later in the day, after the café closed, Millie arrived with Finn Anderson. The wine guy. *Are they a thing?* Rose watched them chat to Meggie and Harriet for a moment, before taking a flyer from Melanie and walking into the school building. *I think they are a thing. Good.*

Rose was hoarse by the end of the day. She must have spoken to every resident in the shire. Harriet stood with her while the men packed up the barbecue. A few last-minute stragglers came through the gate.

'If my exit poll is right, Rose, then you're in. Jill too and Ben and Drum. Steve feels confident but that old rascal Brenton Davies, who stood at the last minute, might have a few votes. But I'm hopeful.'

'Jamie!' Rose turned to see Jamie with little Warwick holding his hand. Harriet walked across to him and hugged him hard. Jamie gave her a lop-sided grin.

'I'd better go in, the booth closes in a few minutes.' He patted Rose on her arm. 'You've got my vote Rose. Always.' He smiled then and Rose felt some small relief. Jamie was trying. If not for himself, then for Warwick.

Millie and Finn were still there, chatting with Melanie and Ben, when Jamie came out. Warwick saw Tiffany, Billie and Tommy at the swings and shot off, his chubby legs pumping hard while he called Tommy's name. Jamie and Rose stood together as Tommy jumped off the swing, picked Warwick up and swung him around in a circle. His laughter could be heard across the play-ground. The girls joined them and they took Warwick to the slide.

'He won't remember her, will he?' Jamie's voice was quiet. Rose looked at him for a moment, her eyes filling with tears. 'But we will Jamie. All of us. And we'll tell him all about her. What a wonderful mother she was. And wife. And all the things she did for this town.'

'The café.' Jamie jerked his head toward Millie, still talking with Melanie and Ben. 'I need to make some decisions about the café.' He shook his head then. 'I don't know what to do.'

'What would Debbie want, do you think?' Rose's voice was gentle.

'Honestly? She'd want it to stay open. I know that much. But I can't run it Rose. And Millie has advised Douglas that Cathy is retiring.' Jamie shook his head. 'I don't know how long Millie plans to stay. She's been great though.'

'Have you spoken to Douglas about this? He may have options you can work through.' Rose closed her eyes for a moment. Frances was deteriorating, quickly. Ben had told her earlier today, in confidence, that Douglas may sell the whole building and retire. She didn't want to mention this to Jamie, it may not be public knowledge yet. She looked across at Millie. *Would she stay? Take on the business?*

'Come over to Melanie and Ben, Millie's with them now.' Rose led Jamie across. Melanie hugged him, Ben shook his hand. Millie smiled a hello and said it was lovely to see him and Warwick. She asked Jamie if he knew Finn. Both men nodded and shook hands, said they'd met a couple of times.

'Millie.' Jamie put his hands in his pockets as she focussed on him. 'I want to thank you. For everything. The way you run the café.' He looked across the playground to the children for a moment and they all waited until his gaze returned. 'I heard what you did, the day after. The first few days. Feeding people at the cafe, making it a place they could come.' He swallowed. 'Could come and talk about Deb, share their stories. Their grief.' He couldn't stop the tears then and Rose saw Millie step forward, like it was the most natural thing to do, and put her arms around him. He hugged her back, and Rose was standing close enough to hear him say, 'it's just what Debbie would have done, for any of us. It's exactly what Debbie would have done.'

The children ran over, and Mille stepped away from Jamie, but not before Rose saw her eyes were glistening too. They all turned to walk back to the gates, and as Millie and Finn walked through Jamie said to her, 'I'll be in touch. Very soon Millie. And thank you again.'

Rose looked across at Angus, who gave her an almost imperceptible nod. 'They'll start counting the vote at six. We may have an early result in a couple of hours. Let's wait together, at Barrington Homestead.' She turned to Angus. 'Are there any sausages left? I have salad fixings.'

Jill Tait joined them, and Steve and Rachael Webb. Jill laughed. 'Everyone raid your pantry and take something over to the Homestead. It'll be pot luck tonight.'

66

HARRIET

May – Barrington Book Club – Meeting 9
Present: Harriet (Hamish), Millie, Meggie, Laura, Nicole,
Melanie (Bronte), Rose (Harper).
Apologies: Frances
Book: *The Drowning* by Bryan Brown

'Hi Rose, I see you made the news at your first official Council meeting.' Harriet chuckled as she waited for Rose to extract Harper from the car. They walked into the café together and Harriet was happy to see everyone there. Only Frances was absent and Douglas was unsure if she would attend book club ever again. Harriet hoped Frances would be back, they'd talk about it tonight.

'You made headlines this week Rose. The local paper had a field day!' Laura led them to their usual table and Harriet saw Rose try to smother a grin.

Harriet put her hands on her hips. 'Rose Gordon Hamilton. Was it just a publicity stunt? Really?'

Laughing, Rose shook her head. 'The media thinks so. But really, Harper was beginning to fidget and I knew she'd scream any minute. We were in the middle of the budget discussion and I didn't want to leave the chamber. So I fed her. End of story.'

Melanie clapped her hands. 'Go Rose! Women should be able to breastfeed when and where they choose. On my, the comments in the paper and on the radio, especially from Jeffries and Stevens, were outrageous! And I loved that Debbie's dad threw them out of the chamber for making such a fuss about it. Mayor Steve is doing a great job!'

Harriet saw Rose sigh. 'They'd already questioned me about having Harper in the room and wanted to vote on it. But with Drum, Ben, Jill and Steve on my side, they got nowhere.' She glanced at Harriet briefly. 'I fed her before the meeting started and topped her up in the first break, in a private room.' She lifted her chin. 'But when she began to grizzle during the budget discussion, I wasn't going to leave the room. I had questions and I wanted my vote to be counted.'

'Absolutely Rose.' Nicole looked at the others. 'You won't get any argument from any of us. I watched the meeting online and it was a show of strength against the bullying tactics those two had employed in the previous Council term. They need to know there is no place for misogyny in local government.'

They found their places around the table and Laura poured wine for those who were drinking. Millie had brought coffee to the table for the others and had set out an array of delicious looking snacks.

'Before we start on this month's book, I just want to check in with everyone.' Laura's tone was softer than usual. She paused for a moment. 'It's a month since we lost Debbie. I feel like so many things in town have changed in that time. A new term of council and a new Mayor. Steve will be progressive, I think.' She drew in a sharp breath.

Harriet gazed at her friends around the table. 'I've often thought that Debbie was the heartbeat of this town, perhaps due in part to the café.'

'I wondered how I'd feel, coming in here, knowing I'll never see Debbie smiling at me from behind the counter ever again.' Meggie's gaze fell on Millie as she spoke. 'But Millie, you and your team have kept everything running and I love coming in here. It's almost as if Debbie is still with us.'

'The café is Debbie's legacy. I feel close to her when I'm here too.' Rose wiped her eyes with a serviette. 'But it's Millie's smile I look for now.'

Everyone turned to Millie then, and Harriet noticed she was flushed and her eyes bright with unshed tears. Millie shook her head, sadly. 'No one can replace Debbie and I would never try. But I'm happy to continue here, as long as Jamie permits.'

'Has Jamie discussed the café with you yet Millie? Do you know what his plans are?' Laura reached for a mini quiche.

'We have a meeting next week, upstairs with Douglas.' Millie shook her head. 'In the interest of transparency, I'm not in a position to buy it myself. The best I can hope for is that Jamie doesn't sell, and I stay on as manager until I can make him an offer.'

'Oh.' Rose touched Millie gently on the shoulder. 'I didn't know that. I had hoped you'd buy it.' She frowned then, saying more quietly, 'Jamie told Angus he'd like to sell it. Says he doesn't know enough to keep it himself.'

Millie nodded. 'I thought as much, and I don't blame him. He has the farm and little Warwick to take care of. But I do love it here and hope I can stay, whatever happens.'

The group was quiet for a moment.

Laura opened her iPad. 'Let's talk about the book shall we?' The energy in the room lifted slightly as they took out their copies of the book, some paperbacks and others with eBook devices.

'Okay, I'm just going to put this out there.' Nicole pushed a copy of the book to one side. 'I adore the cover and that alone would have encouraged me to buy it. And the story was good, a mystery and very Australian. Tick and tick. But overall it was a four-star read for me. The first time.'

'The first time? Did you read it twice?' Harriet was confused. If Nik had said it was a five-star read, she'd understand reading it twice.

'I listened to the audiobook version the second time. Bryan Brown read it himself. It was brilliant. And funny. I loved it.' Nicole glanced around, 'I think I'm going to do more audiobooks. I listened to it while I was gardening.'

'I've never tried an audiobook.' Harriet looked at the others. 'But I listen to podcasts quite a lot. Especially on long drives. I'm going to do that too. Try an audiobook.'

'There are audiobooks, and audiobooks.' Rose cleared her throat. 'So many publishers and indie authors are using artificial intelligence to create audiobooks, and frankly, I'm dead against that. It's putting creatives out of work. Creatives like me. Except they're narrators and maybe actors and professional voiceover people. I'm planning to have my books narrated, but I'll be using human-narration. Yes, it's more expensive, but the result is worth it.'

'I've heard this too.' Meggie spoke firmly. 'And I agree with Rose. Human narrators are so much better.' She grinned at Nicole. 'And now I want to listen to Bryan Brown reading The Drowning. I enjoyed it. It wasn't quite a five-star read for me either, but it had *something* that kept me intrigued.'

'I loved it.' Laura took a sip of wine. 'But I'm going to get the audiobook version so Ben can hear it when we take our next trip. Actually, I can see this one as a movie too.'

The discussion continued and Harriet held Hamish on her lap when he woke. He seemed happy enough to just look around and she let the conversation wash over her, just enjoying the warmth of the conversation, between a bunch of women she really cared for.

If she squinted as she looked towards the coffee machine, she could almost picture Debbie there.

67

MILLIE

Finn asked Millie if she'd heard about the future of the café. He'd told her he wanted her to stay. He'd even said she could work with him, at the winery, if she needed a new job. Millie loved him for suggesting it, but it was too early in their relationship to work together. She'd done that with her ex-husband, and it hadn't ended well.

Walking upstairs to Douglas's rooms, Millie weighed up her options. Perhaps she could get a business loan, but she had done her research, and she calculated the price would be beyond anything she could borrow in her present circumstances. It may take time for an alternative buyer to be found, and in the meantime she was confident Jamie would keep her on.

Douglas met her in reception, and told her Jamie was already there. For a moment she wondered where Frances was, but then remembered Harriet had mentioned she was with their daughter and her family for a week.

'Hello Millie.' Jamie smiled at her, but his eyes were sad and he had dark circles under them. Millie's heart broke for him. She knew time would help, but in her heart she wondered if Jamie would ever fully recover from the loss of his wife. Rose had told her that Debbie was his first and only love. They all hoped that he would learn to live without her, for his son's sake at least.

'Hi Jamie. How's Warwick?' The question brought a spark of light to his eyes.

'He's such a funny little bloke. Goes everywhere with me. Loves being outside on the farm.' A half smile lit up Jamie's face and for a moment Millie caught a glimpse of the happy young man he was. Before.

'That's great, Jamie.' She smiled at him, hoping he felt the sincerity of her words.

'Thank you for coming, Millie. Jamie has made some decisions about the café, the business.' Douglas always sounded so considered, his tone warm. Millie simply nodded. She was too worried to speak.

Jamie turned to her. 'I'm sorry Millie, but I can't keep the café myself. I have to sell.' He looked away for a moment, then turned back to her. 'I want to take over the farm from mum and dad, and I need funds to buy them out. Selling the café business will go towards that and will give me security for myself, and Woz. They're not in a hurry, but I think it's best to put it on the market now.'

Douglas handed some documents to Millie. 'The café business has been valued. This is the price and the inclusions. Jamie wants you to have first offer to purchase. As you know, the building is owned by me and Frances, so the rent will remain the same for the next six months, at least.'

Millie looked at the document and blinked. It was beyond her own resources. She had wondered if she could borrow from her parents, but although they owned their home, she didn't think they had a lot of savings.

'Thank you Douglas.' Millie smiled at Jamie warmly. 'And thank you too Jamie, for keeping me on as you have. The offer is generous, but I need to tell you that buying it is beyond my current resources. I will make some enquires about a business loan, but it may be best, for you, to place it on the market to achieve your ends. It's a fabulous business and I wish my circumstances were different.' She folded the paper up and put it in her bag. 'But I am keen to stay on while you go through the process, if you'll have me.'

'I'm truly sorry Millie.' Jamie looked devastated. 'I had hoped you would be the one. To continue on in the business.'

Millie stood up. 'Me too Jamie.' She smiled brightly at him, not wanting him to feel bad. 'But I am sure you will find a buyer and I will be here, until you do.'

'Thank you Douglas, for your time. I'll leave you to finish your meeting.' Millie left the room quickly, returning to the café downstairs.

'News?' Cathy looked at Millie expectantly.

'It will be sold Cathy. But I'll stay until it is.' Millie gave the older woman a quick hug. 'Our jobs are secure until then.'

'I'm thinking end of June, to retire Millie.' Cathy half smiled. 'But I won't leave you in the lurch if it hasn't sold.'

'Thank you. I think it will sell. It's got a great reputation and the figures are good.' Millie sighed, then jerked her head towards the door. 'The tennis ladies are coming in, let's get to it.'

68

FRANCES

Where am I? I don't know this house. Where is Douglas? Frances turned around in the bedroom. The room was unfamiliar, although very pretty. She walked to the window and looked out. She recognised the Sydney Harbour Bridge and knew she was on the lower north shore. Maybe Mosman. Sitting on the bed for a moment, she concentrated on her breathing. and pictured Douglas. And their house in Barrington. She relaxed slightly.

'Good morning Mum, did you sleep well?' The young woman looked familiar and called her mum. But this couldn't be her daughter Anna. This woman was middle-aged.

'I think I slept well.' Frances was confused. 'Where is Douglas? I want to go home. To Barrington.'

The young woman sat on the bed next to her. 'It's me, mum. Anna.' She picked up her hand and Frances turned to her. 'Last night we talked about the time we had the bonfire, at home in

Barrington, when we made damper in the coals and all my friends came for my birthday.'

Frowning, Frances remembered the night clearly. She also remembered how Douglas had caught their daughter Anna, kissing a boy around the side of the house. He hadn't become upset, but she had. She'd argued with Anna then, but two weeks later, when the boy broke her heart, she'd comforted her too.

'Anna?' Frances questioned, looking into the woman's face. And suddenly she knew. 'Anna!' she wrapped her arms around her daughter and hugged her tightly. 'I forget things sometimes, darling girl.'

'I know you do mum. But we love you. Dad loves you. We all love you.'

They sat together for a little while, then Anna took her hand. 'Come and have a cup of tea mum, and some breakfast. Dad, er Douglas, is coming to get you this afternoon.'

Frances felt her chest swell with happiness. She clapped her hands. 'Douglas? Douglas is coming? I can't wait to see him!' She touched her hair with her free hand. She'd have to get ready if Douglas was coming.

69

MEGGIE

June – Barrington Book Club – Meeting 10
Present: Harriet, Millie, Meggie, Laura, Nicole, Melanie, Rose.
Apologies: Frances
Book: *The Wattle Island Book Club* by Sandie Docker

'A book about a book club. Loved it. Good choice Millie.' Laura arrived with a bottle of wine in one hand, her nose red from the cold. She shrugged off her coat and unwound the scarf from her neck. Millie took them, placing them on a chair near the entrance.

'And we all adore a dual timeline these days.' Rose laughed as she walked in, then spun in a circle, hands in the air. 'Look girls, no baby!' She dropped her coat on a table then hung her bag over the back of a chair. 'And a regular handbag. Not a massive holds-everything-a-baby-could-possibly-want bag!'

Meggie giggled as Melanie almost ran in, jumping around in her excitement. 'Jeans, jacket, scarf and no baby!' She pointed to her feet. 'Ugg boots. I'm wearing Ugg boots and they're so cosy-warm.'

Harriet was with her and also child free. 'Let's not get too excited. The men said they'd take charge so we can be child-free at book club.' She grimaced. 'But this may be a one-night-only deal.' Laughing loudly she pulled a bottle of red from her bag and waved it in the air. 'It's that one that Finn makes that we all like. And Hamish has just weaned himself.'

Millie whistled. 'Book club, with wine. I'm on board.' Quickly setting out more glasses, she said, 'so who is *not* drinking tonight, is really the question.'

Rose sighed. 'Me. I think I'll be breastfeeding until Harper starts High School at this rate. She'll take a bottle of breast milk I've expressed, but turns her nose up at formula.'

Meggie patted her tummy. 'I'm not drinking. And I'm six months and all is well.' Everyone spoke at once then and Meggie felt warmed by the laughter and friendship in the room. She'd been anxious in the early months that something would go wrong, but now she'd reached six months she began to feel more confident. Her doctor said he had no concerns, the baby was doing well.

They settled at the table, chatting easily together over drinks and snacks. When they finally turned to the book, Rose picked hers up. 'I adore the cover. All of Sandie Docker's books have the same look, but different colours. It's so easy to find them on the book shelf. Clever.' Turning to Millie, Rose asked, 'What made you choose this one Millie? It's been out since 2021, but I admit I hadn't read it.'

'It was the title. The book club title and I've read two of her earlier books and loved them. And we've been enjoying the ones with dual timelines, so it seemed to fit.' Millie looked pleased with herself.

'I loved it, and I've read her earlier ones too. There's a new one coming out soon, we need to put it on our list.' Meggie nibbled her bottom lip. 'Did anyone else cry. Her books always have a thread of sadness, but this one really got me in the feels. Of course, it could just be pregnancy hormones.'

'Howled like a baby. Robbie couldn't work out what was wrong.' Nicole sipped her wine. 'But for me, after everything that's happened here.' She waved an arm around at the café, 'it was cathartic. I needed to cry.'

Laura raised her eyebrows. 'Not a big crier myself. But this book moved me. It really did. Having said that, I couldn't back right up with another one of hers. I need a palette cleanser for our next read.'

'A palette cleanser. Hmmm. Anyone fancy a bit of spice in the next one?' Meggie flipped through her phone, then glanced up. 'There's an Aussie author called Davina Stone who's written a series called Laws of Love. There are four or five books and they all have a bit of, uh, sexy-time in them.' She waggled her eyebrows as she passed her phone around with the book covers on the screen and smiled to herself at their various reactions. Laura laughed out loud and Melanie put her hand to her mouth. Rose and Harriet looked at each other and grinned. Nicole simply said, 'I'm in.'

'Should we start with the first one or can they be read as stand-alones?' Rose demanded.

'I've read most of them, and yes, they can be read as stand-alones. I'm up to *The Felicity Theory*, so I'd love it if we picked that one.' Meggie clapped when they all agreed.

'May I choose the one after that? Julie Bennett's new book

will be out. *The Lost Letters of Rose Carey*. I'm really keen to read it.' Harriet made notes on her phone, then looked up. Everyone spoke at once then, about the author's first book. Meggie leaned back in her chair with her hands on her baby bump. Despite all that had happened, she was looking forward to the future.

70

ROSE

'Do you know if there's been much interest in the café? It's been for sale for a couple of weeks now.' Rose and Meggie were having a lazy lunch out at the homestead. Charlie was at day care and little Harper was on the floor, now able to get up on her hands and knees and rock, although she hadn't quite worked out the crawling bit yet.

'Ben's had some enquiries. A young couple came in a few days ago, they're working at a place in Forster at the moment and want their own place. But they haven't made a firm offer. I think there's three separate groups doing their due diligence.' Meggie took another sip of hot chocolate, the days were really cool now.

'It's a shame Millie's not in a position to buy it.' Rose reached for a brownie. 'I have to stop eating these. I'm still carrying an extra few kilos of pregnancy weight.' She closed her eyes for a moment. 'But they're so good.'

'And as far as I can see, most of the interest is from people who won't need a manager. So there's a real chance we'll lose Millie.'

Meggie didn't look happy about it. 'But she's definitely seeing Finn. His car was parked outside her place when I called in to work early the other day.'

'Well that's good isn't it? Maybe he will have job for her at the winery.' Rose knew she was speculating, but Millie had become part of their group. They were connected by Debbie and she didn't want to lose her.

'Yes, he probably could. But I get the feeling Millie wouldn't go for that. She worked with her husband and it ended badly. And I can see that she's very independent. I don't know Rose. Jamie wants to sell. He has every right to sell.'

'He does.' Rose felt like crying as she said the next words. 'But what if someone buys it and changes it. You know, takes all the Debbie-ness out of it.' She wiped her eyes. 'I couldn't bear it Meggs.'

They sat silently for a moment. Rose gazed out of the window, remembering happy moments with Debbie. *She shook her head. Sometimes the last image she had of Debbie was the only one she could picture.*

'Rose! Rose look!'

Whipping her head around, Rose saw Meggie pointing at Harper. 'She's crawling Rose. Six months and she's crawling.' Rose laughed aloud, tickled pink. Harper was crawling steadily towards her favourite stuffed toy, a dog that looked a bit like Woof.

'Oh there'll be no stopping her now. Life as we know it is over. She'll be everywhere!' Rose leaned forward. 'Angus will be so proud. Charlie didn't crawl until eight months.'

71

MILLIE

'Any news on a buyer for the café?' Finn was lying on his side with one hand under his head and the other laying across Millie.

Millie sighed. 'There are now four groups doing their due diligence, but the very young couple dropped out. Barrington is too far from their family and friends, they said.' Millie sighed, then met Finn's gaze. 'The groups that are still in contention are all couples or partners and won't need a manager. Ben has told me they're all keen for me to stay on, but in Cathy's role. Um, with the pay drop, it would be hard for me to stay.'

'I've asked before and you've said no. But Millie, I can offer you a job. And accommodation. If not with me, if you're not ready, then in the empty apartment downstairs we use for staff when the grapes are ready to pick.' Finn sounded frustrated. She liked that he was keen to keep her here, but she truly believed it was too early in their relationship to work or live together, and rather than making it stronger, may well ruin it.

Shaking her head, Millie leaned close and kissed him quickly. 'I adore that you want to keep me here. I want to stay. But we've talked about this Finn. If I have to move back to the coast, it won't end what we have.' She waggled her eyebrows. 'It might even make it more fun, only seeing each other once a week or so.'

Finn laughed and drew her to him. 'It's just so *easy* with you Millie.'

'Easy? I'm easy you say?' Millie tried to look serious.

'You know what I mean. My ex-wife and I didn't share any interests except the kids of course, and frankly, we pushed each other's buttons. All the time. But not you Millie Tucker.'

'Perhaps you haven't found my button Finn Anderson.' Millie put her hand to her mouth, she'd shocked herself with her words.

He growled in her ear. 'Oh, I know I've found *that* button. But let's talk about that, shall we?'

Millie shook her head, laughing. 'No. We won't be talking about *that*. Not now, not ever.'

'You're all sweet-smiley-goody-two-shoes on the outside Millie. But I know better. You're a wild woman.' He gave her a faux-creepy grimace. 'Between the sheets. And on the sofa. And that time on the rug at my place.'

Millie playfully slapped him away, extricated herself from the bed and stood up. Naked and not caring that he could see her. *All of her.* 'I'm going to take a shower now, I suggest you do the same.' She wrinkled her nose and he was off the bed, following her from the room.

Finn was ready first and by the time Millie had dressed and dried her hair he'd made the bed and washed up the dishes they'd left on the sink the night before. Millie found him sitting on the couch, her copy of *The Felicity Theory* in his hands. He raised his eyebrows and read aloud, *'all Oliver could do was stand there, chest heaving and his boxer shorts suddenly too small...'* He looked up at her then. 'This is smut. Is this your *book club* read? Really? Naughty girl. Grrrr.'

Millie giggled. She'd told Finn this one had a bit of spice. She hadn't expected him to open it to the place near the end where her book mark was. But then she had an idea. Plonking herself on the sofa next to him, she asked in her sexy-don't-stop-now voice, 'read the rest Finn. Out loud. It's only a couple more pages. And I love your voice, so much.' She lay back and closed her eyes as Finn obliged. She loved his speaking voice and having him read aloud was better than an audiobook. *Her own real-life audiobook.*

———

TWO HOURS LATER THEY WERE AT THE WINERY together. Lucas had driven into town to watch the football with friends. Millie had helped Finn in the stockroom, although he told her to relax, it was her day off, but when the clouds came over and it started to drizzle they ran back to his apartment. He had a wood fired heater and the loft apartment was cosy.

'It's your day off Millie and you've been helping me here for hours. What would you like to do? We can drive across to the coast for dinner and a movie if you fancy?'

Millie knew Finn would do that, if she asked, but she really just wanted to relax here with him. 'Is it too early for a glass of wine? I fancy staying in tonight.'

While Finn poured the win, Millie looked around the room. She spied two guitars hanging on the wall in the area he used as a study. She'd never noticed them before. Pointing, she asked, 'do you play guitar Finn? You've never said.'

'A little bit. For my own pleasure really.' He shrugged.

Millie sipped her wine, then looked at him over the rim of the glass. 'Will you play something for me?'

Finn seemed to hesitate, then shrugged again. 'Sure.' He walked over to the guitars, chose one and returned. 'This is a Maton acoustic. My favourite.' He settled himself on a chair, facing her, the guitar in his lap. He looked sheepish for a moment, then said, 'I've been learning a new song. For you. It's, ah, an Elvis tune.'

He began strumming and Millie raised her eyebrows. The guitar sounded mellow and she knew the tune. It was from one of his movies. Finn began to sing, 'wise men say only fools rush in, but I can't help falling in love with you..' *His voice. Gosh, if she closed her eyes he could be Elvis. And the song. Was he really singing that song? To her?* Millie watched his face as sang the whole song, how he strummed the guitar and how his expression changed on certain words. She was mesmerised and when he finished she had tears in her eyes.

'That. Was. Beautiful. Oh gosh Finn!' Millie had her hands to her face. A flush raced up her torso, her chest, neck and face. *Darn peri-menopause. Why now?*

Finn looked away for a moment. Then he moved to the sofa and took Millie's hands. 'I could say, *they're just lyrics.* But Millie, I've been learning this song, to sing to you.' He stopped, looked away, then turned back to her, his lips gently meeting hers. 'The lyrics are true.'

Winding her arms around his neck, Millie kissed him thoroughly. Finally she stopped. 'I have questions.'

'Yes?' Finn raised his eyebrows.

'Your voice. Why have you never done anything with your voice? It's superstar-quality.' Millie was confused.

Shaking his head, Finn grinned. 'I think you're biased. And I was keen when I was really young. Sang in a band for a while. I learned to play guitar much later. But I married young and my ex, well, she wasn't a fan. It became something I just did by myself. Sometimes with the kids. But mostly just for me. I'm happy you enjoyed the song.' He set the guitar against the chair.

'Don't stop! Now that I know, wow, I want more! What else do you know?' Millie clapped her hands in excitement.

Reaching for the guitar, Finn grinned as he strummed another tune. 'This one reminds me of you too.' He began singing To Sir With Love, except when he got to the second verse he changed the lyrics and sang *who has taken you from full briefs to g-strings* and she fell about laughing.

'Stop it! Too funny. But also, wow! You can change your voice. Not just Elvis then? Who else can you do?' Millie topped their wine glasses up as Finn belted out a Johnny Cash song, sounding just like the star himself. Then he did a Kenny Rogers number - her dad would love that one. Just as quickly he transitioned to Bruce Springsteen. Millie was amazed. *What a talent!*

'I have to stop or I won't be able to speak tomorrow.' Laughing, Finn strummed again, and Millie recognised the song. Another Elvis love song. He looked into her eyes as he sang and that was when Millie knew. *He loves me! He really loves me!* When he finished the song she threw her arms around him and whispered, 'I love you Finn.' He held her tightly. He didn't have to say a thing.

72

———

HARRIET

July – Barrington Book Club – Meeting 11
Present: Harriet, Millie, Meggie, Laura, Nicole, Melanie, Rose.
Apologies: Frances
Book: *The Felicity Theory* by Davina Stone

MEGGIE DROVE ROSE AND HARRIET, AS THEY WERE baby-free for the second time at book club and Harper was beginning to self-wean.

'Brrr, it's cold out there tonight. Just as well you have ducted heating in here Millie.' Harriet removed her coat, scarf and beanie as the others arrived, all at once. Bottles of wine were opened and Millie produced steaming portions of freshly baked lasagne.

'Good choice Millie. Something warm is just the ticket.' Laura held one foot up. 'Ugg boots. Like Melanie. My first pair. So warm.'

Harriet giggled. 'You know you're a redneck if you wear them out. They are strictly for wearing at home only.'

'Pffft. I admit, they're not a fashion statement. Bu my feet have never been so cosy.' Laura tossed her head back. She never bothered about what others thought anyway. 'And being in the café feels like home to me.'

Rose clapped her hands. 'It does. Thanks to Millie, it really does feel like home.'

Harriet saw Millie's cheeks flush with pleasure. 'By the way Millie, is there something you need to share? We all know you've been seeing Finn. But I bumped into his son Lucas the other night, when we were having dinner at the pub. He mumbled something about, and I quote, 'dad and Millie, all loved up at home.' Is this true. Is it, you know, a thing?'

They all turned to Millie who blushed, then waved her hand in front of her face in a cooling motion. 'Peri-menopause. It's the worst.'

'Don't change the subject Millie. We want to know about Finn.' Meggie steepled her hands under her chin, her face innocent, waiting for a response.

'Okay. You've got me. It's a thing!' Millie laughed and shook her head as they began asking questions. 'Stop it. A lady never tells.' But then she placed her hand on the paperback in front of her. 'But ...'

'But what?' Harriet was curious and loving the happy energy in the room.

'This book.' Millie giggled. 'Loved the story. And definitely a bit spicy. Not that I minded.' She leaned in. 'Have any of you noticed the timbre of Finn's speaking voice?'

'Yes. Now you mention it.' Meggie chuckled eyebrows raised. 'I asked him to make an announcement at a noisy elopement function, to get everyone to sit for their meal, and he spoke into the microphone. He could be on radio.'

'Radio. Yes. But the other day he was flicking through this,' Millie pointed to the book again, 'I was close to the end and he began reading it aloud.' She fanned her face, flushed again. 'Oh my, I had my own personal audiobook narrator. And he was good. If you know what I mean?'

Nicole put her hands to her face. 'Lucky girl. Maybe we should do another one by this author and ask him to come to book club and read it aloud.'

'Oh no. For my ears only.' Millie looked delighted. 'He sings too. And plays guitar. He sings like Elvis.'

'What? No! Really?' Harriet looked at Meggie. 'Why did we not know this? We could pay him to do wedding gigs.' Meggie shook her head, holding her hands up in an I-had-no-idea gesture.

'The book was fun. I read a couple of bits out to Robbie. But now he's questioning what we do at book club.' Nicole grinned. 'I told him it's book-chat and paperbacks and that's all he needs to know. I love book club nights.' She nodded firmly on the last words.

'Oh me Too Nik. Maybe I should read a bit to Ben. But you know. His heart.' Laura laughed loudly as she spoke and Harriet felt something shift in the room. It seemed warmer somehow.

They ate and chatted together for an hour and all had ordered the next book. 'Do you think we should try to get Frances here next month? I'll ask Douglas if he thinks she'd be okay with us. I miss her.' Harriet glanced around as the others nodded.

Quietly, Rose said, 'Douglas told me a few days ago that she is slipping quickly but has moments of lucidity. They're still juggling her meds, trying to make those moments more frequent, or last longer.' She shook her head. 'It's a terrible disease. For the sufferer and their loved ones. Douglas has aged these last few months.'

'He has. I've noticed it too. He's put the building on the market. Frances doesn't like being with anyone but Douglas. She always knows him, but sometimes doesn't recognise their kids. He wants to be with her, provide the best care and quality of life for her that he can. He's a good man. He's hoping a Solicitor will buy it, but there are no guarantees.' Harriet sighed. 'Douglas has been an institution in this town. He will be missed. Although he said he'll continue to practice, just for existing clients, from home.'

Turning to Millie, Harriet continued, 'but no contract on the café yet?'

'No it's strange. I really thought it would have sold by now. Some buyers have expressed interest in owning it freehold, but they'd have to buy the whole building and with Douglas planning to vacate his rooms upstairs, it may not value up until there's a new tenant. Horse before cart situation, I think.' Millie smiled then. 'I know Jamie wants it sold, but honestly, I'm grateful for the extra time here.'

'We are too Millie.' Nicole reached for her hand. 'I'm hoping it will still work out for you to stay.'

'We all are, Millie.' Laura raised her glass, then finished the last mouthful of wine in it.

They began clearing the table, and slowly drifted out the door. Harriet and Rose waited in their car for Millie to lock up and walk across the road to her apartment. As they drove away, Harriet glanced in the rear-view mirror. Finn parked his car outside the post office and stepped out, entering the building holding Millie's hand.

73

FRANCES

'YOU LOOK BEAUTIFUL LOVE, AS ALWAYS.' FRANCES turned as Douglas spoke and smiled. Today was a good day. She'd had a few lately. They'd fiddled with her medication. She turned back to the mirror and patted her hair, then dabbed Chanel perfume on her wrists. Sometimes she was shocked by her own appearance, how old she looked. In her mind her marriage to Douglas had only just begun.

'Rose and Harriet are here to pick you up.' Douglas walked with her to the hall, where two gorgeous young women stood. One tall and auburn. Rose Gordon. Rose Gordon Hamilton, she corrected herself. And the other petite and fair. That was Harriet. She was married to Drum Murray and both women had babies.

'Hello Rose, Harriet.' Frances smiled and let herself be enveloped in their hugs. 'Thank you for picking me up.' She paused then, wanting to tell them everything. 'I wasn't able to read the book. The one with the gorgeous cover. I wish I had been able to.'

'We've missed your company at book club Frances.' Rose leaned down, her mouth near Frances' ear. 'It's as much about the company as the books. But never tell Douglas that.' Then she straightened and laughed, her young face glowing with health and cheerfulness.

Frances felt young and alive, just like these women. Her friends, Rose and Harriet. She waved goodbye to Douglas, who held a look of fondness on his face. So much that for a moment Frances thought about staying home with him. But she was keen to have an hour or two out in the company of friends.

74

ROSE

August – Barrington Book Club – Meeting 12
Present: Harriet, Millie, Meggie, Laura, Nicole, Melanie, Rose,
Frances
Apologies: none
Book: *The Lost Letters of Rose Carey* by Julie Bennett

EVERYONE WELCOMED FRANCES WHEN THEY ARRIVED, and Rose hoped they wouldn't overwhelm her. She had to ask who Millie was and couldn't remember Nicole's name, but no one minded.

The nights were still cold and Millie had made a feast of hot snacks. A few drank the wine Laura and Melanie had provided and the others chose chai lattes and hot chocolates.

'This book.' Harriet held her copy up. 'What can I say about it. This writer is amazing. The research, the locations. Everything. I loved everything.'

'The dual timeline got me, and the mystery of the letters. And it's based on a true story.' Meggie frowned, as if recalling something. 'I remember learning, somewhere, that Australia was very early to adopt movie-making. A lot of silent movies were made here. But really, I didn't fully understand just how involved we were in those early days. I love a book that makes me want to do my research. You know, do some fact-checking.'

'Fact-checking Meggie? Or google checking? Not always the same thing.' Nicole grinned.

Rose felt the same. 'It was that. The story, the research, the recreation of the time, the romance. But even more for me, it was the words.' Rose tapped her copy. 'this beautiful cover and the words.' She shook her head then. 'This author painted such a vivid picture in my mind that I savoured every chapter, every paragraph. A triumph.'

Laura had noted some paragraphs on her iPad and read them aloud. 'These were so lovely, that I marked them to read again. You're right Rose. This writer wields words with a delicate touch.'

After returning from the bathroom for the second time, Rose raised her eyebrows at Meggie. 'Not long to go now Meggs. Six weeks? How are you feeling?'

'Just under six weeks. And I'm doing well and so is baby.' She tried not to laugh then. 'But Max, well, he's a whole other story.' Meggie snickered.

'Max? Why? He's been there before, with Tommy.' Laura offered Frances more wine bus she shook her head.

'He's funny. Treating me like I'm made of glass, fussing about. He's been worse since we found out the gender.' Meggie's eyes were twinkling.

Rose was surprised, she hadn't heard about this. *Why didn't Meggie tell me?* 'Well don't keep us in suspense, are we allowed to know?' Rose tapped her fingernails on the table.

'Yes. We're having a girl!' Meggie beamed and Rose jumped up and hugged her. They all began talking at once, until Harriet asked about baby names.

Meggie was quiet then. 'I've been doing some research. Did you know that Debbie is the shortened version of Deborah, which is Hebrew for honeybee? The meaning is all about hard work, organisation and sense of community. I've been thinking about using that, perhaps as a middle name for this one.' She patted her baby bump. 'And my other favourite is Anne, with an E. It was my grandmother's first name but also *Anne of Green Gables*, the book that started my love of reading.' She had tears in her eyes. 'So do you think Jamie would mind if we call her Debbie-Anne? The sense of community bit really gets me. I want to honour Debbie. And in a way, book club. All of you. The book-club posse.'

Rose looked at the others. She wasn't the only one crying, but they were all smiling too. But it was Frances who moved closer to Meggie, taking one of her hands, her words gentle and kind. 'I don't remember everyone. Or everything. But I do remember Debbie. Your little girl will be a beautiful reminder of our darling friend. I'm sure Debbie's family will be honoured by your choice.'

Before they left, at the end of the meeting, Rose held up her hand, and they stopped chattering and looked at her. 'Next meeting, does anyone have a book suggestion?'

'I do.' Harriet looked Rose in the eye. 'One of yours Rose. I'd like to read one of yours.' She gestured around the table. 'Together. Tonight was our twelfth meeting, and a lot has happened in a year. Our next meeting marks the start of a new cycle. Let's start right and read one of our own.'

Rose flushed and looked at her friends. She nodded. It felt right.

'Um, before you all leave, I have news too.' Millie was standing at the end of the table. Rose had wondered about this. Harriet said earlier that Ben had sold the building, and the café business, but she didn't know who the buyer was. Rose hadn't wanted to ask Millie in case she hadn't yet been told.

'The contracts will be signed tomorrow, but I asked if I could share the news. The building has been sold. The café has, effectively, a new landlord.' Millie didn't look anxious, so Rose hoped it meant she might be able to stay.

'Do you know who the buyer is Millie?' Nicole asked the question, but they all wanted to know.

'I do. Steve and Rachael Webb, Debbie's parents, have bought the whole building and the café too.' Millie nodded happily.

'Rachael and Steve Webb. Mayor Webb?' Rose smiled. 'He'll be familiar with the building, he was the bank manager here for years before the bank left town and Douglas bought it. Well, that is good news.' She looked at Millie. 'So you'll be working for Steve and Rachael then? You'll stay?'

Millie wiped a tear from her eye. 'This is the good bit. They're selling me the café, vendor finance. The café will be mine. Well it will be, in about two years, so I'm staying!' Her voice rang out loudly on her last words and they all cheered. 'There is one proviso. It's written into the contract.' Millie looked at Rose. 'In fact, I think they're using your words for this clause.'

'My words?' Rose was mystified.

'They want to be sure the café maintains its *Debbie-ness*. An easy promise for me to keep.'

They were all standing now, hugging each other, hugging Millie. Even Frances joined in. Rose turned to get a tissue from her bag and movement near the coffee machine caught her eye. *For a split second, she could have sworn she saw Debbie there.* Shaking her head, she joined the others, gathered around Millie.

75

MILLIE

MILLIE CALLED FINN THE NEXT DAY. 'HI FINN. I KNOW it's a week night, but can I drop by after work? I have news.' Millie held the phone to her ear. She'd just signed the contract to purchase the café.

'Sure. Come for dinner. I'll cook.' Finn paused then. 'Is it good news Millie?'

'It isn't bad news Finn. I'll fill you in when I get there. Around six?'

'Okay. Looking forward to it.' Finn rang off and Millie returned to the café.

At five past six Millie knocked on Finn's door. She knew he was alone, she'd passed Lucas driving into town. Millie wondered if Lucas had a girlfriend, he seemed to go into town a lot.

Finn opened the door with a tea towel over his shoulder. A delicious aroma wafted out through the door with him. *Something spicy?* He opened his arms and Millie walked into them, loving the way his strength seeped into her core. 'Dinner won't be long, Millie.'

Millie leaned back and looked into his eyes for a moment. *She felt good. More than good. Happy and sexy all at once.* She stood on tiptoes and kissed him. Gently at first, then with all the love and happiness bubbling inside her. He tightened his embrace. Her voice was husky as she placed her lips near his ear. 'I'm not here for the food, Finn.'

THE END

THE BARRINGTON BOOK CLUB
READING LIST

1. ***Apples Never Fall*** by Liane Moriarty
2. ***The Quarantine Station*** by Michelle Montebello
3. ***The Stationmaster's Cottage*** by Phillipa Nefri Clark
4. ***The Work Wives*** by Rachael Johns
5. ***Runt*** by Craig Silvey
6. ***A Stranger in Featherwood Falls*** by Heather Reyburn
7. ***The Understudy*** by Julie Bennett
8. ***Buried in Between*** by Leanne Lovegrove
9. ***The Drowning*** by Bryan Brown
10. ***The Wattle Island Book Club*** by Sandie Docker
11. ***The Felicity Theory*** by Davina Stone
12. ***The Lost Letters of Rose Carey*** by Julie Bennett

I hope you enjoy this story and take a moment to check out the books read by the Barrington girl-posse.

Please consider leaving a review, it really helps indie authors build their following and keep writing. A simple star rating and a couple of words - (loved it!) - is all that's needed. If you choose to write a longer review - thank you very much - but please don't give away the what/who of the tragedy.

Susan Mackie

SUSAN MACKIE

A voracious reader, Susan dreamed of becoming a writer from the age of eight. Career advisors told her it wasn't a real thing and suggested journalism. So she became a journalist, then took a zig-zag path to publish her first book in 2020, via a varied career in publishing, marketing, tourism and small business. Susan even worked in State Government for a few years (but she doesn't talk about that much).

Nervous about the release of Charlie's Will, she told Bloke while sitting on the sofa one night, that she'd be happy if she sold fifty. Charlie's Will quickly reached Number One in its genre on Amazon - motivating Susan to crack on with more stories and take her writing seriously. Finally. Now Susan is a happy Indie Publisher and offers services to other writers (editing, formatting). She is also the publisher of the Love in a Sunburnt Land Anthology series, co-authored with four (quite brilliant) Aussie women.

Susan loves engaging with fellow authors and readers, and she discovered something she thought was kinda funny. A lot of authors tell her they're introverted. It's a writerly thing, apparently. But (and here's the funny bit), Susan isn't. Introverted. Not one bit. Not at all. Speaking and presenting at writers festivals, conferences and libraries is totally her thing.

So it's okay to send Susan a message, ask a question and chat on social media. She thrives on it and will always respond. Send her a photo of one of her books 'in the wild' and she'll share it. Everywhere.

If you enjoyed this book, join our Facebook group - The Barrington Book Club - and visit Susan's website on the link below.

www.susanmackie.com

ALSO BY SUSAN MACKIE

Charlie's Will

A Place to Start Over

The Bee Whisperer

Ragged Mountain Ranges

Meggie & Max

Something in the Water

Coffee is my Calling